BROKEN SILENCE

NATASHA PRESTON

Visit my website at www.natashapreston.com
Cover Designer: www.luminosgraphics.com
Editor and Interior Designer: Jovana Shirley,
Unforeseen Editing, www.unforeseenediting.com

For Shawn

acknowledgments

Thank you to Sofie Hartley for saving my butt and creating the most gorgeous cover refresh at such short notice. You rock, lady!

To my talented editor, Jovana Shirley, thank you for taking my manuscript and making it SO much better.

And last but not least, a huge thank you to a good friend who is always there to help. Kirsty, I literally don't know what I'd do without you!

one

OAKLEY

Everyone said that getting over somebody just took time and that, one day, it would stop hurting and the door would open for you to move on. We were also told that love was eternal, something extraordinary that would stay with you forever. However, after a breakup, suddenly, love became something you should get over once a little time had passed. The contradiction was immense.

Right now, I was somewhere in the middle.

I walked my usual route along the beach, holding my sandals in my hand so that I could feel the soft golden sand between my toes. Every night, I would walk along the beautiful Australian coast. It was so tranquil here. It was what I needed after everything had come out. The air was still warm, and the moon reflected off the ocean, creating rippling shadows on the water's surface. I sighed, smiling at the breathtaking sight.

A couple ahead of me walked hand in hand, gazing happily at each other. The man leant over and kissed the side of his partner's head. He reminded me a little of Cole with his messy hair and flirty smile. I gulped and quickly strolled past them, keeping my head down.

My heart gave a small squeeze as my mind drifted back to Cole. Again. That was no surprise though; most things reminded me of him. His eyes were the same shade of blue as an early night sky. The tree outside our house that had one branch leaning to the side, creating an L, was the same shape as the one he had fallen off while trying to rescue a cat. Our neighbour's dog had a light-brown patch of fur on its white tail that was the same colour as Cole's hair in the summer when the sun lightened it a fraction.

After I'd first left, we'd texted, but it'd become too hard to keep turning him down, so I'd cut off all contact. It was one of the hardest things I'd ever done. All I'd wanted was to tell him to get on the first plane out here. But he had so much in England. I didn't want to get in the way of his university and career dreams, and making him move away from his whole family would be too selfish. I loved him far too much to be selfish.

For the last four years, I hadn't spoken to him at all. It never got any easier. I'd still find myself almost dialling his number every day.

I knew Mum and Jenna, Cole's mum, still spoke. Well, they emailed because it was easier with the time difference, so I knew Cole was doing well. He had gone to the university he had always wanted to go to, and he'd landed his dream job straight after. Mum never mentioned if he had a girlfriend—or worse, a fiancée or wife. I didn't want to know. It would hurt too much, but I hoped with all my heart that he was happy.

As soon as I went back inside our house, Jasper practically pounced on me. Since the truth had come out, he had barely left my side. He had gone from overprotective to almost suffocating. No one could come within ten metres of me without Jasper being there to check them out. I didn't need a babysitter. I'd moved halfway across the world to be *free.*

He stood in front of me and bent his head to look into my eyes, checking if I was okay. "You all right?"

"Yes, Jasper." I sighed and headed into the kitchen.

Mum stood at the counter, making three mugs of hot chocolate. That was our little routine now. Every night, after my walk on the beach, the three of us would sit in the lounge, drinking hot chocolate and chatting. Even Jasper would make it every night. Four years ago, he would have laughed at the idea and gone out clubbing. We were really close now. I loved it but hated that they'd both lost so much for me.

"So, have you spoken to Miles today?" I asked Mum, smiling innocently, as I leant on the kitchen island.

Jasper shot me a warning look, his eyes narrowed. He was trying to get me to drop it, but I wasn't going to.

Mum had met Miles at work three years ago, and they really liked each other, but she wouldn't give him a chance. I understood why she found it hard to trust again, but anyone could see that she was as in love with him as he was with her.

She sighed. "No, I haven't, Oakley."

I bit my lip. "Well, why don't you invite him over for dinner tomorrow?"

"Please, honey. Nothing is going to happen between us. Give it up."

I stared down at the steam rising from the hot chocolate. "Not every man is like Dad, you know," I whispered.

"Don't call him that," Jasper snapped, speaking through gritted teeth. His knuckles turned white as his grip tightened around the handle of his mug.

Since knowing what had happened, on the rare occasion when Jasper did speak about Dad, he'd only ever refer to him as "that sick bastard."

"I know. Miles is a lovely guy, but I don't want a relationship."

Yes, you do.

She deserved to be happy. I didn't want Dad to affect the rest of her life, too, not to the point where she wouldn't allow herself to be with someone again.

Sighing in defeat, I followed Mum and Jasper into the living room and sat down. I wouldn't give up, not until she smiled properly again.

"You working tomorrow, Oakley?" Jasper asked, turning his nose up.

We both worked at the juice bar near the beach. It wasn't exactly the career either of us wanted, but Jasper refused to quit because so many bikini-clad women would come in, and I had no idea what I wanted to do.

I felt as if I were stuck in time. My life was on hold until the trial was over. Even though I was thousands of miles away, I still needed Dad and Frank to be locked away, so I could properly move on. Well, I hoped that would do it.

"No. You are though, right?"

"Yep. Wanna work for me?" he asked.

I gave him a flat look. "No."

Mum cut in, "Do you have plans, Oakley?"

When do I ever have plans? "No."

"Why don't you meet me for lunch at one? We can go to that sandwich place near my office, the one that Jasper's obsessed with."

"Oh, lovely," Jasper said sarcastically. "I'm bloody working, and you're planning on taking your favourite child to *my* favourite restaurant."

"Are you sure he's older than me?"

Mum smirked. "Mentally, no."

Jasper scowled.

"Oh, we'll get you a meatball sub!" she offered.

Jasper sat back and smiled proudly. "Good. Bring it to work, yeah?"

"I'll drop it off on my way home." I crossed my legs and sipped my hot chocolate.

Conversation quickly turned to the trial, which was only two months away. I was due to give evidence via a video link because I couldn't stand the thought of being in the same room as them, but the more I thought about it—or talked about it in therapy—the more I felt I *had* to go face them.

My therapist, Martha, had gone in depth a million times about finding closure. She'd asked me to think about what it would take for me to be able to put it behind me enough to move forward. Following her instructions, I had been thinking about it over the past year, but I had nothing—not until the trial date was set, and my lawyer spoke about how I could give evidence from Australia.

Martha had seemed to think that facing them could offer the closure I needed, but she'd also asked me to consider what I would do or how I would feel if they got off. Betrayed. Scared. To think that a jury could possibly believe I had made it all up would be devastating.

Dad had said so many times that no one would believe me. If it turned out that he was right, I didn't know how I would handle it.

There was also something else, or more someone else, to consider—Cole.

Sipping my boiling drink, I listened as Mum and Jasper talked about the jury seeing through Dad's charm. No one had for years, not even the people closest to him. *How are strangers going to?* I couldn't think like that. There was evidence on his laptop that proved he had indecent images of children.

I wished it were already over.

After Dad and Frank had been arrested, other girls had come forward. One lady had claimed that Dad had abused her when she was a child, and he was in his early twenties. I believed her one hundred percent.

If those women could face them again, so could I.

Taking a deep breath, I turned to Mum and Jasper. *Now or never.* "I have something I need to talk to you about," I said.

"What's up?" Jasper asked, concerned.

"I want to go back and give evidence in person."

Silence fell upon the room, and I watched on as they thought it through. I didn't expect them to come, not for a second. It wasn't just me that had gone through it; they had, too. I understood if they didn't want to be anywhere near him.

I could go alone. My aunt, Ali, and cousin, Lizzie, would be there for me. My grandparents, too. Mum and Jasper were my biggest support, so, of course, I wanted them to be with me, but I would never ask.

Mum finally nodded. "Okay. If you're sure that's what you need?"

"It is."

She put her mug down on the coffee table. "Right. I'll speak to Ali about us staying with her, and then we'll book the flights."

She wants to come? "You don't have to come, you know. It's fine if you don't want to."

Jasper scoffed. "Like you're going alone."

"I mean it, Jasper. If either of you doesn't want to come, it's fine with me. I understand if you don't want to see them again. It's just…I *have* to."

"We're doing this together, honey. I made that promise to you four years ago, and I'm not going to break it now."

"Thank you," I whispered. I swallowed a lump in my throat.

It meant so much that they would come. I knew how hard it was for them, especially Mum. She blamed herself for not seeing the man she'd married for what he truly was. Dad had had everyone fooled though. What had happened was no one's fault but his.

Jasper clenched his jaw, as if he was trying to hold something in. I knew he didn't want to see Dad again, and I felt guilty that he would because of me.

"Jasper? You okay?" Mum asked. "Oakley's right. You don't have to come."

"I'm going," he replied, putting his mug down and folding his arms over his chest in a stubborn manner. "I just don't know how I'm going to stay in control when I see his face again."

I thought he hated Dad more than I did.

"Maybe you should come to therapy with me. I'm sure Martha could fit us in for a joint session."

"No, thanks," he muttered in response.

Therapy was something that Jasper always refused. I'd started seeing Martha shortly after we'd arrived in Australia, and Mum used to see someone, too. Jasper had his own way of dealing with things—bottling it up and letting it explode in a fight or finding the bottom of a bottle.

"It's not weak to ask for help, Jasper." I said.

He stood up. "I don't need help. I just need to help you two."

My heart dropped. I didn't know what to say.

Jasper walked out, and I wanted to run after him, but I knew he needed to be alone to cool down. He did see therapy as a weakness and wouldn't do it because he had to be strong for me and Mum.

My stupid, sweet brother.

"He'll be fine. I'm sure he'll seek help when he's ready for it."

I nodded. "I suppose pushing it away is easier than facing it."

It had taken me more than a decade of pretending everything was fine before I had spoken up. It would be hypocritical of me to push Jasper into anything.

"Are you going to tell Jenna that we're coming back? I think you should warn them."

I couldn't just turn up and be like, *Hey, Cole, how's it going?* It had been too long for me to spring a surprise visit on him.

Mum nodded and wrapped a tartan blanket around herself. It wasn't cold. It was actually pretty hot, but I thought it was to protect her from the conversation we were having rather than the temperature.

"She emailed yesterday. I haven't replied yet, so I'll mention it. Are you looking forward to seeing Cole again?"

I looked out the window. Hearing someone say his name was like being punched. "I don't want to talk about it."

"Okay," Mum said. "I'll call Ali. You get the laptop and look up some flights."

Within an hour, Mum had spoken to Ali, and our flights were booked. In a week's time, we would be in England. I emailed my lawyer, Linda Rake, to explain that I had changed my mind, and I was going to call her tomorrow to discuss it. She would be pleased. A while ago, she'd suggested that I think about appearing in court in person, but I had said no.

Jasper walked back into the room just as Mum went up to bed. He sat down next to me. "We're really doing this? Going back?"

"Yes." I wasn't a scared child anymore. I could face them.

"What are you gonna do about Cole?"

I hadn't thought he would bring Cole up. He knew I didn't like to talk about Cole anymore.

"Nothing."

"Right. So, you're going back to where the guy you love is, and you plan on doing nothing?" he asked with the most sarcastic tone I had ever heard.

I nodded in reply.

"Oh, come on, Oakley! You've been moping around here for *four* years. I've never even seen you look at another guy. Are you seriously gonna waste your chance at being happy again?"

I sighed.

There had been no one else because I couldn't stand the thought of being that close to anyone else. There was nothing wrong with the guys here or anything. I just didn't feel safe and secure with them. They couldn't make me forget every disgusting thing that had happened to me with one little smile.

"And what? I should just turn up on his doorstep and get back together with him until the trial ends, and we come back? Like you said, it's been four years. He has a whole new life. He could be married for all we know!" The thought of him being married quite honestly felt like I was being stabbed in the heart.

"I think Jenna would have mentioned something like that," he replied as he raised one eyebrow.

Okay, yes, she would have, but that didn't mean there wasn't someone in his life. This was *Cole*. He was the sweetest, funniest, most incredible, beautiful, generous, and caring person in the world.

"Whatever. I'm not gonna do anything stupid and mess up his life."

"Then, maybe you shouldn't have left him behind."

My eyes prickled, filling with tears. That was low.

"Shit! I'm sorry, Oakley," he said.

He grimaced as I pushed myself off the sofa.

I raised one hand, telling him to back off. "It's fine. I'm going to bed. Night, Jasper."

He groaned in frustration as I walked away. The problem was that Jasper was half-right, and that was what stung.

As soon as I finished in the bathroom, I got straight into bed. I hadn't done much all day, but I felt exhausted. Tucked under the pillow on the spare side of my bed was Cole's hoodie—the only thing of his I had. It'd stopped smelling of his aftershave long ago, but it was his, and that meant everything to me.

My throat burned, and I swallowed hard to try to stop myself from crying, but it was no use. I buried my head in his hoodie and cried silently, so no one would hear.

Although we never spoke about my feelings for Cole, Mum and Jasper knew I was still in love with him. On the rare occasion I went out, Mum would encourage me to meet someone else, but I couldn't help comparing guys all to Cole—and they never lived up to him. No one else could make me feel *normal.*

I lay awake in bed for most of the night, thinking about what Jasper had said. I tried not to let any doubt enter my mind, but when he said things like that, I couldn't help it.

Did I do the right thing? Was Mum right when she'd said he could come to a school here? They have the degree he wanted, but it wasn't the university he wanted. All his family and friends are in England, too. If he'd come, would he have ended up resenting me for making him give all that up?

I groaned and ran my hands over my face. Going over it again wasn't helping. I had made the decision. I had to live with it, and so did he. Soon enough though, I'd get to see whether Cole felt I'd done the right thing or if I'd made the biggest mistake of both our lives.

Our suitcases were already in the boot of the car. Mum and Jasper were having a quick tidy before we left for the airport, so I took the last opportunity I had to do something I knew Mum hadn't.

"Back soon," I called from the front door so that I could get out before anyone questioned where I was going.

I walked along the beach, and knowing this was the last time for a while gave me a heavy heart. The beach was my getaway, and I was going to miss it.

His house wasn't too far from ours, so I made it in just over five minutes. Taking a deep breath, I knocked on his door and waited.

"Oakley, hi," Miles said, frowning a little and shaking his head in confusion.

I knew where he lived but had never come round before. "Hi. Can I come in for a minute?"

Miles stepped aside, making room for me to walk in.

"Has she told you we're going back to England?" I asked, deciding to get straight to the point. There had been a lot of miscommunication between them, so I wanted to be clear.

His face fell, and I wanted to slap my mum for being so blind to how much he cared about her.

"No, she didn't. How long are you going for?"

"I'm not sure. However long the trial lasts, I suppose."

"Right. Of course. Sorry, I didn't think."

I waved my hand, making light of the situation. "It's fine. I just thought you should know. Look, Miles, she likes you, but you're gonna have to make the first move. She's scared and stubborn. She needs to see how much you care."

He smiled and nodded, brushing his greying dark hair with his hand. "How?"

I laughed at the thought of giving a forty-something-year-old man love-life advice.

"She's insisting on leaving her mobile here, so she can concentrate on me, apparently. I know she's just kind of petrified though, so here," I said, handing him a piece of paper. "That's my mobile number. The trial's going to be hard for her, too, and as much as she will not admit it, she would really appreciate you calling. Don't email; she can avoid that."

"Right." He smiled. "Thank you. I'll call. I promise." Miles took the paper, slipping it in his back pocket.

"I know you will, or I'll get Jasper to kick your arse when we get back," I joked.

He laughed quietly and shook his head. "I hope everything goes well. Oh, is that the right thing to say?" he asked as he grimaced.

"I'm not sure, so, yes, that's okay. Thanks, Miles."

He breathed a sigh of relief and smiled. "Okay, good. You'll let me know how everything goes?"

I smiled, raising my eyebrows. "Mum will—when you call."

"All right," he replied with a chuckle. "I'll see you when you get back then?"

I nodded, walking back to the door. "See ya later."

"Bye, Oakley."

I really hoped he would call. As terrified as Mum was, she deserved to be happy. Miles was a great guy. Nothing like my dad.

As always, Jasper was waiting for me when I got back. I had been gone only twenty minutes.

"Everything's fine," I told him before he could ask.

"Oh, good. You're back, honey. Jasper, do you have your passport?" Mum said as she locked the front door.

I got in the back of the car because I knew Jasper would probably moan like a child if he couldn't sit in the front.

"Yeah," he grunted as he got in the seat in front of me. "Why didn't you ask Oakley that, too?"

Mum shot him a sarcastic smile that made me laugh.

"Whatever," he mumbled under his breath.

"You emailed Jenna, right? They definitely know we're coming back for a while?" I asked.

"Yes, I emailed."

Okay, that's good. I didn't want to run into them without them knowing it was a possibility.

Part of me was excited at the thought of seeing Cole again. I had missed everything about him for the last four years. I wanted to hear his voice again and see him smile. The other part of me was terrified. The thought of him hating me hurt so much. I was also scared that I might have to watch him be with someone else, and if I had to, I would only have myself to blame.

two

COLE

My so-called friend Ben sighed. "It's pathetic!"

"*No*, it's romantic," Kerry argued, slamming her hand on the table.

At least one of them was on my side.

"Romantic? It's been *four years*, and he *still* mopes around like a teenage girl who just found out Justin what's-his-face is off the market," Ben countered as he pointed his finger at me, as if it weren't clear who he was talking about. "Back me up, Cole. It's pathetic, right?"

"Thank you," I muttered. *I'm glad I agreed to going out with them.*

I wasn't completely pathetic. I had been on a few dates since Oakley had left, but they never turned into anything. No matter how hard I'd tried, I couldn't force myself to want a relationship with any other woman, which fucked me over royally because she'd left. She'd rejected me and then left.

Ben held his hand up as Kerry opened her mouth to argue her side again. "I'm just sayin', maybe it's time to give Chelsea a chance. She's a great girl, and she lives in *England*."

I sighed and rubbed my jaw. Chelsea was a great girl. She was pretty, had a good sense of humour, and was intelligent, but she wasn't Oakley. I'd met Chelsea on the first day of university, and we had been friends ever since. She had hinted a few times that she wanted more, but I didn't want to lead her on just on the off chance that I could grow to like her romantically.

Kerry slapped Ben across the chest with the back of her hand. The sound made a solid thud. "Don't tell him that, Ben! Oakley is clearly his soul mate."

"And she ditched him to move halfway across the world."

That fucking hurt.

"Because she thought she was doing the best thing for him. *He* should have gone after her. They could be sunning themselves on a gorgeous beach in paradise right now."

I tried to go with her. She didn't want me.

"*But* he didn't, and it's been *four years*. She's probably with some other guy now, sunning herself with him on the beach!"

I closed my eyes and pushed away the thought of another man touching her. *Would she even allow that?*

She'd let me, but we had been friends forever. She knew I would never hurt her. Oakley's trust meant everything to me, and the fact that she'd felt comfortable and safe enough to get that close made me feel a thousand feet tall.

Half of me hoped she would never let another man near her, and the other half hoped she would. I wanted her to be happy and for those bastards not to have completely ruined any chance she had of being happy.

Four years later, and I still thought of her as mine.

"Either change the subject, or I'm leaving," I hissed.

The whole conversation was making me feel sick. Kerry was right about one thing; I should have followed her. Staying here was the biggest regret I had, but it'd seemed like Oakley didn't want me to go with her. I was scared to go flying out there and surprise her in case she told me to go back.

For the first few weeks, we'd sent text messages. Well, it was mostly me plaguing her with texts. She'd kept apologising for everything and saying that I should forget her. Forgetting her wasn't going to happen; she was a huge part of my life and had been since we were both kids.

I understood completely that she couldn't be here anymore. After what those fuckers had done to her, of course she wouldn't want constant reminders, but she was wrong about my life being here. I hadn't gotten enough time to convince her; she'd just left. It was too late now, of course.

"What are we talking about?" Chelsea asked, taking a seat next to me and grabbing the menu.

I hadn't even seen her come in.

"How romantic Cole is," Kerry said, and at the same time, Ben came out with, "How pathetic Cole is."

Kerry and Ben were made for each other. Obviously, "change the subject" meant something completely different to them than it did to me.

"Right." Chelsea laughed and shot me a brief smile. "So, are we going out tonight?"

"Oh, definitely," Kerry said.

She launched into a conversation about where we were going. Thankfully, that ended the topic of my patheticness over Oakley.

By the time I joined their conversation, everything was planned. We would all be meeting at my place at eight and going into town.

"See you all later," I said as we parted in the car park.

"Bye, loser!" Ben shouted.

Great.

My parents, my sister, Mia, and my niece, Leona—or Fifi, as we often called her due to her obsession with *Fifi and the Flowertots*—were sitting on the sofa, watching *Cinderella.*

"Hi, sweetheart," Mum said, struggling to hold Leona still as she bounced around on her lap.

One thing I had learnt since Mia had had Leona was that children were loud. They also often made a huge mess and wouldn't keep still.

"Hi," I replied, frowning at being called sweetheart at twenty-one

I walked into the kitchen to make a cup of tea, and Mia followed.

One, two, three…

"You've got the I'm-thinking-about-Oakley face on again."

I'm pretty sure that's just my usual face.

"I don't want to talk about it. I want to go and murder a bunch of people on the PlayStation until I go out later."

She gave me a sympathetic smile. "Who are you going out with?"

"Kerry, Ben, and Chelsea."

"Chelsea, too, huh?"

"We're just friends, Mia," I said as I rolled my eyes.

"I know that. Does she?"

"No, I thought I'd string her along until I stopped thinking about Oakley all the damn time." I started out being sarcastic, but the end of that sentence was honest—*too* honest. I still thought about Oakley constantly. It had just ended so suddenly. One minute, she had been there, and the next, she and her family had taken off to Australia with no warning.

"Aw, Cole."

I held my hand up. "Don't."

I didn't need the pitying looks or sympathetic words. I would be fine. There wasn't any other choice. I wished Oakley had lied and told me she didn't want me and she didn't love me. That way, I would have known it was a definite end, and there would be no chance of us getting back together.

Mia opened her mouth again to talk even though I had told her not to, but thankfully, Leona skipped into the room, brushing her fringe out of her eyes.

"Untle Ole!" she yelled as she ran at me.

I managed to sweep her up just before she smashed into my crotch. Again.

Leona still had problems pronouncing her Cs, so I was Untle Ole.

I smiled at her and said, "Can you say *C*-ole?"

"Ole," she chirped proudly, making me laugh.

Close enough!

I took her into the lounge to escape another Oakley conversation with Mia. Leona wriggled in my arms, waving her doll around and almost smacking me in the face with it.

"Maybe you could actually fix it, David?" Mum said dryly, hitting her laptop, as if that were magically going to make it work.

"It's not that simple, Jenna," Dad countered, matching her tone.

Well, at least this argument isn't about how romantic or pathetic I am.

"Oh, how hard can it be? Just call the Internet people. There must be someone in charge of the Internet!"

I laughed. Mum turned and glared. Leona giggled along, too, even though she had no idea what she was laughing at. Mum had no fucking clue when it came to anything technical.

"It's the router, Jenna, not the entire Internet!" Dad said, shaking his head. He walked off to his study where the router was.

As I held Leona over the sofa, she started laughing and squealing immediately, knowing what I was about to do.

"Ready?" I said slowly, making her squeal louder.

I dropped her on the cushions, and she screamed like she was being murdered. Kids were so easy to amuse; all you had to do was chuck them around a bit.

Leona had been with Chris the Dick all morning, so she was on a sugar high. All it took was smile at him, and he would give her whatever she wanted—usually, sweets. At least Chris the Dick had stuck around. He'd surprised everyone there. As much as I hated to admit it, he was a good dad. I still wouldn't piss on him if he were on fire though.

Grabbing my mail from the side table, I escaped to my room. Having Leona around was great, but at the end of the day, I was exhausted. She had too much energy.

I flopped down on the bed and ripped the first envelope open. *Please have something decent in here.*

The estate agent had sent me a few new houses. I had seen about six already, but they were shitholes. Refurbishment, I could handle, but I didn't want to do anything structural.

Two out of the five were okay, and I would make an appointment to view them; the rest I threw in the bin.

House-hunting was something I was meant to do with Oakley. When we had been together, I'd thought about stuff like that. We were eventually supposed to move in together. I hated that I would now be living alone.

Oakley had been on my mind more than usual lately. The trial would be starting soon. I hoped those scum would rot in prison for the rest of their lives. At first, I hadn't wanted to go. I didn't want to hear the details. I had given a full statement of what had happened the day she called me, and it was going to be read out loud in court.

Now though, I wanted to be there. I needed to watch them go down, and I wanted to see her again. It would only be on a screen, but it would still be better than old photos. I would get to hear her voice. I'd only have two weeks of hearing her speak again, and that just wasn't enough.

"Hey," Chelsea said, letting herself into my room.

Damn, it is a quarter to eight already. Moping around in your own self-pity really passes the time.

I smiled and sat up. "Hey. You look nice."

She wore an extremely low-cut, extremely tight black dress. It looked painted on. I wasn't used to seeing quite that much of her, but I wasn't exactly complaining. Oakley would never wear anything like that. It wasn't her style, and she certainly didn't need to do anything to get herself noticed.

Chelsea laughed and playfully slapped my shoulder, running her hand down my arm. "Thanks. You look the same as earlier!"

"Yeah, I should get changed." I got up and grabbed a pair of jeans and a black shirt.

Normally, I would change in my room, but Chelsea sat on the bed, clearly going nowhere. She was a great girl, but she was becoming more forward, and I didn't want to lead her on.

After changing in the bathroom, I walked back in my room to get Chelsea, so we could go downstairs to safety. Kerry and Ben would be here soon. She was lounging on my bed, as if it were hers.

Make yourself at home. "We should wait downstairs; they'll be here in a minute," I said, nodding toward the door.

"Sure." She swung her legs off the bed and pushed herself up.

Sighing, I followed her downstairs. Thankfully, my parents were out to dinner, and Mia was probably trying to get Leona to sleep.

"They're here," Chelsea said, peering out the window.

Good.

Kerry was sitting in the back of the car. It was as if she had known I'd want to escape any awkward scene with Chelsea because she rarely let me have the front seat.

"Ready to get smashed?" Kerry said the second I was in the car.

"Beyond ready," I replied. I wanted to get so off my face that I wouldn't even remember Oakley's name.

We walked into the club, and I headed straight for the bar with Ben. After ordering a beer, JD and Coke, glass of wine, and a disgusting blue WKD, Ben and I carried the drinks to the table that the girls had managed to get. It was still quite early, so the club wasn't very full, yet there weren't any free tables now.

Chelsea shot me another flirtatious look and sipped her WKD. She knew that I didn't want more than friendship from her; I had made that clear. *Does she think I'll change my mind if she shows off more skin?*

The few dates I had been on since Oakley ended in fuck all. I'd felt as if I were cheating, which pissed me off so much because she was the one who had left me behind. Oakley had left me, and I felt like I couldn't see anyone else.

Everyone had been telling me to move on—everyone but Kerry anyway. She wanted me to wait for Oakley.

"When the time is right, you'll be reunited and live happily ever after," she'd told me multiple times.

I knew that was crap, but I couldn't help hoping.

Three beers, two JD and Cokes, and five shots later, I was wasted. The women were more attractive, and I wasn't a mess, waiting for someone who had fucked off and was staying fucked off.

"Cole," Chelsea slurred, gripping my arm to hold herself up, "come dance with me?"

I shook my head. "No. I like the bar." I slumped against the wooden counter and raised my hand for the bartender. "Double JD and Coke, please. Want anything, Chels?"

"No, thanks." She huffed and spun around, storming off.

"What are you laughing at?" Ben asked, sitting down on the stool next to me.

I waved my hand. "Don't worry." My body was heavy. I hadn't been this drunk in a while.

"Drinking your problems away." Ben shook his head. "You have to face the problem. Head-on."

"You're right, man. I'm pathetic."

He sighed. "True. You either need to get over her or go get her."

"I can't do the first one 'cause I love her," I said, waving my finger at him to try and make him understand. "I'm going to America."

"Australia," he corrected.

Laughing, I shook my head. The room spun, making me feel sick.

"She's in *Australia*." I frowned. "That's not funny actually. You know why?" I waited for his reply.

He rolled his eyes and gestured with his hand for me to continue.

"Because I love her, and you know what you do when you love someone? You follow them to Australia. I'm right, right?"

"Yes, Cole, you're right," he muttered.

"I knew it!" I said, slamming my fist down on the bar. "All right, let's go."

"Whoa." Ben grabbed my arm and pulled me back. "You need to sober up first. I'm taking you home to bed."

I swayed and gripped the bar.

"No more alcohol for you. We need to find the girls and get you home," he said.

Kerry and Chelsea were dancing at the edge of the dance floor. They looked possessed, throwing their arms up in the air. I chuckled. They were drunk, too. Chelsea looked over and rubbed her body against some stranger behind her. I shrugged. Trying to make me jealous wasn't going to work.

"We're leaving!" Ben shouted over the music.

Chelsea glared. The random behind her moved over, grabbing another girl.

"Fine," she snapped, shoving past a group of girls with the longest fake eyelashes I had ever seen. They looked like spiders had died on their eyelids.

I sat as still as a statue in the front of Ben's car. Movement made me want to hurl. I could already tell that I would feel like shit tomorrow. The alcohol hadn't even done what it was supposed to do; I'd still had a bloody Oakley conversation!

"Ben, for fuck's sake!" I hissed.

It seemed like he was hitting every bump on the road on purpose.

"I can't help it! Stop being such a pussy!"

Groaning, I pressed my forehead to the cold window. *Kill me.*

Ben pulled into my drive and walked around to my door. I leant against him as we walked to the front door.

"Tomorrow, I'm going to Australia," I announced as Ben turned the key for me and shoved me inside.

He snorted and closed the door, saying, "Enjoy."

Mum, Dad, and Mia gaped at me. Dad opened his mouth, but I held my hand up.

"I'm not going right now; don't worry. I need to sleep first," I mumbled, staggering toward the stairs.

The journey to my room took longer than usual. The hallway had stretched.

Collapsing on my bed, I squeezed my eyes shut, effectively stopping the room from spinning. I felt something dip on the bed and knew it was one of them coming to ask me, *What the hell?*

"Good night?" Mia asked.

"Australia's really far away, isn't it?"

Sighing, she placed her hand on my shoulder. "Yes. Are you serious about going, or is it the alcohol talking? I don't think it's a very good idea just to turn up there."

"I don't know." I shrugged. "She left me. She wouldn't let me go with her. It hurts," I admitted.

"I know it does, but you need to make a choice, Cole. You have to either try getting back together with her or move on."

"That's what Ben said."

"It's been too long. This isn't healthy. Whatever you decide, I'll be here for you, but you have to decide soon. I hate seeing you like this. I'll leave you to sleep."

She left my room, closing the door behind her. I thought about her words.

I had to get her back or move on.

I'd tried the second option, but it was too hard. Oakley hadn't broken up with me because she didn't love me anymore. If she had, at least I would have known we had no chance, and I could have moved on.

Oakley had left because she couldn't be here, and knowing that made me unable to move on.

three

OAKLEY

We approached our old neighbourhood, and so many memories flashed through my mind. Most of them included Cole and things we had done together. My heart skipped. I was so close to him. We turned the corner, and his house came into view. Butterflies swarmed in my stomach. My old house was just past his, but I refused to look at the place I had grown up in.

"Oakley, you can say no if you want to," Mum started. She lifted her foot off the accelerator, and the car slowed.

My eyes widened as I realised what she was asking.

"What are you doing?" I asked, trying not to show the panic in my voice.

"We've not seen them in almost four years. I've missed Jenna," she whispered. "But, if you don't want to, honey, we can do it another time. I will understand."

I knew she didn't mean to make me feel guilty, but that was exactly what she had done. It was my fault that she missed them. My fault that she hadn't seen her best friend for four years.

Gulping, I tried to push my fears away.

"No, it's fine. I miss them, too." I could suck it up and let her see her friend again. *Cole's probably not even in.* "Jenna wouldn't be happy if we were in the area and didn't call in anyway."

Mum smiled at me in the mirror as she stopped outside their house. "Thank you."

Jasper rapped on their door. He was obviously as excited as Mum to see them all again. I was terrified and felt like running as I heard someone on the other side of the door.

Thankfully, it was Jenna. She gasped in surprise and threw the door wide open. "Oh my God!" she shouted.

Mum stepped forward, and they hugged, laughing like teenage girls. It was nice to hear Mum laugh like that again.

"When did you get back? How long are you here for?" Jenna asked, ushering us inside. She hugged me and then Jasper with as much enthusiasm as she had Mum.

Why is she asking that? They know.

My heart dropped as I realised she hadn't received Mum's email.

Out of the corner of my eye, I saw Mum frown.

"Didn't you get my email?"

Jenna huffed. "No, our Internet's been down for a while now. I've told David to fix it, but you know what he's like! It's so good to see you again."

Oh God, this isn't good.

"You look great, Oakley. You're so grown-up," she said, pulling me into another hug.

I smiled, trying to hide the panic rising inside. Cole couldn't see me for the first time like this. A surprise visit was the last thing he needed.

Jasper laughed humourlessly. "She's still just as immature."

"Coming from you, Jasper? Really?" I replied.

Jasper was a man-child and one of the most immature people I knew.

He narrowed his eyes and wrapped his arm around my shoulders. He shoved his hand in my hair, ruffling it up.

"Get off!" I shouted, batting his hand away with my own. Now really wasn't the time to mess around.

I needed to find out if Cole was around, so I could figure out how to meet him again for the first time. There was no getting around the fact that we would meet, but I wanted to do it properly.

I shoved Jasper, and as I looked up, I froze. It was too late to leave. Cole was standing in front of me, staring, open-mouthed.

No, no, no!

My heart soared. Seeing him again was such an incredible feeling that it took my breath away.

He hadn't changed much. His hair was the same style but an inch or two shorter. My memory hadn't done him justice at all.

Beside him was a girl I didn't know. I felt a chill, and my heart plummeted to my toes. *His girlfriend? Of course.* I knew he'd probably found someone else, but I sure as hell didn't want to see it.

Jasper touched my arm just as I felt like I was going to faint. My legs were weak. I wanted to leave before this girl was confirmed as his, but I couldn't move.

"This is awkward," Jasper muttered under his breath.

I wanted to hit him, but I still couldn't move. The girl, who I unreasonably hated, clearly recognised me. She looked at me with wide eyes, surprised to see me, too.

Does Cole talk about me to her? Am I the bitch ex who left him and she's the angel, the current girlfriend? That wouldn't be far from the truth.

"Oh my freakin' God! Oakley!" Kerry screamed, bursting into the room.

She bounced over to me, and I was wrapped in her iron grip. Ben stood behind her, looking between me and Cole.

"You're really back! I can't believe it. For how long? God, I missed you," Kerry said.

I mumbled a breathless, "Hello," as she squeezed the air from my lungs.

"Ooh, you have a sexy, husky voice!"

I didn't really know what to say to that, so I said nothing. It must be so strange for her to hear me speak. I hadn't seen her since everything had come out.

"Ben, say hello," she ordered, but before he could, she continued. "Oh, and this is Chelsea, our *friend*."

I smiled at Kerry and her not-so-subtle way of telling me that Chelsea wasn't with Cole. Relief flooded my system. "Hi, Chelsea."

"Hey," she replied.

I looked back at Cole, who was still a statue. He hadn't looked away from me this whole time, and I didn't know if that was a good sign or not.

"I wonder if it's possible for this to get any more awkward," Jasper said.

I glared at my idiot brother.

"Beach party, Jasper," I hissed. "Beach party."

He shot me a dark look but backed down, as I had known he would. It worked every single time I needed him to shut up.

"What happened at the beach party?" Kerry asked. Ben wrapped his arm around her and shook his head, discouraged at her gossiping.

"Nothing happened at the beach party!" Jasper yelped. "Now, come on, let's leave Cole and Oakley to talk."

And to think I've gone almost twenty years without having any real murderous thoughts about my brother!

"Sure. I wanna see your mum anyway," Kerry said as she ushered them all into the kitchen.

I chewed the inside of my cheek as I desperately tried to think of something to say. Something that wasn't, *I love you. Please forgive me.*

Giving myself a little pep talk in my head, I took one step forward. It was only right that I be the one to speak first.

"Hi," I whispered.

His lips pulled up into a small smile. "Hi."

My stomach flipped over. I had missed the sound of his voice so much. Let's face it; I had missed everything about him.

With that brief exchange, we fell into silence. I stood still and stared at him, and he did the same. There was so much I wanted to say that I couldn't figure out what to open with. His eyes bored into me with such intensity that I felt naked. Looking at him again, I had no idea how I'd managed to leave him behind.

His eyes flicked over my shoulder, and he glared at something behind me. I looked around and saw Jasper and Kerry peeking around the kitchen door. It was Jasper's idea to give us some privacy, yet he was the one snooping.

Cole looked back at me and nodded toward the French doors leading to the back garden. I moved toward the door, and he followed. *At least he's coming, too, and not just telling me to get out.*

He closed the door behind us and sat on the step from the deck to the grass. I sat beside him and looked forward, too scared to make eye contact straightaway. When his aftershave mixed with his natural scent hit me, I felt safe again—something I hadn't felt in four years.

Finally, he turned his head and looked at me. "How long are you back for?"

His question wasn't what I had expected first.

"Um, I'm not sure. It depends on the trial, I suppose."

He frowned, looking out at something in the garden.

What?

"I didn't think you were coming back for it."

I shrugged. "I wasn't going to at first. But, now, I feel as if I have to. You know, to put it all behind me and move on."

Maybe I shouldn't have come back? Am I just making this harder for him?

"Sorry, we should have called first. I didn't want us to meet like this. I wanted you to know before you saw me. Mum did email Jenna, but your Internet's not been working, so obviously, you didn't get it. I'm sorry again. We should have made sure—"

"It's fine," he said, laughing and shaking his head at me.

I had missed the sound of his laugh, too. I could hear it in my head, but the real thing was so much better. "What?"

"Just haven't heard you ramble like that since we were little kids."

I nodded and smiled, relieved. "So, what was university like?"

He raised his eyebrows. "You really wanna talk about school?"

Not really, but school was a safe subject. I nodded, wrapping my arms around myself, now feeling the cold.

Cole sighed sharply. "Uni was fine. The course was good. Could have done it anywhere."

I dropped my eyes to the ground. *Could have done it in Australia, is what he meant.*

"Sorry. I shouldn't have said that. What's Australia like?" he asked, changing the subject.

The small-talk thing was awkward. We were way past that, and I could tell he wanted to say something else. There were a million other things I wanted to say.

"Hot." *Beautiful. Tranquil. Safer.*

"You're cold now," he said, nodding toward the goose bumps that covered my arms.

I should have dressed for the English weather better. He pulled his hoodie over his head and handed it to me. I bit my lip and took it. Our fingers brushed against each other's, making my heart skip a beat.

"Yeah, England's not so hot. Thanks for this," I said. I put it on.

His mouth thinned as his expression turned serious. "Do you know when you have to give evidence?"

"Not for a few weeks yet."

He nodded once. "You staying at Ali's?"

I turned my nose up. "Yeah."

"Lizzie's still the same then?" he asked, chuckling.

"Yep. She calls me now, too. Wants all the 'goss' on Australia's 'hot' surfers."

Cole frowned. "Right…surfers. Wait, can you surf?"

I laughed and shook my head. "I tried once, but it didn't go well. I practically drowned and had to be pulled out of the water. Jasper's pretty good though. Surprisingly."

It was strange that he could do it. Jasper could drown in a puddle but ride a wave like a pro.

After a few minutes of awkward silence, Cole said, "You finished school in Australia then?"

"You really wanna talk about school?" I asked, using his words.

His mouth twitched into a smile. "Touché."

"I did, but I had to stay until I was seventeen." I had never liked school and having to stay for another year compared to high school in England wasn't ideal. Although I was never bullied in Australia, so it wasn't that bad.

"That's rough."

I nodded, chewing on my bottom lip. "Please just say whatever is on your mind, Cole."

"I honestly don't know where to start." He lowered his head, looking hurt.

It made my heart ache. I was responsible for that look.

"You made the wrong decision," he said.

I tried to force down the lump rising in my throat. "I did what I thought was the best thing for you. I didn't want you to have to give up everything."

He scoffed and shook his head. "But that's exactly what you made me do. For fuck's sake, Oakley! How many times did I tell you how much you mean to me? How much I love you? How you are everything to me? I don't get how you came to the conclusion that I would be better off without you!"

Present tense. He said everything in the present tense. Does that mean he still feels that way?

"I'm sorry. I thought you'd be fine and that you'd get over us and go to the university you'd always wanted to go to. I thought you'd find someone else and be happy." As much as him being with someone else would hurt me, if he were happy, I could deal with it.

"Well, I didn't. I'm not fine. I'm not over you. There's no one else, and I'm not happy. I haven't been properly happy in four years…but thank you for letting me go to university," he said sarcastically.

The snippy tone in his voice broke my heart. I had never heard Cole sound like that before. I didn't blame him, but I hated it.

I found it harder to breathe as I replayed his words in my head even though I was hurt at how he had said it. There was no one else, and he wasn't happy. I opened my mouth to say something but couldn't find the words.

"I guess it doesn't matter to you though. You've got your perfect little life halfway around the damn world."

That snapped me out of it. Australia was pretty perfect to me, but my life sure as hell wasn't.

"You think I have a perfect life? You think I don't feel the same way? God, Cole! There's not been one second that I haven't thought about you. Every single thing reminds me of you or something we've done. Every morning, when I wake up, I still expect you to be there, and every morning you're not, it breaks my heart."

"You did it, Oakley! You. I *wanted* to come."

"I couldn't have asked you to move to the other side of the world."

"I would've moved to the fucking moon!" he shouted.

I flinched.

"Why can't you understand that? You knew I wanted to be with you, so why did you do it?"

I groaned in frustration and blurted out, "Because you deserve better than me."

He fell silent. My words hung over us like a dark cloud.

Cole finally spoke first, "What? What do you mean?"

I lowered my head and wished I hadn't said anything at all.

"Oakley?" he prompted.

Sighing, I turned my head, looking away from him. I didn't want to see his face when I confessed what I really thought. I knew now that what had happened to me wasn't my fault, but it didn't change how I felt about myself.

"You deserve someone who isn't like me…someone who isn't used, dirty, and—"

"Don't finish that sentence," he snapped, making me jump.

I kept my eyes firmly fixed on one particular blade of grass that was slightly longer than the rest.

"Look at me, Oakley. Please."

I took a deep breath and followed his instruction. He was closer than before. His eyes pierced into mine. My breath caught in my throat, and my heart went wild. I didn't really expect him to kiss me, but I wanted him to so much.

His face slowly softened. The hard line of his jaw disappeared. "What happened wasn't your fault," he said.

"I know, but I can't help how it makes me feel." I blinked a few times to stop the tears from falling.

The only time I had admitted that out loud was in therapy. It wasn't something I spoke about with Mum or Jasper because I didn't want them to feel guilty.

"You—"

"Cole, please. I can't talk about this now."

Seeing him after four years and having *that* conversation so soon would be too much. I seriously didn't want to get into what *they* had done or how I felt about it.

He sighed heavily, and I could tell he wanted to talk about it. He probably wanted to try to make me feel better.

"Okay," he said.

I knew he would let it go for now, but he would definitely bring it up again.

"I'm so sorry, Cole. I *really* did think I was doing the best thing," I whispered.

By leaving, I had thrown away my chance at a future with him, but he did deserve better.

Cole laughed, but there was no humour to it. "You know how many times I wanted to come out there?" He ran his hands through his short hair, lightly tugging it. "I shouldn't have listened to you. I tried to date again, but I compared every woman to you, and no one ever came close."

A metallic taste filled my mouth. "I'm sorry," I repeated as I wiped my eyes.

"Doesn't matter anymore," he muttered.

That was a lie. It still mattered, and he knew it did.

"It does matter," I said. Fresh tears rolled down my cheeks, and I swiped them away.

He roughly rubbed his hands over his face. "I can't do this, Oakley."

I nodded. It was too much for me, too. Before I completely broke down and cried like a baby in front of him, I got up to go find Mum and Jasper.

I needed to leave. This was all too hard.

Just as I opened the French doors, Cole said, "Do you regret it?" I turned back to face him, and he continued, "Not letting me come with you?"

"Every day," I replied before I walked into the house.

I wanted him back. I wanted to put everything right, but I had no idea how that would be possible or if he even wanted me to. He was still too angry to forgive me, and I wasn't sure if he could ever get past it. Whatever happened though, I knew I was still completely in love with him.

four

COLE

I watched Oakley walk back into the house, and I couldn't move off the step.

She's back. My heart threatened to leap out of my chest. *I can't believe she's here.*

All I wanted to do was kiss her.

The door closed, shutting her off from me, and I felt sick. Jumping up, I followed her into the house.

Maybe I shouldn't have said all that, but I needed to tell her. I hated when she was upset, and knowing I'd caused it made me feel like shit, but at least it was out there.

Oakley stood with everyone else in the kitchen, her back to me. She was taller, just a little though. Since she now wore makeup, she looked older. I suspected if she took it off, she would look exactly the same. She still had the angelic face and soft, smooth skin. Her hair was down to her waist and streaked with lighter blonde highlights.

"Where's Mia?" Oakley asked my mum.

The sound of her voice made the hairs on the back of my neck stand up. She really did have a *very* sexy, husky voice. I wanted to grab her, carry her to my room, lock the door, and make up for lost time.

"She'll be back soon. She's just taken Fifi to Fun to Play."

Oakley turned, following Mum as she moved to the fridge. She frowned. "Taken who to what?"

I laughed and stepped forward, just a little bit closer. She turned around and took a deep breath.

"Leona. She's taken Leona to one of those indoor soft play centres," I replied.

Oakley nodded, biting her bottom lip. Her beautiful blue eyes were slightly glazed over from crying.

"I don't think they'll be long. Are you staying to wait for her?" Mum asked.

I carefully watched Oakley's reaction. She looked so torn.

Sarah, Oakley's mum, touched Mum's arm and smiled. "We have time. I'd love to see Mia again and meet Leona."

I could have kissed her.

Oakley smiled at her mum, that fake little smile that didn't reach her eyes.

She doesn't want to stay.

Not that I could be surprised after our conversation. She had to know that she was wrong, and I was never better off without her in my life.

What she'd said about not being good enough for me was just ridiculous. I hated that she felt that way about herself. I should have killed Oakley's father, Max, and his bastard friend, Frank, when I'd had the chance. They deserved to rot in prison for what they had done.

"Dude, your hair looked better before," Jasper said, staring at my head.

"Thanks, Jasper. Missed you, too."

Jasper's eyes flicked to his sister. They looked like they were having some weird silent conversation. Finally, she nodded and rolled her eyes.

And that means what?

Four years ago, it was me and Oakley that could have a conversation without words.

"Oh my God! I'm so glad you're staying for a bit. We're gonna watch a movie, so come sit," Kerry said, pulling Oakley and Jasper toward the sofas.

Over the past four years, the only thing that had changed about Kerry was the length of her hair. She was still the same slightly crazy, overtalkative, hyperactive girl.

I sat beside Oakley without thinking about it. It still felt natural to be close to her. She sat awkwardly; her body was tense. It was like she was nervous. My leg almost touched hers, and I could feel the heat radiating from her.

"What's the movie?" Jasper asked Kerry, blatantly staring at her cleavage.

He hasn't changed a bit!

"*Piranha*," Ben replied.

Oakley's head snapped to Jasper, and he smirked, about to say something.

"Beach party," she said quickly.

His mouth closed, and he looked back at the screen.

"Okay, *what* happened at that party?" I asked.

It must be good if Jasper stopped taking the piss out of someone because of it.

"Nothing, Cole. Shut up, Oakley," he snapped. He frowned at his sister.

Oh, I was going to ask her about it later. *Maybe that could be some sort of icebreaker?*

We needed to talk more, but I didn't want it to end in an argument again. Everything had just spilled out at once.

She laughed quietly, making me smile. That was the first time I'd heard her laugh properly in fifteen years. I couldn't help smiling like an idiot.

"You won't be laughing when you're screaming like a girl in the middle of the night 'cause you're dreaming the little fish are eating you!" Jasper replied.

"Jasper performed a striptease to 'Poker Face' at a beach party," Oakley announced, folding her arms over her chest and raising her eyebrows at Jasper.

"A *striptease*?" I repeated.

"It wasn't a striptease! What the hell is wrong with you, Oakley?"

"It was a striptease. Although I don't know if he actually went all the way. I left when his hands reached the top of his boxers." She shuddered in disgust. "He sang and everything though."

Jasper mumbled a string of swear words under his breath.

"Repeat performance, please?" Kerry asked.

"I don't think so, puddin'."

"Did you just call me puddin'?"

Oakley shook her head. "You know nothing about women, Jasper."

"I know enough to get what I want."

"Pig," Kerry scoffed.

The movie started, and everyone shut up. I was suddenly really aware that my arm was almost touching Oakley's and that I could smell her hair. It smelled of raspberries. My heart was going to explode.

Be cool. Don't make yourself look like a dick!

Oakley glanced at me out of the corner of her eye. I smiled, and she smiled back. It was almost too intense. The atmosphere around us felt like…I didn't even know how to explain it. Everything just felt like it was on fire. The inch or so of air between us was too much.

Across the room, I saw Chelsea looking at Oakley. It was like she was trying to figure Oakley out, and occasionally, she'd clench her jaw. I really hoped Oakley wouldn't notice. I knew it would make her feel awkward if she did, and I didn't ever want her to feel awkward while at my house.

I didn't know what to do about Chelsea. We weren't together, and I had never led her to believe that we ever would be. She didn't really have the right to act like a jealous girlfriend.

I sat uncomfortably and forced myself to look at the screen. I should have sat somewhere else. I couldn't concentrate on anything but the beautiful little blonde beside me. All of a sudden, never having another relationship didn't seem that pathetic. Being a sad twat for four years was worth it.

Kerry waved the empty bowl of popcorn at me and raised her eyebrows. "Your turn, Cole."

Sighing, I grabbed the bowl and made my way into the kitchen. I was actually glad to leave that room for a minute. I needed some time to pull myself together.

How can she still affect me so much?

Grabbing the popcorn bag from the table, I turned around and almost slammed into Jasper. He'd just been standing still behind me like a psycho.

"What the hell, man?" I said.

He smirked and cocked his head to the side. "Sorry, dude. Did I scare you?"

The sarcastic bastard.

I glared for a second but then shook my head. There was no point in even trying with him.

His face turned serious, losing that cocky edge. He took a step closer to me and was uncomfortably close, but I thought that was the point.

"What happened? What did you do to her? She's been crying, and I don't like it when she's upset."

"I didn't do anything to her," I replied, frowning. *How the hell can he think I'd do something, anything, to her?* "We talked. There were things that needed to be said."

"Couldn't it have waited?" he asked, folding his arms over his chest. "She's my sister. Don't upset her, okay?"

"She's my…" I trailed off, managing to stop myself before I said *girlfriend.* She wasn't my girlfriend, and she hadn't been for a long time. *So, why do I still think of her as mine?*

Jasper smirked. "Your…" he prompted.

I gritted my teeth. "Nothing." Shaking my head, I roughly threw the popcorn bag into the microwave and punched the Start button. "If you keep giving me that look, I'm gonna punch you, Jasper."

"What's the deal with the new chick? Are you screwing her? Tell me now, so I can make sure Oakley's not around to see it," he said bluntly.

"Not that it has anything to do with you, but I'm not *screwing* her. Even if I were, it would be Oakley's fault. She left me. She moved ten thousand five hundred fifty-five miles away!"

"Right, because she *really* wanted to!"

"She still did it!"

He sighed loudly. "Just don't hurt her."

What? is he really saying all that shit to me? "*Me* hurt *her*?"

"Yes. Don't, or I'll cut your balls off." He looked at me with hard, serious eyes.

I stared at him in disbelief, and he shrugged.

"Well, big-brother bit over. How've you been?"

"Jasper, has anyone ever diagnosed you with anything? Personality disorder or…"

He rolled his eyes but grinned, too. "Not you, too."

"I think, if more than one person has commented on it, you should make an appointment."

His grin widened. "There's nothing wrong with my personalities. They're all awesome."

"So, you all grown-up and settled down yet?"

He looked at me as if I'd grown a second head. "You're kidding, right? Have you seen how hot the girls are in Oz? *And* we live near the beach. Bikinis, baby! I'm never settling down—ever."

"Okay then."

"You got over my sister?"

I glared. Jasper had no boundaries.

"That'll be a no then. So, what *is* new around here?"

"I can't keep up with you!"

One minute, he was the protective big brother, ready to rip my head off, and then he was back to normal, if Jasper could ever be described as that.

He shrugged. "Women have that problem, too."

Raising my hands, I started to walk out of the room. *Screw the popcorn.*

"She's been miserable, you know," he said.

I stopped and turned around. I needed to hear that she'd missed me, too, and not just from her. "What?"

"I thought she'd be okay after a while, but she never stopped looking sad. I hated seeing her that unhappy every single day. Just do me a favour; don't give her too much of a hard time. She didn't want to leave. She was going through a lot of…stuff." He frowned.

"Yeah, I know she was." Well, I didn't know. I would never know what she had gone through; none of us would.

Jasper got the popcorn out of the microwave. "Ouch, popcorn bitch!" he hissed as the bag burnt his fingers.

Grinning, I went back in the lounge. "Talking to popcorn. Your brother hasn't changed one bit," I said to Oakley as I sat back down.

"What did he say?"

"Something about bikinis."

She laughed. "Yeah, he really likes the beach."

I would have liked it, too. Hanging out in the sun with Oakley all day sounded pretty perfect to me.

"This is getting scary, so don't go anywhere," she said.

I'm not the one who goes anywhere.

Shortly after the film finished, Mia and Leona pulled up outside. They never usually took so long, but I was grateful they had. At least there'd been time for things to relax a little between me and Oakley.

Mia's jaw dropped as she walked in. She dropped Leona's bag and ran to Oakley. "Oh my God!"

There was a lot of hugging after that. Leona took to Oakley straightaway and refused to leave her side.

"We should get to Ali's now, kids," Sarah said. "Maybe we can meet up soon though?"

"Tomorrow?" Mum said as she hugged Sarah.

Oakley smiled.

Everyone else said good-bye. I wasn't quite sure what to do. Well, I knew what I wanted to do, but it would be completely inappropriate in front of an audience.

Screw it. I stepped forward and wrapped my arms around Oakley.

She gripped ahold of me and buried her head in the crook of my neck. I felt like I could breathe again. I had missed this so much. She clung on to me, as if she were afraid I was going to disappear. I gently pressed my lips to the top of her head and held her tighter. I didn't want to let go, even when her arms loosened around my waist. She had to leave though.

Gritting my teeth, I let go. When she took a step back, I felt like I was being kicked in the gut.

She stared up at me with those sky-blue eyes and said, "See you soon?"

"Yeah. Tomorrow." *Twenty-four hours away. Man up, Cole!*

"That sounds good," she replied. She nervously bit her lip before releasing it and smiling.

I groaned internally; she was sexy as hell.

"Oakley, get your tiny backside in the effing car!" Jasper shouted, breaking our probably not-even-a-moment moment.

She rolled her eyes. "That's my cue. Bye, Cole."

I nodded once. "Bye."

Mum closed the door.

Mia turned to me. "Well, well, well…"

Holding my hand up, I said, "Don't say a word."

five

OAKLEY

I felt as if I had been in the boxing ring with Mike Tyson. I had been travelling for almost a day, but that wasn't the exhausting part. At leas my first meeting with Cole again was over, and hopefully, things would be okay the next time we saw each other.

"How did it go?" Mum asked as soon as I was in the car and closed the door.

"Better than I'd expected actually. I thought he would shout and chuck me out."

Jasper turned in the seat. "He was never going to chuck you out."

Yeah, I had known that really. He would have had every right to though.

"So, he still loves you then," Jasper said.

My jaw dropped open. *Seriously, Jasper does have absolutely no respect for anyone's privacy?* "You listened?"

"Yeah, of course I listened! Well, I tried to. I only heard that bit before Kerry repeatedly hit me. You wanna do that girlie thing where you overanalyse every little detail? What did it *mean* when he sat so close to you? Did it mean *anything*? Was it accidental or—"

"Shut up, Jasper," I snapped. "What's wrong with you?"

"Isn't this the kind of shit girls do?"

"You're not a girl."

"Yeah, but you have no friends, so I thought I'd try cheering you up."

I blankly stared at him, hiding how much I wanted to shove him out of the car. "Thank you; that really helped," I replied dryly.

He wasn't wrong. I didn't really have friends. I'd speak to a few girls at work, and occasionally, I'd go out with them, but I wasn't particularly close to them. I didn't want to get close to anyone.

"Enough now, Jasper," Mum said, shaking her head at him.

Jasper was stuck inside a teenage boy's mind, and I wasn't sure he would ever grow up.

"Was it nice to catch up with Jenna?" I asked to change the subject.

I saw her smile in the mirror. "It was. I was worried that it would be awkward at first, but it was like we'd never been apart."

See? That was true friendship. I envied Mum a little for having that. But then it was my own fault that I didn't.

We pulled into Ali's drive, and nothing about their house had changed from the outside. She was still planting the same flowers and had the little water fountain in the front garden. It was nice to see.

The front door burst open, and Ali came flying out. Mum jumped from the car and ran into her sister's arms.

"Great. I forgot how crazy those two are together," Jasper said, opening the car door.

Like he can complain about anyone else being crazy…

"Oakley, sweetheart," Ali whispered as she tugged me into a hug. "Are you okay?" She pulled back to watch my response.

I smiled. "I'm fine. Just a little tired from all the travelling."

"Oh, come in, come in."

Inside, we were hugged by Lizzie.

Just as I was hoping to go to bed, Lizzie grabbed my hand. "We have so much to catch up on."

I shot Jasper a desperate look. It had been a long flight. I was tired and ever so slightly emotional from seeing Cole. I did not need to deal with Lizzie as well.

"Go on," he said. He smiled smugly.

I mouthed, *I hate you*, and turned, letting Lizzie drag me upstairs. I supposed getting it over with now meant I wouldn't have to dread her gossip-filled conversation tomorrow. I didn't like gossip.

The second her bedroom door was closed, she pulled me to her bed, and we sat down. "How was it, seeing Cole? Did you have one of those romantic reunions, or was he pissed at you?" she questioned.

How does she even know we've been at Cole's house? Unless Mum had called them to explain why we were running late.

"I'm tired, Lizzie. I don't want to talk about that right now." I got off the bed and flopped onto the futon that I'd be sleeping on by the wall.

She sighed in frustration. "At least tell me if you still love him."

I paused. *Oh, what the hell?* "Yes, I still love him."

"I knew you did! Oh God, this is so romantic. Reunited after years apart," she gushed, making little squealing noises that made me want to slap her. She wasn't helping. And it certainly didn't *feel* romantic, just draining.

"Yeah," I replied sarcastically. I buried my head under the pillow and prayed that either sleep or suffocation would happen soon, so I wouldn't hear her anymore. It was getting late, and I just wanted to sleep.

"Fine. I get it. I'll go see Jas then."

Wow, don't let him hear you call him that!

I woke up to the sound of Lizzie spraying hairspray. She kept going, holding her finger on the can and spraying it all over her head. Christ, that hair was going nowhere, ever.

I hope she doesn't go near a naked flame.

My mind drifted back to Cole. *Will I really see him today? Or at least hear from him?* He didn't have my number, so he couldn't call even if he wanted to, which he probably didn't. I sighed. Obsessing wasn't going to get me anywhere.

"Hey, you're awake," Lizzie chirped, sounding surprised even though she had created all the noise. "So…have you spoken to him yet?"

I'd been up for five seconds, and she thought I might have spoken to Cole already. It took everything I had not to reply with some silly comment.

"Not yet. He doesn't have my number." *Why haven't I given him my number? Because he probably doesn't want it? He said he'll see me today though. Oh great, I'm obsessing again!*

Something hard hit my leg, making me jump. Jasper was standing by the door, smirking at me.

"What's wrong with you?" I protested. *Why can't he call my name to get my attention, like any other normal person?*

He nodded to whatever it was he'd thrown at me—his mobile phone. "It's Cole."

I sat up, almost giving myself a head rush. *Oh God!* I grabbed the phone and stared at it. Cole's name was on the screen along with the time ticking by. He had already been on for almost five minutes. *Crap, what's Jasper said to him?*

I gulped. My throat was dry.

"I'd open with hello," Jasper said sarcastically, winking at me before walking out of Lizzie's room.

Slowly, I raised the phone to my ear. Cole's quiet laughter made me smile.

"Cole."

"He told you to open with hello," he said.

"Yeah, well, he's an idiot."

"Agreed. So, do you wanna go get some ice cream?"

Wow. How easy was that? A huge grin stretched across my face.

"I'd love to."

I couldn't wait to get ice cream again. It was something we'd done all the time when we were younger.

"Great," he said.

As if I'd said no.

"I'll pick you up in an hour? Will you be ready then?"

"Yeah," I whispered, gripping the phone tight. My stomach was doing flips.

"Okay. See you in a bit." He hung up.

I smiled to myself. That conversation had been a little awkward, but I didn't care. Hopefully, things would be normal between us by the end of the day.

Lizzie wiggled her eyebrows. "I'm outta here. Have a good date."

Before I could correct her, she was out of the room. It wasn't a date. Even if Cole wanted anything, it was too early for that. Life wasn't a fairy tale. Things took time and effort, and even then, there were no guarantees.

Jumping up, I grabbed my clothes and ran into the bathroom to have a quick shower and get dressed. My morning routine took a little longer since I'd started wearing makeup. My dad never let me wear it, but that was my decision now. I didn't particularly like the stuff, so I'd only use a little mascara and a natural eye shadow. It wasn't about making myself look better; it was about having the choice.

As soon as I was ready, I went downstairs to find Mum. The smell of coffee wafted through the hallway, and I knew she was in the kitchen. She smiled as I walked in.

"Morning."

"Morning." I smiled.

"You look nice. Are you going out?"

I froze. *Nice? Trying-too-hard nice?*

I had on a navy-blue maxi dress—Australia clothes!

Maybe it's too much to meet Cole in? Should I go more casual?

"You're meeting Cole, aren't you?"

I nodded numbly, mentally searching through all the clothes I'd brought with me.

"What's wrong? I thought you'd be happy."

"Should I change?"

She smiled, and I knew, inside, she was going, *Aw*.

"No, you look beautiful. Stop worrying, Oakley. You could turn up in a bin bag, and he'd still love it."

"That's not helping." I sipped a glass of water, trying to calm my nerves. "Yeah, I really need to change."

Before I could take a step closer to the door, the bell rang. That would definitely be Cole. It had been almost an hour since we spoke.

"Too late." Mum grinned, amused.

"No, it's not. Get the door. I'll be back in a minute," I called over my shoulder as I ran out of the room.

Her laughter rang through the house. I was being stupid, but today was extremely important, and even the small details mattered. I grabbed a pair of light-blue skinny jeans and a long T-shirt. Much more casual.

As I dressed, I heard muffled voices downstairs. I prayed they were catching up, and Mum wasn't telling him I was changing again. He was so close to me, and that made me feel dizzy with nerves and excitement.

Taking a deep breath, I slowly crept downstairs. His eyes landed on mine as soon as I stepped into the lounge, and my heart started beating wildly.

"Hi," I said hoarsely, chewing on the inside of my cheek.

He smiled, his eyes lighting up. I loved seeing him like that.

"Hi."

"Have a nice time," Mum said as she walked into the kitchen, giving us some privacy.

"You ready to go?"

I nodded in response to his question. I could barely talk.

We drove in a comfortable silence. I watched as he pulled his lip between his teeth every so often. He was nervous as nervous as I was. It seemed too good to be true. I was still waiting for him to get angry with me again. He wasn't being honest about how he felt. This going for ice cream was incredible, but it was masking the conversation we needed to have. It was as if we were papering over the cracks, and that would get us nowhere in the long run.

"I'll warn you now; it's different," he said as we parked in front of the diner.

"Different how?"

"You'll see."

As he always did when we got out of the car and I followed him. Cole held the door open for me, and I walked in. I turned my nose up. It was completely different now. Not one thing was as it used to be.

"From that look on your face, I take it that you don't like it?"

"No. Why did they change it?" Frowning at the new decor, I walked toward the counter.

"To 'move with the times,' apparently."

I much preferred the old traditional-style diner to this ultra-modern, minimalistic look. The walls were a warm caramel shade with large mirrors hanging from them. The tables and chairs were white glass and boring.

"I don't like it either. Ice cream's still good though. Want your usual?" he asked.

I turned and grinned. Those three words made my whole day.

"Want your usual?"

I hadn't heard that in four years.

"Please."

Cole ordered, and we sat where our old booth used to be. The seat was comfortable but not falling-onto-a-cloud comfortable.

"I wanted to say I'm sorry for yesterday. I didn't mean to upset you, but I needed to say that stuff."

I shook my head. "Please, don't apologise. I guess you've waited a while for the opportunity to say it. I'm the one who's sorry. I should have given you the choice. I was too wrapped up in what was going on. I didn't want your life to be messed up, too."

He raised his eyebrow, and I knew exactly what he was thinking. His life *was* messed up because of it.

"I would have come with you, Oakley."

"I know," I whispered, looking down at the table. "Can we get past this? I don't want things to be weird between us."

The waitress arrived, cutting into our conversation. She balanced the tray on the edge of the table and passed us our milkshakes and ice cream. My lungs started to burn, and I realised it was because I had been holding my breath, waiting for him to answer.

We both muttered a polite, "Thank you," and I turned my attention back to Cole.

He smiled, and before he could even open his mouth, I knew we could get past anything.

"Yeah, but only if you give me some of that ice cream," he said, reaching out and digging his spoon in before I could answer.

I slapped the back of his hand with my spoon, laughing. Finally, I was laughing properly again.

"So, when do you think you'll move out of your parents' house?"

It was weird, thinking of Cole living on his own. He didn't seem old enough, but he was twenty-two now.

"I'm actually looking at a couple of places next week. As soon as I find somewhere that's not a shithole, I'll be out."

I shook my head. "How are you going to survive on your own? Do you even know how to work a washing machine yet?" I teased.

"No, but both houses I'll be looking at are close to home, so I can just take washing to Mum," he said, shrugging his shoulders and chuckling.

"I bet you would, too."

"Definitely! She likes to feel needed. I'd be doing this for her."

I laughed. I was sure Jenna would love receiving bags of her grown-up son's washing every week.

"Do you have any plans to get your own place?" he asked.

"No. I don't think I can live alone, not yet anyway." I hated being on my own. I didn't feel safe.

Cole's face fell, but he soon turned it around and smirked. "No one to remove the spiders? You'd have so many glasses dotted around the house with spiders trapped inside 'em," he teased. "Does Jasper catch them for you?"

Frowning, I shook my head. "No. Jasper throws them at me, and the spiders in Australia are bigger than cats." Well, perhaps not quite, but they were a lot bigger than the spiders in England, that was for sure.

"You wanna come with me next week?" Cole asked, changing the subject before he started laughing. "I could use another opinion. Apparently, I'm too negative when house-hunting."

"Yeah? I'd love to," I replied. I knew it wouldn't be a date or anything, but I was still excited to spend more time with him.

"Good. Then, if it falls down, I can blame you."

We stayed in the diner long after we'd finished eating and drinking. I managed to drag everything out for as long as I could, just wanting a little bit longer. Eventually though, there was nothing more I could do, and Cole paid the bill. Nothing had changed; he never let me pay for anything.

His arm brushed against mine as we walked to his car. My breath caught in my throat. This was so nice, so normal, for us. I didn't want the talk to come even though I knew it had to. I was enjoying things being as if I had never left.

Cole opened the car door for me, and I suddenly realised how close he was. Our faces were inches apart. My lungs deflated as he stared into my eyes. *Is he going to kiss me?* I could barely breathe. He still had the same effect on me.

His eyes flickered to my lips, and my heart soared. Everything else disappeared, and all I could see was his beautiful face.

Is this a good idea?

We'd only just managed to get back to being friends, and I really didn't want to mess that up. I hated that he was angry with me. Kissing would only make things worse and make leaving him again a million times harder on us both.

"Thanks," I whispered, very reluctantly taking a step back.

That seemed to snap him out of it, and he smiled, nodding for me to get in the car. I closed my eyes and took a deep breath. That hadn't been easy to do. I wanted to be with him again so much.

Cole got in the car and started the engine.

"Er, Leona said you have to come back and play with her," he said, nervously scratching the back of his neck. "I can get you out of it if you want. I mean, you—"

I shook my head a little too enthusiastically. "No. I'd love to spend time with her." *And you.*

"Yeah? Okay, good."

"You're close?"

"Really close. Mia couldn't afford to move out, so she stayed home with Leona. The kid is loud, and I barely got any sleep when she was really little, but I wouldn't change it."

"How is Chris with her?"

Cole made a distasteful face. He still wasn't a Chris fan then.

"He's a good dad; I'll give him that. Would still love to punch him in the face though."

I laughed.

"At least Mia realised what an arsehole he is," he said.

We drove home, catching up on family things. Neither one of us dared to touch the subject of how much I'd hurt him again. That was fine.

As soon as we walked through the door, Leona ran toward me. She looked just like Mia had as a child. Thankfully, there wasn't Chris in her at all. She was beautiful.

"Oaley," she chirped, mispronouncing my name. Her tiny little arms shot out for me to pick her up.

Balancing Leona on my hip, I followed Cole into the kitchen. He made a comment about how Leona would normally have gone to him first and that I was her new best friend. I couldn't help smiling a little at that; it meant a lot to me that Leona liked me. I'd missed so much of her little life, and I had a lot to make up for—and not just with her.

"Hi, sweetheart," Jenna gushed, giving me an awkward hug around Leona. "Come and sit. I'll make you a hot chocolate." She smiled wide, showing her straight white teeth.

"Can I have some, too?" Leona asked.

Jenna leant over and stroked her cheek. "You can have whatever you want."

Leona was so sweet and so innocent. It broke my heart that, one day, she would watch the news or overhear adults talking, and she'd understand that the world wasn't some happy, perfect place.

I sat at the table between Cole and Leona. It was so cute, watching them interact. Leona looked up at Cole as if he was her hero. He would be a great dad one day.

"Why are marshmallows squishy?" she asked Cole.

"Because they're made from clouds," he replied.

She gasped and looked into her marshmallow-topped hot chocolate with amazement.

"Clouds?" I asked.

He shrugged and mouthed, *I have no idea how they're made.*

I loved being at Cole's house; I always had. Going back to Ali's wasn't what I wanted, but I knew I couldn't stay here. "I should probably go now."

Cole stood up. "Right, come on then."

In the car, I sank back in my seat and looked over at him driving again. "You really didn't have to drive me back, you know. I could have someone pick me up. Or I could walk."

"I don't mind. I'm not letting you walk, Oakley. You don't know what psychos are out there."

I *did* know what psychos were out there though. The world was not perfect. It was dark, evil, and full of monsters in human disguises. The world was a horrible place, and you were no safer surrounded by family than you were wandering the streets alone.

Instead of voicing my opinion, I smiled and received one in return.

Yes, I definitely want him back.

six

COLE

It was Saturday, and I was spending the first day of the weekend with the girl I couldn't stop loving, no matter how much time and distance she'd put between us.

I drove to Ali's house at a snail's pace. Oakley probably thought I had turned into an old-man driver, but I just wanted to get a little extra time with her. God, if Ben were in my head right now, he would definitely tell me to man up. I could admit, my patheticness had progressed to a completely new level, but I was in love with her. *That entitles me to act like a teenage girl, right?*

As we approached the street, I slowed down a little more.

"The accelerator is the one on the right," Oakley teased, biting on her bottom lip.

I loved it when she did that.

"Very funny," I replied flatly. I pulled up outside the house and sighed quietly. *This is where she leaves.* "So…I'll see you on Tuesday? You'll come view the houses?" That was only three days away. *Great. Now, I'm back to counting down the days until I can see her again!*

She smiled, and her eyes lit up. "Yes, definitely."

I watched her like a stalker as she got out of the car and bent over to look back in. "Will you text me when you get home?"

"I would, but I don't have your number. Obviously, I'm not one of the privileged ones."

I pouted my lip, and she rolled her eyes.

"Give me your phone then, Mr Dramatic," she said, holding her hand out.

Sighing, faking annoyance, I handed her my phone. This was how we used to be, teasing each other.

This is how it's supposed to be.

My fingers brushed over hers as she took the phone. There was a small smile on her lips and a blush on her cheeks as we touched. It was good to know that she felt the same. I watched her closely as she punched her number in my phone.

I couldn't believe I'd actually survived four years without her.

Nice. Very melodramatic!

"Done," she announced, handing me the phone back.

I made sure my fingers touched hers again, and like last time, her cheeks flushed.

"Feel special now?"

I pretended to think about it for a minute. "Um, no. You're gonna have to do a lot more than that to make me feel special."

She raised her eyebrow and tried to stop herself from smiling. "Really?"

I nodded, my eyes lingering over her lips.

"All right," she said, giving me a cute smile that made my heart stop. "I'll buy the ice cream on Tuesday."

Oakley didn't look back at me as she walked into the house. *Is that deliberate? I think it is.*

Damn, I'm in some serious trouble.

I had a feeling she would still be able to wrap me around her finger. In fact, I knew she could, and I think she knew it, too.

I drove back to my house with the biggest smile on my face. This day couldn't get better. Well, it could if she turned up naked in my room. *Stop it.*

I pulled into my driveway—behind Chelsea's car.

Did we have plans?

Mum and Leona walked out of the door as I started up the path.

"Oh, hi, sweetheart," Mum said. "Chelsea's inside. I'm just taking Leona to get her hair cut."

I knelt down to Leona's height and flicked her hair. "You having it all cut off like mine?"

Her mouth dropped open, and she looked up at Mum. "I not, Nana!" she shouted, looking a little terrified.

"No, you're not, sweetie." Mum frowned. "Cole," she scolded.

"Sorry." I chuckled. Sometimes, I couldn't help myself. Leona's reactions were funny. "You tell the hairdresser to keep it long."

Leona nodded and skipped off to the car.

I expected Chelsea to be in the lounge or kitchen, but she was in my room.

"Hi," she said, looking at the picture of me and Oakley that still sat on my desk.

"Hey. What's up?"

She sat down on my bed. "You seem happy."

I nodded slowly. This was going somewhere I didn't want it to go.

"It's good. You haven't smiled like that since I've known you."

I hadn't smiled properly since a good while before that. "I am happy."

"You know, at one point, I thought I could be the one who made you smile like that, but I get it now. You need her."

She was right; I did need Oakley.

"Sorry I didn't want more from you?" It almost sounded like a question with the way I'd said it. I had no clue what I should say. I was not good with situations like this.

Chelsea laughed quietly. "Don't worry about it. You're not the only good-looking guy in the world!"

I shook my head in mock disbelief. "Liar. Look, we're good, right?"

Chelsea was a good friend and had really been there for me over the last four years. I didn't want to lose her friendship.

"Yeah, of course we are." She dismissively waved her hand, and I knew that was over. "So, what's going on then? You back together?"

I frowned. "Not yet. Well, I don't know if we ever will be."

Chelsea cocked her head to the side, sceptically looking at me. I'd told Chelsea the whole story of Oakley and me many years ago.

"I'm serious, Chels. Say we got back together, and everything's great. As soon as the trial ends, she's going back to Australia. I don't think I could do that again," I admitted. Actually, I *knew* I couldn't do it again.

"You're dumb, Cole."

That took me by surprise. *So, I'm dumb now?*

"You can ask her to stay with you, and if she can't, then go with her."

Yeah, I've tried telling her I'll go with her before.

"Look, if you find someone who makes you this happy, then you need to make it work. Life is way too short. Tell her you love her, kiss her, and get her back. You'll regret it if you don't. Anyway, I gotta go. Good luck with Oakley. You should invite her and her weird brother along tomorrow night."

Did she just come here to say all that?

"Yeah, thanks."

Chelsea skipped out of my room, waving her hand over her shoulder.

I should invite Oakley tomorrow. I had never seen her on a proper night out before. *Does she drink now?* I couldn't imagine it. Chuckling to myself, I dialled her number. *Wait, should I ring her so soon after dropping her off? Damn, am I the stalker ex now?*

"You made it then?" Oakley said on the phone, sounding amused.

"No hello?"

"Hello, Cole," she replied sarcastically.

Thankfully, she couldn't see me because I was smiling like an idiot again.

"You and Jasper are coming out with us tomorrow night."

I didn't give her an option. She needed a night out, and I needed to see her.

"If it's a strip club, I'm walking straight out of there."

I could practically see her grinning. It was still a little strange, hearing her speak. I would usually just look at her expressions and reactions to know what she was thinking.

"Prude!" I teased. "No strip club, I promise. We're just going to a couple of clubs."

"Okay, we'll come."

"I'll pick you up at eight. Wear something short," I said, hanging up and laughing to myself. I'd bet she was blushing.

Less than a minute later, I received a text message from Oakley, a one-worded text that made me smile from ear to ear.

Behave!

The rest of the day, I spent with Leona, helping her draw princess castles. I didn't even care that I was wearing a pink tiara while we drew. Nothing could remove the smile from my face.

Once I'd finished drawing the princess in front of the golden castle, I gave it to Leona for her approval. "What do you think, Fifi?"

"It's Princess Oaley," she chirped, smiling at me with one of those wide smiles where you could see all her teeth.

Oakley? I looked down at the picture, and Leona was right. I'd drawn the princess with long blonde hair and blue eyes.

"Er, yeah." *Damn it. Now, I'm drawing her!*

"Do you love Oaley?" Leona asked bluntly.

I loved how kids had absolutely no tact at all, kind of like Jasper.

"Yeah, I do."

"Tan I be bridesmaid? Jessa was, and I want to be one, too."

God, the bridesmaid thing again.

Leona was absolutely devastated that her friend Jessa was a princess bridesmaid, and she hadn't ever been one. She'd even tried convincing Mia to get married, so she could be a princess for the day.

Leona looked up at me with hopeful big eyes, the ones that expected me to magically make all her wishes come true.

How do I tell her that I don't think I'll ever be lucky enough to get Oakley back, let alone marry her?

I pulled her on my lap, and she immediately started rearranging the stupid tiara on my head.

"When I get married, you can be the princess bridesmaid."

She squealed and threw her arms around my neck, squeezing tight.

Leona distracted me for a while, but as soon as she went to bed, my mind wandered back to Oakley. Again.

So that I wouldn't call her for any reason, even to just hear her voice, I showered and played the PlayStation until I was tired enough to go to sleep.

I gulped, raking my eyes over Oakley's outfit. She was wearing a sexy little dark blue dress. It sat just above her knees and clung to her body, but unlike a lot of girls clubbing, she didn't look like she was trying too hard. She actually looked so beautiful that I could barely breathe.

"Put your tongue away, Cole," Ben joked.

My fucking tongue isn't out! I shot him a dark look then went back to staring at Oakley just as she and Jasper got in the car.

Jasper sat in front of me, and Oakley sat beside me.

"I thought I said short," I whispered as she put her seat belt on.

She glared.

"I'm kidding. You look amazing."

"Thanks. You look all right." She shrugged and smirked.

We got out of the cars at the club and went straight to the bar for the first of many, many drinks.

Tonight, I learnt something new. It only took three drinks to get Oakley drunk.

She clung to the bar and was laughing at God knows what. We had lost Kerry and Ben a while ago. Chelsea was dancing with some random guy, and Jasper was chatting up everything with a pulse.

"You're such a lightweight." I gently nudged Oakley in the ribs.

She gasped. "Let's do shots!"

What? I shook my head.

"I've never been this drunk before. Can we do Sambuca? I haven't had that one." She waved her hand to get the barman's attention before I even had time to reply.

I made eye contact with Jasper and gestured for him to come over. He was beside us in seconds.

"Jas, we're doing Sambuca," Oakley announced to her brother.

His mouth dropped open. "*You're* doing shots?"

Oakley nodded enthusiastically. "We all are. Three Sambucas, please," she said to the barman.

Since when has Jasper been okay with people shortening his name?

"Is this a good idea?" Jasper asked.

She handed him a shot. "Yes. Drink."

I tipped the disgusting liquid in my mouth and swallowed. She might not have had it before, but I had, and it tasted like piss. Oakley slapped her hand over her mouth, her face scrunched up in disgust. *It was worth it!*

"I don't like that," she slurred, slamming the shot glass down on the bar.

"What the hell are you looking at?" Jasper suddenly shouted at some guy who was standing beside us.

What's that guy done?

"Jas, don't." Oakley pushed him toward the exit.

I followed. *What the hell have I missed?*

Outside, they had a quick argument, and I barely picked up one word.

"Watch her," Jasper mumbled before walking back inside.

Huh? I looked around in utter confusion.

"Er, what was that about?" I asked.

Oakley glared in the direction Jasper had disappeared in. "Jasper gets ridiculously overprotective if someone even looks in my direction."

That guy was looking at her? I wanted to go punch him.

"Anyway, forget about him. Wanna go back in and do another shot?" She raised her eyebrows and smiled, but she wasn't fooling me.

"You don't want to do another shot, Oakley."

"Yes, I do. The next couple of months are gonna be really hard. I want to get drunk."

So, that's what this is about.

She was drinking away her problems. *Not happening.*

I shook my head. "It's going to be okay."

Reaching out, I touched her arm, and she started crying.

Shit! I stepped into her, wrapping my arms around her beautiful body, and held her tight. It made me feel sick, seeing her upset. I just wished there were something I could do to make it better, some way of turning back time and protecting her from those sick bastards.

She buried her head right into my neck and clung on to me.

This would have happened at some point though. She had been trying to be strong and pretend everything was fine, but it wasn't. Even if Max and Frank got the maximum sentence, it wouldn't be fine. This was never going to go away.

"I'm scared, Cole," she admitted as she sobbed on my shoulder.

I held her tighter and kissed the side of her head. *I'm scared, too.*

seven

OAKLEY

Cole held me tight, and I felt safe. It was a huge relief to get it all out rather than holding it in. I couldn't do it in front of Mum and Jasper. Well, I could. They would always listen, but I didn't want to make any of it harder for them.

I took a deep breath and pulled away from Cole. It was time to be strong again. If I were with anyone else, I would have pulled it together much sooner, but Cole always could drag my true emotions out of me.

"Sorry," I mumbled as I swept my tears from under my eyes. Thankfully, I had waterproof mascara on, but I had cried a lot. No doubt I looked like a panda.

Cole kept one of his arms around me. I liked that too much.

"Don't be sorry. You're not the one who has to be sorry. Not ever."

I managed a smile.

"You okay now?"

"Yes." I smoothed down my hair, hoping that would be enough to make me look human again. "We should get back inside."

Cole shook his head. "No, we shouldn't. You want to talk."

He was right to be confident. I did want to talk about it. A few years ago, talking had been the last thing I wanted, but with time, I'd realised that ignoring the problem wouldn't make it disappear.

"There's a crappy little cafe down the road. We can go there."

"Crappy cafe? That's not very gentlemanly. If that's what you say to the ladies, then it's no wonder you haven't had any since—"

"Yeah, all right. Very funny," he replied.

I grinned. My happiness was almost overwhelming. I loved being near him again, talking, joking around, and knowing that there hadn't been anyone since me.

"Let's go. I could really do with a coffee."

"How crappy is this café then? I'm not going to get food poisoning, am I?" I asked as we walked along the street.

"That depends."

I raised my eyebrows. "On?"

"Whether you're eating anything or not."

"Okay, that will be a not."

"Good choice."

Cole held the dull red door open, and I walked inside. He wasn't joking; it was crappy. The patchy magnolia paint had started peeling off the walls, and the white blinds were turning a light yellow. Four rows of dated metal tables and chairs stretched from one side of the room to the other. I wasn't sure if I even wanted to sit down.

"Want a hot chocolate?" Cole asked, leading me to a table in the corner.

Most tables were empty. Only a few people were dotted around, sipping tea and coffee from chipped mugs.

"Is that a good idea?" I asked him. I had no problem with going somewhere cheap and cheerful, but I at least wanted to drink from a clean cup.

"I've been here before, and it's not done me any harm."

Sceptically, I arched my eyebrow.

Cole shook his head and pointed to the chair. "Sit and behave."

I did as he'd said and watched him walk to the counter to order. I couldn't believe how lucky I was that we were friends again. Being back was hard, but Cole made it so much easier.

He returned to the table and sat opposite me. His face turned serious, and I knew the messing around and teasing had stopped for now.

"So…how are you really feeling about it all?"

I shrugged. "I'm honestly not sure. Everything's a little hazy. One minute, I really want to give evidence in person, and the next, I just want to run away. I've gone back and forth so much that I feel dizzy."

"You don't have to, you know? I'm sure they'll let you do it by video or whatever here."

"They probably would." I nodded. "But then I wouldn't face them."

"You *want* to?" he asked. His eyebrows rose in shock.

"Yes. I don't expect anyone to understand, but I want to look them in the eyes and show them that they haven't won. I want to watch as they're taken away to prison—hopefully, for the rest of their lives. I think, then, I'll be able to move on properly."

Cole didn't say anything. He stared at me, making me feel uncomfortable.

"What?"

"You're amazing, Oakley."

"See? That's what you should say to the ladies," I joked, hoping it would lighten the mood.

Cole grinned. "Yeah, but I would have gotten a slap for calling them the wrong name."

I laughed for a second—until his serious expression returned.

"I mean it though. I don't know how you do it."

"I don't have any other choice," I answered honestly. "I want my life back. They took so much away from me—my childhood, my innocence, even my voice. There's no way I'm letting them have my future, too."

Our drinks slammed down on the table. I jumped in surprise, having not even seen the waitress approach. She nodded and walked off.

"Thanks," Cole sarcastically mumbled under his breath. "Do you think you'll be okay, seeing them again?"

"Not really. The thought of seeing them, especially seeing Frank's empty beady eyes, makes me sick."

Cole balled his hands into fists, his knuckles turning white, and his jaw tensed. Maybe saying this to him wasn't a good idea.

"Do you want to talk about something else?" I asked, staring down at my steaming mug of hot chocolate.

Making him feel ill was the last thing I wanted.

Out of the corner of my eye, I saw his hand reach across the table, and then it covered mine. I looked up and smiled.

"We can talk about this whenever you want," he replied.

I knew he was telling the truth. He would let me talk, and he would listen, but I could tell he didn't really want to. I couldn't blame him. If it were the other way around, I wouldn't want to hear it either.

"I'll always be here for you."

Always couldn't happen though. We didn't have an always. Once the trial was over with, I'd be back in Australia, and we'd have a world between us again.

Smiling at him, I squeezed his hand. "Thank you. Mum and Jasper going to be there, too. They're are going to watch me give evidence."

"And you don't want that?"

"No. They don't know everything, not all the details. I don't want them to know all of that."

The statements I had given the police revealed absolutely every disgusting last detail. It was torture, reliving those years and years of hell, and I was not looking forward to doing it all over again, especially in front of my family.

Cole sucked air in through his teeth. The hand that wasn't wound around mine clenched back into a fist. He looked like he was going to explode.

"Right. I didn't think about that. Do you...do you want to talk about that with me?"

He looked absolutely terrified that I would say yes.

I shook my head. "No." There was no way I was going to talk about it with him. Even him knowing it'd happened was too much. "I just wish it were over already."

"So do I."

But I also didn't want it to be over. Thinking of leaving Cole and returning to Australia left me with a heavy heart. I couldn't hurt him again.

I took a sip of my drink. "Well, the hot chocolate isn't too bad."

He smirked. "Just don't use the sugar."

I looked down at the ashtray-looking pot of sugar on the table and turned my nose up. "No danger of that."

"Are you nervous about court? What are you going to say about them."

"The truth." The truth was all I had. No one could trip me up because I wasn't going to hide anything.

"What if they ask you what kind of person Max was? You know, in public."

"Then, I'll tell them he was generous, charming, honest, loyal, and trustworthy. Everything everyone believed. Cole, he played the perfect husband, father, and friend. That was why he was able to get away with it for so long. He was my hero until the age of five, and that's exactly what I'll say."

"How can you say nice things about him?"

"Because it's the truth, and that's what makes what he did so much worse."

He nodded and picked up his drink.

I finished my drink shortly after he had.

"You don't wanna go back to the club, right? I'll take you home," Cole said, reading me like a book.

"Thank you. Sorry I ruined your night."

He chuckled, shaking his head. "Seeing you drunk was definitely worth it!"

I didn't feel drunk at all anymore. The world was moving slightly slower than normal, but apart from that, I felt fine. Our conversation topic had sobered me in a second.

"Well, thanks. I can get a taxi back alone if you want to stay though."

"No, it's fine," he replied.

As we sat in the back of a taxi together, I snatched a few moments to really look at him. To me, he was flawless. There was nothing I didn't love about him.

"How did you get that?" I asked, noticing a faint small scar on his jaw. That definitely hadn't been there four years ago. If I hadn't been looking so closely, I would never have noticed it.

"Ben. We were paintballing last year, and he shot me in the face. It bled like a bitch."

"Don't you have to wear protective gear for that?"

"You're supposed to, but apparently, that's pussy paintballing. Ben changed his mind after I'd shot him in the forehead for revenge."

"Mature."

He shrugged. "It's Ben, and it hurt!"

The taxi pulled into Ali's drive, and I suddenly wished we had gone back to the club.

"I'll see you on Tuesday?"

I nodded. "Definitely. You still want me to view the house?"

He smiled. "I'll pick you up at eleven."

"Great." I bit my lip, staring into his eyes.

Cole shuffled on the seat. The air thickened.

"Bye," I whispered, fighting every urge to stay in the car and kiss him.

"Bye, Oakley."

My heart beat like crazy, and my stomach was in knots. I thought we both wanted the same thing, but I knew it wouldn't be a good idea. I hoped he still wanted me too.

The taxi drove off, taking Cole farther away from me.

As soon as I got inside, I texted Jasper to tell him that Cole had brought me home, and then I went to bed.

All I could think about was seeing Cole again. I had turned into an obsessive teenage girl, and although things were about to get hard, I couldn't have been happier.

After picking the key up from the estate agent, Cole and I arrived at the house. The agent was Cole's uncle's new wife, so we were trusted with the key. Plus, the house was empty and in some serious need of some TLC.

The window frames had to be replaced because the wood was rotting and falling apart, and it needed a new door. I hoped Cole wouldn't be put off because, even from the outside, I could tell it was perfect.

The entrance hall was large with an old-style black-and-white-tiled floor. It had a high ceiling and a dark oak staircase to the side. Past the square entrance hall and staircase was a long corridor with three doors off it.

"This is incredible," I whispered, still looking around in awe. For a second, I forgot myself, and I imagined living here with Cole, walking through this door, clutching our shopping bags or stumbling up those stairs after a night out.

Cole stepped forward, his chest pressed against my back. I bit my lip.

"We're only in the entrance hall, Oakley. The rest of the house might be a craphole," he whispered in my ear.

"So? This room's huge. Just camp in here."

He chuckled and nudged me forward, toward one of the doors. "Let's go in this one."

I didn't pay any attention to what he'd said. All I could concentrate on was how close he was and how my body felt alive again.

Cole reached around me and opened the door.

"Wow," I said.

We stepped into the most amazing kitchen. It needed a lot of work. The units were old and falling apart, but it was huge, perfect for parties and entertaining.

"Cole, buy this house."

He rolled his eyes. "You've only seen two rooms, and one was a hall."

"But if it's all like this—"

"Broken and falling apart?"

"Even the things that look broken beyond repair have a chance at being whole again. It just depends on how much you want to rebuild it."

His hand reached out, and he stroked his thumb along my jaw. "Why do I get the feeling you're not just talking about the house?"

"Because I'm not." I frowned and stepped away. "Let's check out the other rooms."

Grabbing his hand, I pulled him out of the kitchen and into the lounge next door. It was just as gorgeous as the rest of the house—large, tall ceiling, chunky wooden floor, and in need of some work.

"All right, if you don't buy this place, I'm going to."

Cole smirked and looked around. "I do like it, but I want to see the rest first!"

"Come on then. Oh, and promise me you won't replace the floors. Have them restored."

"Yes, boss!"

After making our way through the house, checking out the three bedrooms, box room, and bathrooms, we went out in the garden. Outside was also quite large but overgrown. The patio was broken up and covered in slimy green moss.

"So, what do you think?" I asked, watching Cole look around the garden.

"I like it." He got his phone out, and I knew he was calling the estate agent. "Hello, Margaret. Yeah, I really like it, but is the work just cosmetic? I mean, I'm not gonna move in, and it'll fall down or anything?"

I held my breath as they discussed the structural damage, or what seemed to be a lack of damage.

"Okay then, I don't need to see any other properties, I want this one."

Yes! I didn't even know why I was so excited. I wouldn't be living in the gorgeous house. Soon, I wouldn't even be in the same time zone.

Cole hung up and slipped his phone in his pocket.

"You're buying it?"

He nodded. "You're helping. You're staying here until stupid o'clock in the morning, painting and tiling. You're working for hot chocolate and ice cream."

I laughed. "Deal. Wait, how quickly can you move in?"

"Fairly quickly. There's no chain, so I've just got to wait for all the legal shit to be completed." He shook his head and smiled. "I can't believe I've just bought this hole!"

"It won't be a hole!"

"I know. I wanted a project, and I've certainly got one." He looked up at the house—at *his* house. "Man, I can't wait to move in now."

"Well, let's get started. You drive to some boring DIY store, and we can pick up paint charts. Ooh, and look at kitchens and bathrooms!"

We were getting way ahead of ourselves. The sale should be quick since Cole had the funds in place and the house was a straightforward sale. Still, this was a bit premature. But it would be fun to plan with him for a little while.

He groaned. "You're going to be a nightmare, aren't you?"

"Absolutely. Come on."

We arrived back at Cole's house—well, his parents' house—loaded with brochures and paint charts from every brand.

"How did it go?" Jenna asked as we walked in his soon-to-be old house.

"Great. I'm a hundred and twenty-three grand poorer," he replied sarcastically.

It was a steal at that price—although he was going to spend quite a bit doing it up.

"But you have an amazing house," I countered.

"First, I have a project. A damn time-consuming expensive project."

"You're so negative, sweetheart. We'll all help you decorate and do whatever else it needs," Jenna said.

"What are we detoatin'?" Leona asked, rubbing her eyes.

"Uncle Cole's new house."

Leona's bottom lip stuck out, and she looked up at Cole with pleading big eyes. "I want you to live here."

Cole rolled his eyes at his mum and picked Leona up. "I'll come see you all the time, and you can stay at mine whenever you want, okay?"

She nodded and flung her arms around his neck. I didn't blame her for getting upset. I would hate not seeing him all the time. I *did* hate it.

I spent a little more time with Cole, Leona, and Jenna, talking about the house, before going back to Ali's. I wanted to stay longer, but I didn't want to push it.

Mum's hired car was the only one in the drive, so Ali and Lizzie had obviously gone out.

Cole left once I got to the front door.

"You back with him yet?" Jasper asked as soon as I walked in the house.

"Hello to you, too."

He cocked his head to the side, waiting for an answer.

"No, Jasper."

"You two are stupid."

I glared at him and walked away. I wasn't in the mood for Jasper's Cole talk.

"It's gonna happen eventually," he said.

I had an hour before I would have to leave to meet up with my lawyer, Linda. So that I wouldn't have to spend it arguing with Jasper over what I should do about Cole, I grabbed a magazine off Lizzie's desk and lay on the futon to read it.

When I couldn't put it off any longer, I went downstairs. Mum and Jasper had offered to come with me, but I honestly didn't want them to. I was still hoping they would change their minds about being in court while I gave evidence. I understood they wanted to be there—hopefully, to watch *my father* go down—but I hated the thought of them hearing everything that had happened with Frank.

"Hi, honey," Mum said. Her voice was soft, the same one she'd used for me as a child.

I smiled. "Hey."

"Are you sure you don't want us to come?" Jasper asked, getting straight to the point.

"I'm sure."

Mum sighed. "We don't mind. We want to be there for you."

"I know, but the best way you can help me is by letting me do this alone. Please?"

Mum nodded, agreeing, as I'd thought she would. Jasper frowned, but I knew he had given in. Running away would be easier, and I wanted nothing more than to be back in Australia, but that would solve nothing.

The doorbell rang, breaking me from my thoughts.

"I got it!" Jasper shouted even though we were all in the same room.

Jasper soon returned to the kitchen, followed by Cole. I immediately felt a little better.

"Call me if you need anything. Jasper, you can come and help me at the supermarket," Mum said.

"What?" Jasper said.

Mum started to usher him out of the room.

"Ah, you're giving them time alone," he said.

I sighed.

"Love you. Call if you need me." Mum kissed my forehead.

"Shouldn't you be working?" I asked Cole.

Cole had taken a half-day holiday to view the house, but he was supposed to go back in the afternoon.

"So, you've given up on the hello thing altogether," he teased, leaning on the breakfast bar.

I smiled. "Only with you! Seriously, why aren't you at work? Did they finally realise what they'd done, hiring you in the first place?"

"Ha-ha. I've actually come to take you to your appointment. Jasper told me about it."

He held his hand up as I was about to tell him it was unnecessary.

Did my mother ask him to?

"Shh, no arguing. I'm taking you. I'll wait outside if you want me to, but I'm going. If I have to, I'll just stalk you there."

"Creeper."

"Shut up, and get in the car." He tried to sound stern, but a little smile let him down.

I grinned. "Fine."

We drove in silence, and I was fairly relaxed for what I was about to be discussing. However, when we parked outside Linda's office, I felt sick.

"It's gonna be okay," Cole said, rubbing the back of my hand with his thumb. "If you want me to come in, I will."

"Thanks." My throat was dry, making my voice hoarse. I could do this though. It was just about what was going to happen. I wasn't actually going to see my father or Frank in my lawyer's office. "Okay, let's just get this over with."

I got out and followed Cole inside, sticking to him like glue. He was safety, and I didn't want to let him go.

Linda stood by the reception desk, putting blue files in a wooden tray. She looked up. "Hello, Oakley. Come on through."

She was a petite lady with prematurely greying long hair. She looked like more of a teacher than a lawyer, but her looks were very deceiving. The woman was like a shark in court, apparently. I had every faith that she would get both of them sent to prison.

"Thank you." I looked up to Cole, nervously biting on my lip. "Come with me?"

He squeezed my hand. "Course I will."

Cole and I sat opposite Linda. My stomach felt like it was tipping upside down. I was being stupid. I was only here to talk about what was going to happen when the trial started; that was it.

Reaching out, I grabbed Cole's hand, holding it in a death grip.

I took a deep breath. "So, what's going to happen then?"

"Well, as you know, the trial is starting in just under two weeks. I'm not exactly sure when you'll be giving evidence yet though." She frowned. "This is a very complex case, but I predict it'll take roughly three or four weeks; it just depends on how cooperative Mr Farrell is. His lawyer also has a long list of witnesses to call."

"They're still pleading not guilty, aren't they?"

Linda dismissively waved her hand. "Don't worry about that. Their plea is a joke; there's too much evidence against them. The jury can't ignore that. There are five girls, including you, giving evidence against your father. This trial will be a long one, but you have the truth on your side and a lot of people willing to back it up."

Linda was so positive. I supposed she had to be, but we all knew guilty people walked free occasionally.

"So, you have complete confidence then? They won't get away with it?" I didn't know what I would do if they walked free, if they could just carry on with their lives like nothing had happened. I didn't think I would ever be able to come back to England if they did. I couldn't face the possibility of running into them.

"I have confidence, yes." She leant forward. "I believe you, Oakley, and I believe justice will be served, but I can't promise."

"How close will they be to me?" I whispered. A shudder ran through my body. The same room was too close, but there was no way around that.

"They won't be close to you. I *can* promise you that. There is no way they can get near you. You'll be safe, but if at any point, it becomes too much, I can ask for a break."

"Okay. Thank you. What if they try talking to me?"

"They won't be allowed to. They will be severely warned not to. If they attempt to, there will be consequences. It would look incredibly bad on their part if they tried anything like that."

I let out a deep breath. *Thank God.*

"How long are we looking at them getting?" Cole asked, frowning angrily.

"I'm going to ask that the judge considers the maximum sentence."

"Good. Just a shame, we don't still have the death sentence," he said.

I squeezed Cole's hand. He was getting worked up.

Once Linda explained everything, we stood up. I was relieved to be leaving.

"I'll be in touch soon if anything has changed. You can call me if you think of anything else."

"Thank you."

"Thanks," Cole replied.

We stepped out of the building, and I felt more scared than before. It was getting way too real now. I could no longer say it was months off or ages away; it was soon.

I turned to Cole, and he wrapped his arms around me.

I gripped ahold of him and buried my head in his chest.

"It's going to be okay. I'll be with you; I promise." His lips pressed against the top of my head. "I never stopped loving you, Oakley," he whispered into my hair.

I smiled and gripped him harder, needing to be closer. "I never stopped loving you."

eight

COLE

"*I never stopped loving you.*"

Those five words made me feel a thousand feet tall. I knew she hadn't moved on or met someone else, but hearing the words meant everything.

She pulled back and gave me a weak smile.

"You gonna be okay?" I asked, trying to hold off from kissing her.

"I'll be fine," she whispered, still gripping on to my T-shirt.

Her actions contradicted her words.

"I need ice cream. Do you have to get back to work, or do you have some time?"

"I'm yours all day."

Oakley smiled, and that playful glint returned to her eyes. "They did fire you, didn't they?"

"Why would they fire me? I'm a fucking legend!"

She laughed, quickly covering it up with a cough. That was what I wanted though—to make her laugh.

"I took a day's holiday actually."

"You took a day off work, so you could come with me?"

I wasn't sure if I should be a little insulted that she was surprised. Of course I had taken the day off to go with her.

"Yeah," I replied.

"Thank you."

"Anytime. Now, let's go get some ice cream." I instinctively grabbed her hand and led her toward my car.

Her hand in mine felt so natural. When we were together like this, it felt like we'd never been apart.

Oakley scrunched her nose up. "I don't like the new place. They should change it back."

"Yeah, I know. They won't though. I already requested."

"Really? They wouldn't rip out all the new stuff and replace it with the old?" she asked, cocking her head to the side.

"You're so sarcastic now. Australia was a bad influence on you."

She shook her head. "It's not Australia. You just make it easy."

Before I could react, she pulled her hand out of mine and shot around to the passenger side of my car, laughing her beautiful head off. Seeing her smile and hearing her laugh was completely worth her teasing the crap out of me.

"Shut up, and get in the car," I said, repeating my words from earlier.

"Shut up, and unlock the car," she countered.

I tried not to grin as I unlocked the door. As soon as her hand reached out to grab the handle, I locked it again.

"How old are you, Cole?"

Chuckling to myself, I unlocked it again and got in.

"You missed the turn," Oakley pointed out as I purposefully drove past the ice cream parlour.

"I know. We're going somewhere else."

"I knew it! Gay club, right?"

"You're insulting yourself there, Oaks."

She mumbled something under her breath that I couldn't understand. Messing around with her had been fun before, but now, she had the confidence to properly give it back, and I loved it.

I parked in my drive and suddenly felt nervous. *What if she thinks I'm some sort of weird creep?*

"We're having ice cream at your house?"

"Yeah. Come on."

Oakley followed me to the kitchen where I made two milkshakes and two bowls of ice cream.

"Okay, follow me," I mumbled.

She looked at me like I was crazy as I got her to hold the tray while I opened the garage door.

"We're having ice cream in your garage?"

"Trust me."

I took the tray from her and led her around the old wardrobes, car parts, and cardboard boxes. Taking a shaky breath, I walked around the clothes rail and stopped as I saw it. She gasped, and I knew she'd seen it, too.

"What…" Oakley trailed off.

I didn't turn around. I was scared to see whatever look she had on her face right now.

"Why is this here?"

Finding some courage, I turned to face her. "I bought it."

Her eyebrows shot up. "You bought our booth?"

At the back of the garage, tucked away in the corner, was our booth. The owners had sold the old booths, tables, and chairs when they did the remodelling, and I'd bought the one we'd spent so much time in. It was kind of stupid, but it felt like the last little bit of her left to me, and I couldn't let it go.

"Yeah, I bought it."

She nodded, staring at me, dumbfounded.

Okay, this is bad. I shouldn't have brought her here. I should have just kept it to myself.

Finally, after a few of the longest minutes of my life, she smiled. "I can't believe you did that."

She walked past me and sat down on her usual side, and I sighed. She was sitting and not running.

I had not been that scared in a while, not since Mia's water had broken when we were home, alone.

"Well, I didn't want someone else to have their smelly arse on our booth."

"Why would they have a smelly…" She shook her head. "Actually, never mind. Gimme the ice cream!"

Chuckling, I set her milkshake and ice cream down in front of her, doing a little bow.

"You're dismissed," she said, playing along and waving her hand at me.

"What am I? Your bitch?"

Her silence and smug smile said it all.

"So, how much did you pay for it?"

Dilemma. Do I tell her the truth and make her think I'm unstable and a bit of an obsessive stalker? Or lie, so I don't look too bad?

I sighed, not really having a choice. I couldn't lie to her. "I paid two hundred."

"Pounds?" she blurted out, her eyes widening in disbelief.

"No Euros," I replied sarcastically.

She stared blankly and dug her spoon into the ice cream.

"Wow, two hundred pounds. They saw you coming. It's barely worth fifty!"

"I changed my mind. I didn't miss you."

Oakley grinned and shook her head. "Liar."

Every single time I looked at her, I wanted to beg her to give us another chance. We could make it work. I would give up everything and move to Australia if she still wanted to live there. Something stopped me from bringing up the subject, and that was the thought of her saying no. It'd hurt so much the first time. I couldn't do it again. *She loves me, but that wasn't enough four years ago, so why would it be enough now?*

I groaned and sat back in the seat. There was nothing I could do right now. I didn't want to push it.

"What are you thinking? Your face has gone all serious."

"I wasn't thinking anything."

"Of course you weren't," she said, rolling her eyes playfully. "It's fine; don't tell me…"

"You're so dramatic. Anyway, I'm getting the keys to the house one day this week, so I can measure for carpet quotes and stuff. Wanna come?"

"Are you going to carpet shops after?" she asked, smiling hopefully.

I wasn't going to. I couldn't think of anything more boring. I was just gonna call them up and get a quote, but her pleading eyes worked on me again.

I sighed. "Yes."

"Then, I'm there. Oh, do you know what colours you want yet?"

"Something neutral? I couldn't care less really."

Oakley shook her head. "We can have a look in a couple of places."

"Great," I responded with fake enthusiasm. I thought I would actually rather play golf than shop for carpets, and man, golf was boring.

"You have to buy everything, don't you? Like a washing machine, cooker, and all the other appliances."

"Did you think I was joking when I said I was taking my washing to my mum?"

"You're twenty-two years old, Cole! You're doing your own washing."

She held her hand up as I was about to say something. "Don't even think about using, *I don't know how to*, as an excuse. I'm going to show you."

"You just wanna touch my dirty clothes."

She rolled her eyes.

"Kinky," I added, wanting some proper reaction.

"Yeah, I'm having a really hard time not jumping you and having wild sex on the table."

I leant further back, holding my arms out. "I'm not stopping ya. In fact, I actively encourage it."

Oakley rolled her beautiful blue eyes again. "Of course you do."

I looked down at my milkshake and then back at Oakley. Her eyes widened as she knew exactly what I was thinking.

Hmm, it had been a while since we'd had a milkshake fight.

"You're a grown-up now, Cole!" She giggled and grabbed her straw, too, ready to flick it back at me if I started it.

I slowly stirred the milkshake with the straw, watching her the whole time. Her smile grew wider as she waited for the inevitable. I was just about to flick the straw at her when cold milkshake hit my face. My mouth dropped open.

"Too slow," she sang.

Quickly recovering from the shock, I dunked my whole hand in the glass, ready to wipe it across her pretty little face, but she was already on her feet, heading toward the half-open door.

She couldn't move very fast as she had to weave around all the junk Mum had insisted on keeping, so I quickly caught up with her. I wrapped my arm around her waist and pulled her against my chest.

She grabbed my arm, holding it away from her and wriggled to get out of my grip.

"Stop struggling, Oakley. It's happening."

"No! Cole!"

"I'll give up if you say sorry."

"Not a chance," she mumbled, laughing.

I managed to get my arm closer to her face.

"No, no, no! I only flicked a little on you."

"Fine, I'll only wipe one finger across your face."

Again, she started laughing and struggling harder. She was a lot stronger than she used to be. I almost had to try.

"No, Cole!"

Five minutes later, I gave up. We sat back down to finish eating—well, drinking our melted ice cream. She made me feel like a teenager again.

"Jasper wants to go," she blurted out.

Okay…

She had been doing that a lot recently—slipping serious stuff into a conversation. She'd be joking one minute, and then something she obviously found difficult to say would slip out.

"To the trial?"

"Yes. I tried to talk him out of it, but he told me he's made his decision, and he's going."

I wanted to be there, too, when Max and Frank were both found guilty and sent down.

"Why would he want to hear what happened?" she asked, "What Dad did."

"Probably for the same reason as you want to give evidence in person. He wants closure, Oakley."

She sighed and rested her chin on her hands. I knew what she was thinking.

"I feel guilty."

For a few seconds, I was speechless; it was so hard to know what to say. But then I replied, "Why do *you* feel guilty?"

"Jasper lost his dad, and as much as he says he hates him, there must be some part of him that still cares."

"Some part?" *What the hell is she thinking?*

"Yes! The part that remembers Dad teaching him to ride a bike and drive a car. Every Christmas when Dad would make a fort out of the empty boxes. When he took Jasper to the park or helped with his homework—"

"Okay, stop. That man wasn't real."

Her eyes glazed over, and I felt the temperature drop.

"But that's not true. He was real to Jasper."

I moved quickly, sliding in beside her and wrapping my arms around her tiny body.

"The guilt shouldn't be with you. It's not your fault. Jasper might have lost his dad, but that's not because of you."

Oakley nodded against my chest.

"You don't believe me, do you?"

"No one believes you, Cole," she said with a shaky voice, trying to make a joke.

"That's because you all suck," I mumbled against her hair.

Her body shook lightly as she laughed.

Every time I saw her upset, I hated myself. I didn't understand how we *all* could have missed it. Over the years, I had told Oakley thousands of times that she could tell me what was going on, but she never had.

"Sorry. Again. You must think I'm an unstable mess!"

"Not unstable. Although you are getting a little more like Jasper," I joked.

Oakley's moods were about something. She had a good reason, whereas Jasper's were about the most random things. Even when he was a kid, he had always been the joker, and after a while, no one could tell if his reactions were genuine or an act.

"That's the same as unstable."

I chuckled quietly and closed my eyes, pulling her closer. She couldn't feel exactly the same about me as I felt about her, or there was no way she would be able to go back to Australia. *But if I felt leaving her would be the best thing for her, could I do it?* I thought about that for a while. Loving someone meant putting them first. I would have to do it.

"Do you want to go when the trial starts?"

She shook her head. "No. I don't want to be in there any longer than I have to."

"So, you're just going to give evidence and watch the verdict?"

"Yeah."

"Me, too."

"Thanks, Cole," she whispered.

"Stop thanking me."

To change the mood, I started a conversation about our childhood and the time she'd tried to rescue a half-dead bird. She'd kept it in an old shoebox filled with tissue and made me and Jasper bring it worms because she wouldn't touch them. It'd died after two days, and we'd buried it in her back garden.

"He's still there, you know."

"Yep. The new owners probably think Squawk is a cat or dog."

My dad had carved the bird's name into a cross we'd made from lollipop sticks.

"Poor bird. I was really upset when he died. That was the day I stopped wanting to be a vet."

I laughed.

"Yeah, you shouted that you couldn't even save one bird, so you would be the 'rubbishest' vet ever."

She was only four. I thought that was one of the last times I'd heard her shout, too.

I took in every part of her as we spoke. Her light-blue eyes and wavy, long blonde hair. Her full pink lips that I had a hard time not attacking. No one was supposed to be perfect, but to me, she was.

Finally, long after we'd finished eating and drinking, I drove her back.

"Do you want to come in for a bit?" she asked.

"You just don't want to face your mum and crazy brother alone, do you?"

"That's not the only reason."

I was a little taken aback with how honest that was. I'd expected a sarcastic reply.

"Sure, I'll come in." *I don't want to leave you yet either.*

I couldn't help putting my hand on the small of her back as we walked inside. Touching her was too natural.

Oakley grabbed the post from the floor as we walked toward the kitchen.

"Oakley?" Sarah called the second we'd closed the front door. "Honey, how was it? Are you okay? We've been so worried."

"I'm fine. It was fine. Sorry I made you worry, but everything was all right. I was with Cole."

I smiled proudly. Everything was all right because she was with me.

"What's that?" I asked, frowning and turning my head toward the source of the awful noise coming from upstairs.

"Jasper's showering. He sings in the shower," Sarah replied, shaking her head in discouragement.

He was singing very loudly. I couldn't make out every word, but I caught a few "moves" and "Jagger." Jasper was murdering a perfectly good song.

"What's wrong, Mum?" Oakley asked.

I spun around and saw her looking at her white-as-a-ghost mum.

"It's a visiting order from prison," Sarah said. "Max wants to see me."

nine

OAKLEY

I couldn't breathe. My lungs were tight. *He* wanted to see Mum. *Why? Does he want to explain? Is there even an explanation for what he did?* He was going to try to talk his way out of it. If he could get Mum on his side—no, that wasn't going to happen. She would never believe him.

My eyes wouldn't focus properly. I was vaguely aware of Cole's arm around my waist, holding me tight. If it wasn't for him, I probably would have collapsed.

What if she wants *to see him, too?* They were married after all, and she must have things she wanted to say. She never got the chance to talk to him after he was arrested.

"Oakley?" Cole shouted, standing in front of me. He frowned, taking my face in his hands.

Shaking my head to clear my thoughts, I desperately tried to think of something to say.

"Oakley? Are you all right?" Mum asked.

"I'm fine, Mum," I muttered in reply.

"I'm not going. You know that, don't you? I don't ever want to see that man again."

Mum pulled me away from Cole and into one of those hugs that made me feel like a little girl again. She held me tight and stroked my hair. She used to hug me like that if I'd had a bad dream or hurt myself. It made me feel safe and like nothing bad could happen to me. I'd stopped feeling completely safe like that from the age of five.

The night she'd found out, she'd held me, and for the first time in eleven years, I'd believed that eventually it would be okay. That night, I'd felt like I'd gotten my mum back.

"You-you can if you want. I understand if you do."

This trip was about Mum and Jasper getting closure, too, not just me.

"No, Oakley. The only time I want to lay eyes on him again is when he's being carried away to rot in prison."

I flinched at how much hate was in her voice.

"Okay," I whispered.

"What's going on?" Jasper demanded, thudding down the stairs, hair dripping.

"*Max* wants to see Sarah," Cole explained, making Max sound like a dirty word.

I watched Jasper's eyes tense and his jaw clench.

"What?" he growled disbelievingly. His face turned red with anger.

Mum held her hand up. "I'm not going, Jasper. Of course I'm not."

"Good! Why can't that sick bastard just fucking leave us alone?" Jasper paced the room, shaking his head. "What the hell does he want anyway?"

"It doesn't matter. She's not going," Cole said, trying to calm Jasper's temper.

"It *does* matter," he countered. "What the hell is going through his sick mind? Does he think Mum would actually want to see him? What was he going to say to her? *Oh, sorry for selling our daughter—*"

I cringed and squeezed my eyes closed, as if that would prevent me from hearing what Jasper was about to say.

"That's enough, Jasper," Mum snapped.

Don't cry. Don't cry. I didn't want to keep crying all the time. I wanted to be stronger than that.

Jasper groaned. "Shit. I'm sorry, Oakley."

"It's fine."

He looked like he wanted to say something else, but I wasn't up for talking about it. I would speak to Mum once Jasper wasn't around. He would get too angry.

"I'm tired. I'm going to bed."

Cole sceptically looked at me. He knew that I just wanted to get away. I was tired though. It had been a very long day.

"Call me if you need to talk," Cole whispered in my ear as he hugged me tight.

As soon as Cole left, I went to Lizzie's room. She was staying at *someone's* house tonight, so I had the room to myself. I had a feeling Ali had made her stay at a friend's, knowing that I would just want some time alone. I also had a feeling that this someone was Lizzie's boyfriend.

I lay on the futon and stared up at the ceiling, waiting to fall asleep. Thousands of thoughts were swirling around my head, making it impossible to drift off.

The scariest one was, *What if they get off?*

Linda had said there was too much evidence, but it wasn't impossible for a guilty man to be found innocent.

Will Dad have some believable excuse or elaborate story that the jury will believe? It wouldn't surprise me at all if he did.

I eventually gave in to the fact that sleep was not going to come anytime soon, and I got up. It was one in the morning, so Cole probably wouldn't appreciate a call now.

I made my way downstairs and into the kitchen. Mum was sitting at the table, drinking tea. I blinked to make sure I was really seeing her.

"Mum?"

Her head snapped up to me. "Oh, hi, sweetheart. Everything okay?"

"Yeah, just couldn't sleep. What about you?"

"Same."

I chewed on my lip and sat down opposite her. Drinking tea at one in the morning wasn't a good sign.

"Can we talk, or are you going to bed?"

"No. Of course we can talk. I'll make us a drink; this one's cold now anyway."

I watched Mum boil the kettle and get the mugs out. She was too calm. That meant something was bothering her—Dad.

"Are you okay, Mum?"

She nodded and busied herself with making hot chocolate. I smiled as she sat back down, handing me a mug.

"What do you want to talk about?" she asked.

"Dad and what happened earlier."

She pursed her lips and nodded once. "I thought so."

"I know you said you didn't want to see him, but if you're only doing that because of me, then please don't. You were married for a long time, so I understand if there are things you need to talk to him about. If you want answers or—"

"Oakley, I appreciate you thinking of me, but I *hate* that man. You won't understand until you're a mother yourself, but when someone hurts your child, you want to kill them." She wiped her teary eyes.

I blinked in shock. I knew that Mum loved me, but I hadn't understood how deeply.

"I stopped loving him the second I found out what he'd done. If I had the opportunity, I would pull the trigger on him myself."

Mum had never said anything like that to me before. It made me want to cry. I finally realised how wrong Dad had been; Mum would never have abandoned me for speaking out. I wish I had known that years ago, but I was a kid, and I'd believed my dad.

"I'm so sorry I didn't protect you." A tear slid down her face.

I instantly got up, moving around to her side of the table and hugging her. *No.*

"Please, please, stop apologising, Mum. There was no way you could have known what was happening," I whispered as I blinked to clear the tears.

Mum had said sorry so many times over the past four years, but it wasn't her who should be sorry.

"I should have," she murmured against my hair. "I don't understand how you're not angry with me."

"Because it wasn't your fault."

She pulled back and wiped the tears from my face. "I'm so proud of you. The way you're handling everything is unbelievable. You deserve to be happy. Cole makes you happy, doesn't he?"

"Yeah, he does."

"I bet he'd come to Australia if you asked him."

I shook my head. "I didn't ask him to do that four years ago, and I won't now."

"You could always move back here."

"Trying to get rid of me?"

"Yeah, you're a pain in the arse. Seriously though, it's something you should consider if you want it."

"I don't think I could live here again."

Her face fell, as she understood exactly why I couldn't be here. Too much reminded me of Dad and Frank, and Cole's parents lived so close to our old house. Although I'd moved on as much as I could and could now talk about it without breaking down, I still wasn't ready for all those physical reminders.

"Don't let those bastards ruin your happiness, Oak. Find a way of being with Cole if that's what you want. He's one of the good ones, you know."

I grinned. "I know he is. I just don't know if it could work. If he moved to Australia and left behind his family, friends, dream job, and now, his house, he'd end up resenting me."

"You're wrong. That boy could never resent you."

"He might, and I'm not willing to take that risk."

Mum shook her head at me and smiled as if to say, *You silly girl.*

I didn't think anyone truly understood my feelings for Cole though. He would always come before me.

"Miles is one of the good ones, too." I held my breath as I waited for her to respond.

She sighed and stroked the handle of the mug.

"Miles and I are friends. That is all either of us wants."

I opened my mouth to argue with her blatant lie. They were both crazy about each other.

"Please," she said. "Not tonight."

"Okay. Another night then."

"Have you spoken to Cole much about the trial?" she asked, changing the subject.

"A little."

"You never speak to me about it." She frowned, hurt.

Why would she want me to talk about it with her? He was her husband, thankfully now ex-husband. No one wanted to hear the man they'd built a life with was a monster.

"I didn't think you'd want to. I didn't want you to feel guilty."

Mum took my hand. "I'll feel guilty whether or not you talk about it. You *should* be able to talk to me. I want you to. There is nothing we can't discuss."

I smiled and squeezed her hand.

She looked me in the eyes. "Will you tell me how it started?"

Instantly dropping my smile, I swallowed hard. *She wants to talk about that?*

"What?" I whispered.

"If it's too hard, I'll understand, but I think we both need to do this before the trial."

"You really want to know now? You're sure?"

I watched her gulp. She didn't *want* to; she *had* to.

"Yes. I need to know."

I had managed to go four years without completely breaking her heart. Now, I was going to finish the job. She was right though. She did need to know. I took a deep breath and launched into everything.

I didn't stop when she started crying or when it looked like she was going to be sick even though I wanted to.

She sat silently as I told her how Dad had watched everything Frank did to me. How scared I was and how afraid I'd become of my own dad. I told her how I'd blamed myself for years, how I'd thought it was all my fault. When I told her that I'd tried to tell her a week after it'd started, but Dad had gotten to me first and told me not to talk again, she sobbed.

"I'm sorry," I whispered.

Mum shook her head. "No, don't. Don't you ever be sorry. Honey, I…" She gasped for a breath and pulled me into a hug. "I-I don't know…"

"It's okay. You don't have to say anything." I sank into her side, trying to disappear. Finally, everything was out in the open, but I didn't feel much relief.

"You are so brave, my beautiful girl."

I didn't feel brave. I'd run halfway across the world to escape from everything. *Tired* and *desperate* were better words I would use to describe myself. I was tired of trying to move on. Tired of seeing their faces. Tired of being scared that they would somehow get to me again. Most of all, I was just desperate to get my life back.

She took a deep breath and wiped her tears. "I keep trying to think of things, anything that I missed, but there's nothing."

"Because we didn't let there be anything. I didn't want you to find out as much as he didn't. Dad told me so many different things over the years. He told me that you would hate me. You wouldn't want me anymore, that it would kill you, and that you wouldn't believe me. I was so scared. As I got older, I realised you wouldn't, but I knew it would break your heart, and I didn't want that. After it stopped, I convinced myself that everything would be okay, so I forced myself to leave it in the past."

"I believe you. I would have always believed you."

"I know that now, and it means a lot."

Mum pulled me into another hug; this one was tighter and almost squeezed the air from my lungs.

"Whoa, whoa, whoa. What's going on here?" Jasper asked, appearing in the doorway. "Oh, I see—having secret hot chocolate moments without me. I'm hurt." He pretended to stab his heart.

Mum sighed and shook her head in discouragement.

"Sit down, Jasper." She got up to make him a drink.

Jasper sat down. "Sorry about earlier. I wasn't thinking. We cool?"

"Yeah, it's fine. Let's just forget it."

"Okay. So, what are you two talking about? How awesome I am?"

Mum snorted, which made me laugh.

"See? This is why I'm unable to love," he said, waving his hand in Mum's direction. "Well, actually, it was Abby whoring herself to my best friend, but you're not helping. When you're sitting in your big death chair in the retirement home, crying to yourself about never seeing your only son get married, just remember it was half your fault."

"Jasper!"

I stared at Jasper with the same dumbfounded look as Mum. These fine words had come from an adult.

"A death chair in a retirement home?" Mum repeated.

From everything in that little speech, that's what stands out to her?

"Yeah. All those old people have a chair they always sit in, and ninety percent of them will die there!"

I shook my head. "Wow."

I wasn't even going to try. Mum opened her mouth but shut it quickly.

Good call, Mum. It was best not to encourage him.

"What are you two doing tomorrow?" Mum asked.

"I'm going to buy some new games because I'm so bored I want to die. I'm guessing Oakley's hanging out with Cole, and they'll make eyes at each other and pretend they're not minutes away from ripping each other's clothes off."

I gave him a tight smile. "Shut up, Jasper."

"I don't think I will. You should just get it over already. We all know you want to."

"I'm tired."

"Of course you are," Jasper muttered sheepishly.

"Okay. Night, sweetheart. Love you."

"Love you, too, Mum." I turned to look at them, and they were both smirking at me. "Whatever!"

I hated when Jasper was right. It didn't happen often, but when it did, we never heard the end of it. The truth was, Cole and I had been getting closer, and it was only a matter of time before something happened. I didn't even want to stop it anymore.

I got back into my bed, and this time, I was tired. It was almost three in the morning after all. My phone was on the futon beside my pillow.

Will Cole be mad if I call him now?

Before I could think myself out of it, I dialled his number. The worst that could happen was for him to tell me to call again in the morning.

"Hello?" Cole murmured on the third ring. His voice was thick with sleep, and it made me smile.

"Hi," I said as cheerfully as I could.

He groaned. "This'd better be good, Oakley. I was having a *real* nice dream."

"Yeah? What about?"

"Wouldn't you like to know?"

I didn't have to see him to know he was grinning.

"Let me guess…you were naked?"

"We both were."

Whoa. That was kind of obvious, but I hadn't expected him to just come out with it like that.

He's probably joking. Say something, Oakley!

"Wanna know what we were doing?" His voice was husky.

I didn't know if it was because he was tired or turned on.

"If you're touching yourself right now, I'm going to—"

He laughed, cutting me off.

"Sorry, that was funny. Just so I know though, what would you have done if I were? Spanked me?"

I sighed. "You're enjoying this, aren't you?"

"You have no idea."

Men!

"Fine. Okay, yeah, I would definitely spank you. Well, after I tied you to the bed and ripped off your clothes."

The line was silent.

Ha.

"Promise?"

"Oh my God, Cole!"

He laughed again. It had turned into a competition, and I wasn't winning.

"You coming over? I don't have any handcuffs, but I think there are some scarfs around here somewhere."

I sighed in defeat. There was no way I was going to win.

"What are you really doing?"

He chuckled. "Lying in bed, talking to a beautiful girl."

"Really? I should let you go then."

"Yeah, you're kinda disturbing us. There's not really another girl, Oakley."

"I know! There's no way anyone would put up with you," I joked, trying to turn the attention away from my jealousy.

"You keep insulting yourself," he responded.

"Oh, very funny. Oakley loves Cole. Oakley insults herself!"

"Say that again," he whispered.

Oh God! I had just told him I loved him.

"Oakley insults herself?" I repeated, knowing that wasn't what he wanted me to say.

"No, the other bit."

"Oh, very funny?"

He chuckled. "Where are you gonna go now? There's only one thing left you said."

"I love you, Cole," I whispered. "You know that."

"Yeah, well, it wouldn't hurt you to say it once in a while."

I laughed, shaking my head.

"I love you, too," he said.

I closed my eyes, overwhelmed by emotion. Those words were worth coming back for.

"So, you're really not coming over to spank me? You've got me all hot."

And…moment gone!

"Good night, Cole." I hung up the phone and smiled to myself.

ten

COLE

I didn't see Oakley the day after *that* phone call. She spent the day shopping with her mum and then had dinner with her grandparents. We spoke on the phone and texted, but it wasn't the same as seeing her. I was very quickly getting used to being around her all the time.

The following day was dragging like a bitch. Every time I looked at the clock, only a few minutes had ticked by. I used to love my job, but right now, it was just a pain in the arse. It wasn't like I could just take the day off either. I now had a house to pay for.

As soon as it turned one o'clock, I left the office and made my way to the diner where Oakley had informed me we were meeting for lunch. Tomorrow, Max's trial was going to start. I would only be working a half-day, so I could spend the rest of it with her, but I was running low on holidays.

I parked outside the diner, smiling like an idiot as I saw her already sitting at a table inside. I opened the car door, but instead of getting out, I sat for a moment, staring at her, enjoying seeing her completely unselfconscious, unaware that I was looking. People walking past would probably think I was a stalker. Her long blonde hair fell down her back in big, loose curls. She turned to the side and started talking to the waitress.

When it got to the point that my obsessiveness was even worrying me, I forced my eyes off her and got out of the car.

"You're early," I said as I sat down.

She jumped and spun around to greet me.

"Sorry. I'll go away for a bit, shall I?"

"So dramatic." She grinned and threw a menu at me.

"I already know what I'm having."

"Burger and chips," Oakley stated.

I smirked. "No, actually, I'm having the chicken salad."

Her eyebrows rose, but she quickly recovered with a poker face. "You're going to have to go through with that now, or I'll know you're lying."

Damn!

"You can always admit that I know you *that* well and have the burger," she sang, pretending to look at the menu.

"I'm having the salad." *And stopping at McDonald's on the way back to work.*

"Great. I'm having the burger."

"Of course you are," I said, resigned to being tormented.

Ten minutes later, a plate of rabbit food was placed in front of me while Oakley received a large cheeseburger and chips. *Why do I always have to win?* This wasn't even winning. I should have just admitted it, and I would be munching on a juicy cow sandwich right now.

Oakley popped a chip in her mouth and sighed, "Mmm."

I glared. *Why does lettuce have to taste of nothing?* "You're really enjoying this, aren't you?"

She nodded. "You have no idea how much. Don't forget your tomato."

"If you're not careful, I'm going to throw it at you."

And then, inevitably, she broached the event looming on the horizon. "So, you're coming over at one tomorrow?"

"Yep, unless I can get off any earlier," I reassured her.

Then, just as abruptly, she shut down the topic.

We ate lunch and chatted about everything but the start of the trial tomorrow. If she wasn't going to talk about it, then I wouldn't bring it up. I didn't feel like I needed to start a conversation about it anymore. If she wanted to talk, she would come to me.

"So, you gonna call me again tonight for some more naughty time?" I asked, leaning against my car, as we waited for Jasper to pick her up.

She blushed, shaking her head and grinning. "Shut up, Cole."

Trying not to laugh, I placed my hands on the glass on either side of her body. Oakley took in a shaky breath as I stared down at her.

"*Sure* you don't want to?"

Whatever she came back at me with, I knew she wanted to; her eyes gave her away.

She gripped a fistful of my shirt and pulled me closer, so our chests were touching. I reminded myself that taking her in a public place would get us arrested.

"What if I do?" she whispered. Her voice sounded even huskier than usual.

My heart hammered in my chest. Every single part of my body was screaming out for her.

I pressed my forehead to hers and tried to control my heavy breathing. "Then, call me. I *really* don't mind."

Oakley grinned and ran her finger along my bottom lip.

Self-control, Cole. Don't grab her.

"I bet you don't mind."

My eyes wandered down to her lips. There was nothing I wanted more in the world than to kiss her.

"Thing is, I'm not that easy," she said, pushing my chest away from her with her hands, making me stumble back.

I'd been so focused on her that I was surprised I hadn't fallen over. "That wasn't nice. You need to make it up to me. And not with ice cream," I added quickly.

"Bet I can guess what you want," she replied sarcastically.

I pulled her back into my arms. "Me. You. Bed. Whipped cream."

"Apart from the whipped cream, that's pretty much what I thought."

She pushed her entire body against mine. Usually, I would prevent certain areas from pressing against her, but this time, it was her fault.

Oakley ran her index finger along the collar of my shirt, and I shuddered.

"Jasper's here," she said, grinning at me just as I had been about to kiss her.

"Hands," Jasper growled at me.

Oakley laughed. "Will I see you later?"

"If you want to. Good. You can come over and play dress-up with me and Leona."

I had promised Leona that I would play the stupid game, and I couldn't let her down, so I would just have to include Oakley.

"Dress-up?" she asked, looking up at me and failing miserably to try to keep a straight face.

"Not my idea."

"Of course not."

"And you're done," Jasper said. "Enough flirting. We need to go."

She smiled sheepishly and stepped away from me.

I hate Jasper right now.

"See you later then. For dress-up."

She wouldn't find it funny when she was covered in pink glitter makeup and wearing fairy wings and a feather boa.

"I'll see you later."

I watched them drive off before getting into my car. Thankfully, I had a few minutes' drive to calm myself down before I got back to work. Being around Oakley was getting harder. She had to see we belonged together. I wasn't going to rush her though. She already had too much to deal with.

The rest of the working day went by smoothly and, thankfully, fast.

The second I stepped in the front door, Leona was there, holding up the damn fairy wings.

Smiling, which probably looked more like a grimace, I picked her up. "Shall we get your dress-up box then?"

"Yeah!" Leona shouted. She squealed in excitement.

Great!

Oakley arrived soon after Leona had forced me into some wings. As soon as Oakley laid eyes on me, she giggled, slapping her hand over her mouth to try and stop. Yeah, I looked like an idiot, but dressing up like a purple fairy was what uncles were meant to do.

"Wow, you look…pretty," she teased.

"Just embracing my inner child. You should lighten up and do the same!"

Her smile grew into a full toothy grin. "Your inner child is a girl?"

I threw Leona's red wings at her. "Shut up, and put those on."

"No!" Leona screamed. "Oaley's wearing the lellow ones."

I held my hands up in surrender. *Christ.* "Sorry!"

"It's like your hair," Leona pointed out, passing the wings to Oakley.

"Thank you. So, do you want to do my makeup?" She bent down to Leona's level and put the wings on.

"Yeah," Leona chirped, jumping up and down.

"Great, makeup time," I mumbled under my breath. This was the part where my balls would shoot back up inside me.

"Shall we do Cole's first?" Oakley suggested, smirking at me.

"Yeah, Untle Ole!"

Perfect.

I sat still, scowling, as they both plastered bright pink crap all over my face. I should get an Uncle of the Year award for letting them do that to me. It was worth it to see Leona giggling and having so much fun though. Oakley, too, although I would be getting revenge on her.

"Done," Leona announced, admiring my messed up face.

Oakley gripped her heart in mock joy. "You look so beautiful!" she exclaimed.

I smiled sarcastically.

"Don't you think Uncle Cole looks great as a girl?" she asked Leona.

Leona nodded and bounced on the spot. "He's pretty."

I stood up, pointing to the chair for Oakley to sit on. I'd had enough of them laughing at me. Time for payback.

The next half an hour was spent painting hearts and flowers on Leona's face and play-fighting with Oakley to add even more glitter on her face. Oakley had pink stuff on her eyelids, bright purple lips, and pink glitter on her cheeks. I'd refused to look in the mirror.

Eventually, Mum shouted, "Dinner!" from the kitchen.

Leona jumped up and sprinted off. She wasn't usually that enthusiastic for dinner, but Mum had promised to make her favourite of mashed potatoes with broccoli sticking out of it so that it looked like a forest on a mountain, sausages, and alphabet spaghetti.

Oakley was staying for dinner, too, so it was like old times. When we were kids, she had often come over after school.

I made sure I sat next to her at the table. I wanted to enjoy having such a relaxed time with her before she had to deal with what tomorrow would bring.

At half past ten, I took Oakley back to Ali's house. I had to remind myself that her being back was probably temporary. She had a whole life in Australia, and I wasn't sure if England—or I—could compete with that.

I woke in the morning to Leona shouting my name over and over.

"Untle Ole! Untle Ole! Get up," she sang, slamming her hands down on my bed.

I loved her, but I was going to install a lock on my door.

Groaning, I forced my head up. "All right, I'm up!"

She grinned, turned, and ran out of the room.

Was there even a point in waking me? She didn't want anything!

I suddenly realised that today was the start of the trial. *Shit!* I grabbed my phone and called Oakley.

"Hello?" she mumbled sleepily.

Great, so not only is today the first day of her dad's trial, but I just woke her up to remind her.

"Hey," I said, wincing at how dumb I was.

"Before you ask, I'm fine, and I will be fine. Mum and Jasper are amusing me until you get off work." Then, softly, she said, "I'm not a child, you know."

"Oh, believe me, I know!"

She laughed quietly. "Behave."

"But I find it so hard around you."

"I bet you say that to all the girls."

"I'm not even going to waste my time arguing over that."

"Go to work, Cole. I'll see you at lunch."

"Okay. I love you."

She sighed, and I could sense her smile.

"I love you, too."

I found it only half-weird that we would say that to each other, but we weren't together. It felt so natural.

We hung up, and I made myself get out of bed, get ready and head to work.

Forcing a smile as I walked into my office, I flopped down in my chair and debated on sleeping for a bit.

Would anyone notice? Hmm, probably…

I wanted the whole day off, but I had a few urgent things to deal with. Usually, I would hang out in the kitchen for a couple of minutes, drinking coffee and chatting to my colleagues, but today, I made a mug of coffee and got straight to work. At a quarter past twelve, I was done.

"It's all finished," I told Glen, leaning against his door.

"Already? I don't think you've ever worked that quickly. I'll expect that every day," he joked.

At least I hoped he was joking.

"Hey, I can work that quickly. I just don't want to make everyone else look bad."

He laughed, shaking his head. "Get off now then. I'll see you tomorrow, Cole."

I nodded once. "Thanks. See you later."

Oakley was on my mind the whole time as I drove back to my house to change, but that wasn't a surprise. I really didn't want to go looking at boring carpets and different shades of the same colour paint, but she was excited about it, so I could suck it up for the afternoon.

As I stopped in front of the house, she came strolling out. Her eyes were tight with stress, and she walked with a clear single purpose—to get away from whatever had been going on inside.

"What's wrong?" I asked anxiously out of the window.

She shook her head.

"If I don't leave now, I'm gonna kill them both, I swear!" She took a deep breath. "And, new rule—don't ask me if I'm okay."

"I take it, you've heard that a lot today. Get in."

She pulled the door open and practically threw herself in my car. "Every *five* seconds I hear it. If I left the room for longer than a minute, one of them would follow me and ask how I am." She laid her head back against the seat, and closed her eyes.

"It's only because they care."

"I know it is, but it drives me crazy! I'm not the only one going through this, but they only focus on me. Anyway, can we change the subject? How was work?"

I shrugged. "Fine."

"That's what you used to say when your mum asked how school was. I thought you liked your job?"

I did until you came back. "I do like it. Just had other things on my mind."

"I would ask what those things were, but I have a feeling I'll have to tell you to behave yourself again."

"Smart girl."

"Do you have the room measurements?" she asked.

"Yep. Ready to be bored to death in a carpet shop?"

"Yep," she replied, mimicking my voice badly.

We parked outside the shop and Oakley took a deep breath before getting out.

Walking into the carpet shop, I fell into my own little version of hell. I didn't know where to start. I didn't want to start.

Oakley laughed at the expression on my face. "What's wrong?"

"There are just rows and rows of rolled up carpet."

Oakley shot me a warning look.

"I know that's what it's supposed to be, but it's so dull. If I worked here, I'd suffocate myself in one of those rolls."

Someone cleared their throat behind me. "Can I help you?"

Oh, shit. I grimaced.

Oakley replied, "No, thank you." She grabbed my hand and pulled me outside. As soon as the door closed behind us, she turned and slapped my arm. "I can't believe he heard what you said! That was so embarrassing!"

"Well, they shouldn't creep up on you then." I linked her arm in mine, and we walked on to the next row, laughing.

The rest of the afternoon was spent in DIY shops. I was instructed not to talk to anyone—ever again actually. By the end of the day, I had—well, Oakley had picked out carpet for my house, and I'd had some say in the paint. Apparently, I'd had to pick *actual* colours.

"Are you coming in?" she asked as I parked outside Ali's house.

"Are you asking?"

"Did that sound like a question?"

"Er, I think so?" I said, laughing. "I don't know. I'm confused, so I'll just come in."

The house was empty. Sarah had left a note saying they were all at her parents' house, and we could join them if we wanted. As I thought, Oakley didn't want to, so we ordered a pizza and sat in front of the TV.

"You're coming out again tomorrow. Kerry's ordered another night of 'getting trashed,' so I'll need you to suffer with me."

Oakley laughed quietly. "Sounds good—although I'm not doing shots." She shuddered. "Never again."

"So, you don't do gymnastics anymore?" I asked, changing the conversation.

She shook her head.

"Are you still really bendy?"

She nudged my side with her elbow. "I should have expected that, shouldn't I?"

Grinning, I tried to discreetly look at her full lips; in reality, I was probably just staring. I had never wanted anything more in my life than to kiss her in that very moment and carry her upstairs.

"Do you want to start gymnastics again?"

"Yeah, I would like to. Maybe, when this is all over, I'll join a class." She smiled sadly. "And, yes, I'm still really bendy!"

Hmm…

"Prove it."

Oakley pushed me down on the sofa. My eyes widened in shock. She sat on my lap with her legs on either side of mine.

Okay, I like where this is going, but huh?

"Um," I mumbled, mentally punching myself. *That's all I can say?*

"I shouldn't have to prove it; you should trust me."

"You're such a fucking tease." I groaned, pulling on my hair.

"And you've got a filthy mind!" Oakley giggled and lay down, settling her body in between my legs and her head on my shoulder. "Not that I mind," she mumbled against the skin of my neck.

My hands automatically tightened in her hair.

"Oakley," I murmured, closing my eyes, as she kissed just under my jaw.

She ignored me and carried on with planting little kisses all over my neck and jaw, working her way across to my mouth.

I moaned loudly in anticipation of *finally* kissing her again.

Just as she reached the corner of my mouth, the sound of car doors opening outside reached my ears.

No. Fucking. Way.

Oakley looked up, and I knew the moment was over.

"Oh, you've got to be kidding me." I groaned. *This* has *to be a joke.*

"Nope." She pushed herself off me. "They're back."

"Someone up there hates me."

Oakley laughed and threw a cushion at me, which I used to cover my lap just before the front door opened.

eleven

OAKLEY

I grinned as Cole's scowl quickly turned into a warm smile just as Jasper, Mum, and Ali walked in the house. I was just as annoyed that they'd come back at the worst possible time, but thankfully, I hid it much better than him.

Jasper glared at Cole for a second. It was as if he knew what had almost happened. Back home, he wouldn't leave me alone with anyone. Cole was different to anyone else though. He was the one who had saved me. He was the only man I felt comfortable with and the only person I wanted near me. If it hadn't been for him, I would still be that silent girl hiding a terrible secret.

"Hi, love. Hi, Cole," Mum said.

"Hey. How are Nan and Granddad?"

"Good. They miss you. We'll have to go over there again soon."

I nodded in agreement. It wasn't actually that long ago when I had seen them, but I supposed they hadn't gotten their fix since we'd come back.

"You two had a good evening?" Mum asked.

"It *was* great," Cole replied, putting a little too much emphasis on the word *was.*

"Where's Lizzie?" I asked before anyone could pick up on his tone.

"Staying at a *friend's*," Ali replied.

"Guess who we ran into outside Nan's?" Mum whispered as Jasper went to the bathroom.

Cole smirked. "Angelina Jolie?"

"How did you know?" Mum replied sarcastically. "Abby."

"Jasper's cheating ex?" Cole asked.

I slapped his arm. Thankfully, Jasper wasn't in the room to hear that.

"How is she?" I asked.

"She's doing well. Working at your old school full-time now. She lives just along the way from Nan, in the house where that crazy old man used to live."

Mr Johnson was a crazy but harmless old man. He used to walk around the village, asking if anyone had seen his turnips. He had been a farmer before he'd become too frail to work. I'd heard he'd died of a heart attack a couple of years after we'd left.

"Was Jasper okay, seeing her again?"

Mum shrugged. "Must've been. They're going out for a drink tomorrow night."

"*What?*" I yelled.

Ali laughed, shaking her head.

Jasper went back into the room, ending that conversation, and Mum walked into the kitchen.

Jasper and Abby had been sort of okay just before we'd left, so I guessed it was good that he was making an effort to catch up with her. I'd spent a lot of time hating Abby on Jasper's behalf, but the past four years had taught me not to hold a grudge. Life had thrown too much crap at us as it was, so why hold on to something negative if we didn't have to?

I snuggled back into the sofa, pressing my side against Cole's. The brief conversation with my family had made it possible for this gesture to be comforting rather than electrically charged. *How far would we have gone if they hadn't come home?*

I didn't want something to happen if it would just end up the same way it had four years ago. Breaking up with Cole was the hardest thing I had ever done, and that was saying something. Neither of us could go through that again. Even knowing all that, I didn't feel fully in control. I knew, if he kissed me, there would be no way I could stop.

"So, how are you doing?" Jasper asked.

"I'm okay," I replied, trying not to get irritated by the question.

He sat forward in the seat. "Have you heard anything from Linda yet?"

"No."

Jasper's mouth cracked open, probably to ask me why, but Cole shook his head, effectively shutting Jasper up.

The truth was, I couldn't deal with it. It was already too much that my dad's trial had started today. I didn't want to keep hearing about it, too.

"You wanna come out tomorrow night?" Cole asked Jasper, changing the subject.

"Er, I have plans."

Of course. Plans with Abby.

"You can bring Abby, too," he said.

Jasper glared at Mum through the door. Obviously, she wasn't supposed to tell anyone.

Cole's jaw snapped shut as he saw the look on Jasper's face. "Oops," he whispered to me.

Jasper sighed. "I might meet you lot after."

I turned to my brother and smiled. "Are you going to bring Abby, too? It would be nice to see her again."

"Maybe."

"She can be a lovely girl," Ali said.

Jasper looked away and repeated, "Maybe."

"Okay." I didn't push it further.

He looked almost sad, talking about her. Jasper had carried on with sleeping around in Australia and hadn't dated anyone. I had a feeling he still liked Abby.

Soon after they'd arrived home, Mum and Ali excused themselves and went to bed while Cole, Jasper, and I continued watching TV.

"What are you guys doing tomorrow?" Jasper asked, filling the silence.

Cole shrugged. "Working. Some of us do that, you know."

I stifled a laugh. "If you can call what you do work!"

Cole's mouth dropped open in protest.

"Oh, come on," I needled him. "You text me loads while you're at work. You can't be doing that much while you're there."

"Have you ever thought that maybe I'm just so good at what I do that I can work and still have time to text you?"

Tapping my jaw, I pretended to think. "Nope."

"Right," Jasper said. "I've had enough of the flirting already. I'm going to bed. Night."

"Night," Cole and I replied at the same time.

Cole gasped in full teenage-girl mode. "Jinx!"

I lay against his side. "How old are you?"

It was getting late, and he had work in the morning, but I still didn't want him to leave.

"Oakley?" Cole whispered against my hair.

"Hmm?"

"I need to go."

"But I'm comfortable," I mumbled, gripping his T-shirt, not wanting to let him go. "You could stay. If you want to?" As I waited for him to reply I felt wide open, vulnerable, and totally bare.

He kissed the top of my head, and I hoped it wasn't in rejection. "I'll stay, but I'll have to leave pretty early."

Lifting my head off his shoulder, I was met by his beautiful blue eyes.

"Thank you," I whispered. "Shall we go to bed then?"

Cole stood up and offered me his hand.

Well, someone likes the idea of us sharing a bed...

Cole followed me upstairs. The closer I got to my temporary room, the more nervous I felt. The futon wasn't very big, so we would be practically lying on top of each other. *Unless he wants to sleep with me in Lizzie's bed?* I shook my head. There was no way he would want that.

Chill out!

I grabbed my oversize T-shirt and a pair of pyjama shorts, and I excused myself to the bathroom. Taking a deep breath, I looked in the bathroom mirror and smoothed down my hair. I grabbed the makeup-removing wipes and slowly swept it across my eyes, giving myself some more time to calm my nerves.

Once I was ready for bed, I forced my legs to walk back to Lizzie's room.

"Hey," Cole said, sitting up in the futon.

His naked chest was staring me in the face.

My eyes widened. "Hi."

Cole lay down, stretching his arm out for me. I swallowed my excitement and slipped into the tiny bed. I laid my head on his shoulder and threw my arm over his chest. His breathing quickened as I ran my fingertips over his soft skin, drawing a figure eight.

"Are you okay?" I whispered in the darkness.

"Yeah," he replied.

I pressed my face into his neck and sighed happily.

"When are you speaking to Linda?"

Safe topic?

"I'm not sure. I'll call her sometime tomorrow if I haven't heard anything."

Cole's lips grazed the top of my head. "If you want, I'll be here when you call."

"Thank you, but you really shouldn't miss any more work unless you want them to fire you."

He chuckled quietly. His chest shook beneath my hand. "What if I came here on my lunch break and you called her then?"

I smiled against his skin. "Really? You wouldn't mind?"

"Oakley, you know me. Of course I don't mind. I want to be here for you."

"Thank you." I kissed his neck.

Cole kissed me and held me tighter. "Go to sleep, beautiful."

Hearing him say those words made me smile. He was so sweet.

"I love you," he said.

"I love you more."

He laughed humourlessly. "Sure you do."

I woke up to Cole shuffling around in the bed. He was sitting up, pulling his T-shirt on.

"Hey," I whispered.

His head snapped around, and he smiled as he looked at me.

"You leaving already? Doing the walk of shame?"

"No walk of shame." He laughed. "I have to get home and get ready for work. Don't want them to fire me now, do I?"

I laughed and rubbed my eyes.

"Go back to sleep. I'll come over at lunch."

I sat up and wrapped my arms around his waist. *I hate his job.*

Cole pulled me onto his lap and kissed my cheek. "I know you're going to miss me, but try keeping it together. I'll only be gone for a few hours."

Narrowing my eyes, I slapped his chest. "I won't miss you at all."

He laughed. "Yeah, I won't miss you either."

Okay, let him go. I got off his lap and lay back on the bed.

Cole tugged his trousers on and pulled up the zip. Gulping hard, I forced my eyes to meet his.

Of course, he was smirking. "I'm feeling quite violated right now."

Heat rushed to my cheeks. "No, you don't. You love it."

"Maybe," he said as he winked. "I'll see you in a bit. Call if you need me, okay?"

I saluted and got an eye roll in return. I smiled like an idiot and stared up at the ceiling when he left.

"Morning," I said as I walked into the kitchen. I yawned and reached for a mug.

Ali had already left for work, so it was just Mum and Jasper again. They both stood up.

"You okay?" Jasper asked.

I turned around. "I'm fine. Please don't fuss over me all day. I'd rather just carry on as normal. Let's pretend this is like any other normal day."

Jasper snorted. "Normal."

Right. Our lives hadn't been normal for so long that dysfunctional was normal to us.

"Do you guys want to talk about it though?" I asked.

Mum shook her head. "Not until we hear from Linda. Fancy a pyjama-and-sofa day?"

"No chick flicks," Jasper said. "Unless it's that dress one. That chick is fit."

"You mean, *27 Dresses*? And you know you're a sucker for chick flicks. You loved *Wild Child.* Although I think that's like a teen flick or something—"

Jasper threw a tea towel in my face. I managed to grab it right before it made contact.

"Shut up, Oakley!"

"Don't worry, sweetheart," Mum said, pinching his cheeks. "There's nothing wrong with being sensitive and in touch with your feminine side."

"I'm going out."

"No, don't!" I grabbed his arm. "We'll stop now."

He frowned. "We're watching *Die Hard*, and I'm drinking beer."

Mum, Jasper, and I spent all morning watching films and chatting about everything that wasn't trial-related.

"What time is Cole coming? Oh, never mind."

I watched Mum walk to the door, and my heart flipped. He was here already. I jumped up and ran past her. Mum laughed and went back to the sofa.

I ripped the door open and pulled him inside. "Hi!"

"Whoa! Happy to see me?"

"Are you gonna call Linda now?" Jasper asked, not giving us any time to catch our breath.

I chewed on my lip. *Do I want to do this now?* I didn't have a choice, it had to be sorted, but I didn't want to do it in front of Mum and Jasper. The way Mum was staring at the floor told me she wasn't ready for news yet.

"Yes, but I'm going upstairs to do it."

"You don't have to…"

Yes, I do, Mum.

"I'll tell you everything after. I just want some privacy."

She nodded and smiled halfheartedly. Her body relaxed. "Okay."

I led Cole to Lizzie's room and shut the door behind us. This was definitely what I needed, too. Making the call away from Mum and Jasper was for the best.

"You ready?" Cole asked, gently pulling me down on the bed and rubbing my back.

"Yeah," I whispered. I dialled Linda's number. Waiting for her to answer the phone was almost painful. I held my breath. *Please say he's changed his plea to guilty.*

"Hello, Oakley," Linda said on the fourth ring.

"Hi, Linda. How's it going?"

She took a deep breath, which didn't sound positive.

"He is pleading not guilty. Apparently, he knew nothing of the images and contacts on his email. His Internet history was deleted daily, which he said he had no knowledge of either."

"Wait. Everything was deleted? There's no evidence?"

"Don't worry. The police retrieved it. There is no arguing it was there, just who put it there. Please don't panic; the trial has only just begun. I've hardly even started, and we have you and the other women to take the stand."

There were many, many more girls out there, but only four others and I wanted to give evidence. One had written a statement that would be read out loud, but it wasn't as useful to the prosecution's case as being there in person. I couldn't blame her though. I nearly hadn't come myself.

I nodded even though Linda couldn't see me. I felt numb. "Okay."

"Sorry, but I've got to run, Oakley. I'll call you tomorrow, but in the meantime, if you have anything you want to ask, I'm free from six on tonight."

"All right. Thank you, Linda."

"Anytime. Bye."

"Bye." I hung up and stared at the phone.

How could he even pretend that he had nothing to do with it?

I turned to Cole and tried to tell him what Linda had said, but no words came out when I opened my mouth.

Letting go of my hand, he wrapped both arms around me. "It's okay. I heard what she said."

My world felt as if it were shrinking.

"He's going to get off, isn't he?"

"No!" Cole was adamant. "No matter what happens at the trial, he *won't* get away with it."

Pulling back slightly, I looked at him to get him to explain exactly what that meant.

"Don't worry about anything."

"You're not doing anything stupid if he gets off."

He smiled and stroked my cheek. "But maiming him wouldn't be stupid, Oakley."

"Right, so you going to prison because of him wouldn't be stupid? That wouldn't be throwing your life away?"

I wanted to slap some sense into him. *How could Cole think doing anything to harm Max would be justice when he'd be the one to get locked up?* I didn't want anyone else to have their life ripped apart because of my father.

"I don't think you have any idea how much I love you," he said.

Pushing his chest away from me, I stood up and glared. "Great. Thanks for loving me so much! Send me a postcard from prison!"

Cole sighed and stood up. "You're overreacting."

"How am I overreacting? That's what happens when you purposefully injure someone, idiot!"

"Oakley, will you calm down?"

"I'll calm down when you stop being dumb!"

"I'm not being dumb."

"Yes, yes, you are! You're beginning to make *Jasper* sound as intelligent as Stephen Hawking!"

My eyes started stinging, and I fought to keep it together. The thought of Cole throwing his life away over my dad was awful. My dad wasn't worth it. *I* wasn't worth it.

Cole laughed and shook his head. He stepped forward and caressed the sides of my face. "I won't let him walk away after what he did to you."

Throwing my hands up in exasperation, I glared at him. *Am I speaking Chinese or something?*

"Fine. Go ahead. Do whatever the hell you want!" I spun around and headed for the door.

"Where are you going?"

"Away from you!"

Mum and Jasper looked up in alarm as I stomped down the stairs.

"Stupid, exasperating idiot."

"What's wrong? What's he done?" Jasper asked. He looked accusingly at Cole, who was coming down the stairs behind me.

"He hasn't done anything—*yet*." I turned to him. "I think you should go home. We're done here."

Cole stared at me. "We're not done. Are you going to talk to me properly or just shout?"

"What's going on?" Mum asked, looking between the two of us.

"*He's* being stupid," I replied, pointing at Cole like a child.

"Oakley, you can't tell me you don't understand."

I ran my hand over my face. "We've been through this before already. I know how angry you are but can we move past this I-want-him-dead thing."

"This is about *him*?" Jasper spit. "You're arguing over that bastard?"

"No, Jasper. We're arguing because Cole can't see how—" I growled in frustration, not even able to finish the sentence without punching one of them. Spinning around, I stormed out of the house and slammed the door closed.

Seconds later, the front door opened, and I heard Cole and Jasper arguing over who should follow me. I didn't want either of them to follow me. Swiping away the tears that had fallen down my face with the back of my hand, I pushed my legs faster to get away from whoever was running to catch up with me.

"Oakley, wait." Cole grabbed my hand and spun me around.

I guessed he had won.

"Look, I'm sorry. I know we've had this conversation before, but…" He shook his head and looked at me with the saddest expression I'd ever seen. "I just…I love you so much, and I hate that there's even a possibility of him getting off. I don't want you to live your life being scared that he could turn up at any minute."

I didn't know what to say.

He stepped closer, stroked my cheek, and wiped the fresh flow of tears away. I closed my eyes.

"Cole, please don't. Promise me, you'll drop it, and if he gets out, you'll stay away. Please? I couldn't stand it if anything happened to you. I need you. Please?"

He sighed in defeat. "Okay, I promise."

"Thank you," I whispered, slipping my arms around his neck and holding him as close to me as I could.

twelve

COLE

Kerry and Oakley chatted in the back of the car, giggling about something I hadn't caught. Every so often, they would whisper something in each other's ear and laugh about it. The fact that I didn't know what it was drove me crazy. It was fucking incredible to hear Oakley laugh so much though.

"Shh," Oakley suddenly hissed loudly.

I turned my head slightly, so I could see them better. *What the hell are they gossiping about?*

As they saw me, they both smiled innocently.

Okay, this is about me.

"You two discussing how amazing I am?" I asked, shooting a glance over my shoulder.

Oakley grinned. "Yeah, *Kerry* thinks you're awesome."

I nodded slowly. "You're lying. You want to jump my bones, and you know it."

She laughed, blushing a little. "You think way too much of yourself!"

"It's hard not to when you're constantly looking at me with those X-ray eyes."

She shook her head and laughed. "So delusional, Cole."

"Paintballing tomorrow?" I asked Ben.

I needed to kick his arse after shooting me in the face the last time we had gone.

Ben's face lit up like a child who had just been handed a bag of sweets.

"Hell yeah. Boys only though. Those two can do something else, like have a pillow fight or whatever girls do," he said, nodding toward Oakley and Kerry.

"Why did you say, no girls? We never go with the girls."

"Since Oakley's been back, you two have been attached at the hip," he moaned.

"No, we haven't."

Have we?

We'd spent a lot of time together, but it had been four years. Surely, I was allowed to catch up properly.

Wait, he wasn't being an arse about it. I was the one being too defensive.

"So, why aren't we invited?" Kerry asked, poking her head between the front seats.

"Cole and I are having a boys' day. You two aren't boys."

"Oh, boys' day," Oakley teased, suggestively wiggling her eyebrows.

"Hey, hey, hey!" Ben shouted. "Don't even be saying things like that, girl. I'm a ladies' man!"

I winced as Kerry slapped his head. I felt the thud.

"*Ladies?*"

"Lady! Baby, you know there's only you," he said as he rubbed his head where she'd hit.

"Good. Love you, sweetie." Kerry sat back in her seat and continued chatting with Oakley, as if they had never stopped.

Their relationship had changed slightly since Oakley's reappearance in our lives. Four years ago, Kerry had had to learn to read Oakley's reactions and expressions, but now that Oakley was talking more easily, neither of them would shut up.

We parked in the club's car park and made our way inside. Oakley slipped her hand in mine as we walked toward the bar.

"What do you want to drink then, little pisshead?" I whispered in her ear as I wrapped my arms around her waist from behind.

She giggled and scanned the bar. I knew she wasn't really a big drinker, so I thought she was trying to read what all the bottles were.

"A shot of that blue stuff and a vodka and lemonade, please."

"Are you getting drunk again?"

Oakley nodded and leant back against my chest.

Kerry pulled her away to find a table. "Shots all around, Cole!" Kerry shouted, waving her hand over her head.

We sat down on the table Kerry and Oakley had found.

"Cheers," Ben said, raising his glass.

I downed mine and almost spit it back up. "Shit, that's disgusting!"

Kerry shrugged. "I like it. I'll get more."

"I'm not going to be able to stand by the end of the night, am I?" Oakley sipped her vodka and lemonade.

"Not if Kerry has anything to do with it."

I was right.

After two shots and her vodka, Oakley was drunk. Kerry was tipsy but nowhere near as bad. Not drinking often had definitely made Oakley a lightweight.

"Hi, guys. Sorry I'm late," Chelsea said as she sat down.

She had some other guy with her, who I vaguely remembered seeing around uni.

"Brad, these are my friends—Cole, Oakley, Ben, and Kerry. And, guys, this is Brad."

I reached across the table and shook his hand. "Hey, man."

"Hey." Brad looked at all the empty shot glasses on the table and grinned. "We've got some catching up to do."

"Yes, you do. It's my round." Ben got up, grabbing the tray that we'd kept, and made his way to the bar.

Oakley groaned. "I don't wanna fall on my face."

Chelsea laughed. "Not a big drinker?"

She shook her head. "Not at all. Tomorrow is going to be hell."

Another two shots, and Oakley was plain wasted. She leant heavily on the table and laughed hysterically at everything.

"He's so old now," Kerry slurred. Her perfectly styled curly hair was messed up after dancing and stumbling around. "But *still* unbelievably gorgeous."

They'd been discussing who was or wasn't hot for the last half an hour. The thing that made my whole night was when Chelsea had asked them who the *hottest* man alive was, and Oakley's eyes had flicked to me for a second. I'd thought she'd almost said me, but that jokish glint in her eyes had given her away. She'd sighed before saying Ian Somerhalder. Chelsea had said George Clooney, and Kerry had said some guy called Philip Glenister. I only knew George Clooney.

"Dance with me?" Oakley asked, pulling at my hand while trying to stand up.

I quickly got out of my seat to stop her from falling flat on her arse.

I remembered the first time she'd ever tried alcohol. She was thirteen, and I had just turned fourteen. We had been on holiday in Spain, and our parents had gone out to dinner, leaving us kids at the hotel with room service. My dad's half-full bottle of bourbon was sitting on the side table, and Mia had dared everyone to try it. Oakley had coughed for about five minutes. She'd scrunched her nose up so much that it looked like she had been sucking on a lemon. That was the first and last time she'd ever had whiskey.

I pulled her to a stop as we got to the dance floor, and I spun her around. "You okay?"

"Shh," she whispered, pressing her finger over my lips.

She had been driving me crazy all night, and I didn't think she even realised it. I was trying to be a gentleman and letting her figure out what she wanted between us, but that was getting harder to do.

"You're being naughty," I playfully scolded her.

"I think I'm a bit drunk," she said, rubbing her forehead.

"You think?" I laughed as she nodded. "I didn't think you could drink, but you sure can put it away."

"You're a bad influence, Cole."

"Oh, so this is *my* fault?"

"Yep." She wrapped her arms around my neck.

Our lips were just inches apart. I groaned as she stared into my eyes. She wanted us to kiss, and so did I. I wanted that more than anything in the world, but I didn't want it to be while she was off her face.

I slightly pulled away and felt like crap when she pouted.

"Not when you're drunk," I whispered, stroking her hair behind her ear.

Nodding again, she laid her head on my shoulder.

I hate myself!

"Abby," Oakley said, pulling away from me.

Jasper and Abby were sitting at our table. Grabbing my hand, Oakley pulled me along.

When did they become such good friends, or is it because Oakley is drunk?

Abby looked up and opened her arms to hug Oakley. They immediately began talking, catching up on what each other had been doing. I'd bet she wouldn't remember anything Abby had said in the morning.

Jasper smiled but not his usual unnerving smile. He looked happy. I knew he and Abby had been on good terms before he'd left. *But is there more happening now?* Whatever was going on, I hoped Jasper wouldn't end up hurt again. As fucking weird as he was, he deserved a decent girl.

"How drunk is she?" Jasper asked, nodding toward his sister.

I chuckled. "Yeah, pretty drunk. Don't worry though; I'm looking after her."

"You'd better because she's already been through too much."

"I know that, Jasper. Anyway, what's happening with you and Abby? You getting back together?"

He sighed like he had the weight of the world on his shoulders. "I dunno. I want to, but I'm going home with Oakley when all this is over. There's no point in starting anything."

It was like taking a bullet. They couldn't go back.

"Have you spoken to Oakley? I'm sure she would want you to be happy."

"I don't need to talk to her. My sister comes before any girl. She always will. Don't you say anything either. I don't want her feeling guilty for me and Abby not being together."

I nodded in agreement, but I couldn't help feeling bad for him. I knew that Oakley would make him stay here and be happy if she knew he wanted to be with Abby, but I also got that he was putting her first. If I had my way, they would all stay in England, but this was never about me.

As Jasper's eyes flickered to Abby for the twentieth time during our conversation, I wondered how he'd managed to forgive her. *Is it because the situation with Oakley has now put everything else into perspective?*

"I need to go home," Oakley mumbled as she slumped down beside me. "I don't feel good, and I don't like drinking."

I wrapped my arm around her waist. "I think that's a good idea." Standing up, I practically dragged her to her feet.

"I should go, too," Jasper said, looking at Abby.

"No," Oakley slurred. "You stay. I'm fine with Cole."

Jasper looked at me for confirmation, so I nodded. Of course she was fine with me.

"I'll get a taxi. You all stay."

Oakley looked up at me and frowned. I knew exactly what that frown was for. She didn't want me to miss out. I had no clue how she could think that I'd rather stay without her.

"I'd rather go with you," I whispered in her ear. "Night, everyone," I called over my shoulder.

"Bye!" she shouted, enthusiastically waving her hand.

Yeah, she is definitely going to suffer tomorrow.

I led Oakley toward the exit, and the second I got her in the taxi, she leant against my shoulder and closed her eyes. *A sleepy drunk then!*

"Can you give me a minute?" I asked the driver as we pulled up outside her house.

I saw him nod in the mirror, not even bothering to reply. I walked to Oakley's side of the car and reached in, putting my arms around her. Getting her out of the car was awkward, but she didn't weigh much, so carrying her wasn't hard.

"What are you doing?" she asked, slapping her hand over her mouth as she yawned.

"Carrying you inside."

"Bye, Mr Taxi Man," she called out, blowing a kiss over her shoulder.

No wonder the guy was a miserable bastard. He probably dealt with drunk people all the time.

Oakley shoved the key toward the lock. "Huh. It's broken."

I tried to keep a straight face. "Oakley, let me do it."

"No, I can," she replied.

Sighing, I leant against the wall, silently hoping the taxi driver would still wait.

"It's broken!" she insisted.

"Okay, give me the damn key."

I held my hand out, and she dangled it in front of my face, smirking. As I thought, the second I went to grab it, she pulled her hand away.

"Oakley," I said warningly, trying not to smile.

"Yes, Cole?"

Wrapping one arm around her waist, I pulled her closer. Her eyes widened in shock, as she hadn't expected it. I used her surprise to my advantage and grabbed the key out of her hand. I unlocked the door.

She gasped. "You fixed it!" She looked genuinely impressed.

I chuckled, shaking my head. "Yes, I fixed it."

Grabbing my shirt in her fist, she pulled me closer. "I have something else you could fix for me," she whispered.

I gulped and rested my hands on her hips, half-holding her up.

She suddenly frowned and looked up at me, worried. "I don't feel good."

"Let's get you to bed then." *Please don't puke!*

I helped her up the stairs and gave her the pyjamas lying on the futon. She stripped down in front of me. Her chest and toned stomach was staring me in the face. My mouth went dry, but I snapped myself out of it. I made sure she got into her bed and had a glass of water ready for when she woke up with a raging hangover.

Her eyes slowly closed, and her breathing evened. She looked like an angel, and I was completely in love with her.

Ben and I grabbed our paint guns and made our way into the forest. We had been there so many times that they didn't bother us with the whole induction and rules thing now. Nigel, the owner, had made us sign our lives away, and then we had been let loose to inflict pain on each other.

"So, what are you doing tonight? Actually, let me guess…you're going to see Oakley?" he asked as we walked out to the *battlefield*.

"I'm not sure what I'm doing."

He chuckled. "Of course you're not!"

I really didn't have any plans to go and see her. We hadn't arranged anything.

"What's going on between you two anyway?"

I sighed. "Not sure. It's complicated."

"How's it complicated?"

Is he serious? "You're not that dumb, Ben. She lives on the other side of the world. We've spent the past four years apart, and she's back for the trial of the men who abused her."

"So? What's your point?"

My mouth opened in disbelief. "Well…all of that."

"That's what you're letting come between you? You need to man up, Cole. If you love her, then all of that other stuff will work itself out. Just grab her and kiss her."

"Man up," I muttered under my breath. It wasn't a case of manning up; it was a case of not knowing what Oakley wanted. "I don't know."

"You're scared of getting rejected again? Like when she left you before."

"Thank you for bringing that up."

"You're a fool, man."

Is he right? Is the only reason I'm not giving us another chance because I'm scared she'll leave me behind again? Of course that scares me, but I'm older this time. I could get my own place in Australia, support myself, so why am I holding back?

After paintballing and losing, epic-style yet again, I dropped Ben off and called Oakley.

"Hey," she said.

"Hey. What are you doing?"

"Nothing much. Everyone's out, so I just had a shower, and I'm now watching reruns of *Friends*. How was paintballing?"

"Fun and painful. Ben, the bastard, shot me in the same place over and over. I need someone to kiss it better."

"Yeah? Your mum's pretty good at that stuff."

"Don't!" I yelped.

She laughed, and the effect it had on me answered Ben's question. I *was* scared of losing her again. Terrified, in fact. But I had to take a chance.

"Look, I'm driving, so I'll call you later, okay?"

"Okay," she replied, sounding confused by the abrupt call.

I was nervous, really nervous, but I couldn't wait anymore.

Oakley opened the door and frowned. "I thought you said you'd call later?"

Her damp blonde hair had just started to curl. It draped down her arms. Her makeup had been stripped off, leaving her fresh-faced. She had never looked more beautiful to me.

For a second, I was frozen. She was perfect, absolutely perfect. I soon snapped out of it. Stepping forward, I slid one hand in her hair and the other around her back, drawing her closer. She opened her mouth slightly to say something but closed it again. I didn't give her a chance to talk. I pressed my lips to hers and kissed her with everything I had.

My heart felt like it was going to rip out of my chest. I pulled her near; our bodies pressed together almost painfully as we both tried getting as close as physically possible.

The kiss became urgent. Her fingers dug into my back, and she whimpered. That was it. I picked her up, and her legs wrapped around me.

I kissed her deeply and walked forward. I'd had enough of messing around. I just needed her again. So, I did the thing I had wanted to do since the second she'd walked back into my life. I carried her upstairs to bed.

thirteen

OAKLEY

My eyes fluttered open, and the first thing I saw was Cole sleeping beside me. The cover was pulled down, revealing his naked chest. He looked so peaceful. I still wasn't used to seeing him every morning.

We had been back together for almost a week, and I couldn't be happier. Everything was so easy with him. We could do absolutely nothing, and I would still have a great time.

Being in Cole's house again felt amazing, but at the back of my mind, I couldn't help thinking of how close it was to my old home, the scene of so many things I wanted to forget. I refused to look at it, but that didn't stop me from knowing it was there.

Cole thought I should look and face it. Every single good memory was overshadowed by the bad ones though.

I should knock on the door and see if the new owners would let me look around.

"Face your fears head-on," was what Cole had said.

But I was doing that with the trial. Seeing the house as well would be too much.

Cole stirred beside me, rubbing his eyes as he woke up. I watched him with a content smile until his eyes met mine. He reached out and stroked my cheek. Touching me was the first thing he would do when he woke up; it was as if he had to make sure I was actually there.

"Good morning," I whispered, closing my eyes at the feel of his fingertips gently gliding across my jaw.

"Morning." He kissed me. "I love spending Sunday mornings like this—and every other morning actually."

I sighed and pressed my head into his shoulder, breathing him in. "Me, too."

"What are we doing today then?"

"You don't have to keep me busy to stop me from thinking about tomorrow, Cole."

His chest bounced gently underneath me as he laughed. "You know me too well. Are you okay about tomorrow though? You've not really mentioned the trial recently."

"That's because I've been too happy."

Cole grinned, making that little dimple show. "What's made you so happy?"

"Watching *Hollyoaks* again. I missed it," I replied.

Suddenly, his fingers gently jabbed in my side as he started tickling me.

"Cole! No!" I squealed and wriggled, trying to get away. "Okay, okay! It's you!"

He stopped immediately. "I thought so."

It occurred to me there was something I needed to do.

"I'd like to go shopping today. I kind of have a feeling that this will be the last time I'll be able to do it in peace."

Once the reporters learnt I was back, instead of giving evidence from Australia, I knew they wouldn't leave me alone. The case had become high profile because shortly after the arrest of my father, the police had uncovered one of the biggest paedophile rings in our area. That was the only thing I was proud of—stopping that.

"Whatever you want," he replied, kissing my forehead.

I got up and pulled the cover off him. "Let's get ready then."

This was going to be the last day that was somewhat normal, and I was determined to make the most of it.

"No trial talk today. It's banned," I said to Cole as we walked downstairs.

After breakfast, I went to have a shower and get dressed. Cole's house was empty, and I didn't ask where everyone was because I had a feeling they had gone out to give me and Cole time alone.

I got out of the shower and dressed in jeans and a T-shirt.

Cole was sitting on his bed when I got back into his room. He frowned. "Why'd you get dressed?"

"Because we're going out now!" I shook my head and sat on the bed. "Do you need to shower first, or are you walking around dirty?"

"I happen to like dirty."

"Shower, Cole!" I ordered. I tried not to grin.

While he was showering, I put on some makeup. Every time I brushed mascara over my eyelashes or stroked lip gloss across my lips, it was like sticking my middle finger up at my dad. I wasn't controlled by him. I could finally make choices for myself.

"Are you ready?" Cole asked as he walked back into his bedroom.

He wore a white T-shirt and dark blue jeans. Even dressed so plainly, he still took my breath away.

"I'm ready."

I got off the bed and set down my compact mirror on his bedside table.

In the corner of his room was a stack of large cardboard boxes where he had started packing. In about two weeks, he would be moving into his first house. His and the vendor's solicitors were currently sorting out all the legal stuff, but because there was no chain, the sale would be going through quickly.

I couldn't wait for him to move in. We already had most of the paint he needed and had chosen a new kitchen and bathroom. The carpets had been picked out, and he was going to order a little closer to the time.

"Where is everyone?" I asked. I couldn't *not* ask anymore. There was no way I wanted his family to feel like they had to go out of their own house because of me.

"Mia's taken Leona to her Tots Music and Movement class, and my dad's taken Mum somewhere."

That didn't really answer my question. I wanted to know if they had planned to do that anyway.

Cole grabbed his keys and slipped his shoes on. "Mall or town?"

"Mall. That okay with you?"

He shrugged. "I couldn't care less, Oakley."

Right, he hated shopping.

Neither of us spoke on the drive to the mall, but we didn't need words. I was content to sit with him and mentally plan what I was going to buy. I didn't really want anything in particular. It would just be retail therapy. We pulled into a parking space and got out.

"Where to first?" Cole asked as we walked toward the entrance.

His hand quickly found mine, and we both squeezed at the same time.

After shopping and one of the best Indian meals I'd ever had, we went back to Cole's parents' house. Their driveway was still empty. Cole must have arranged an all-day thing with them.

"Where is everyone?" I questioned. I felt really uneasy with being the reason they had been kicked out of their own house.

"Still out, I guess," he replied. "Want to watch a movie or…"

"Movie sounds good. Or later."

He smiled. "Definitely *or* later."

I slumped down on the sofa and sighed. "Thanks for today. It was nice to do something normal."

Cole sat beside me. "How do you feel about tomorrow?"

"Uh-uh." I shook my head. We had agreed not to do this. "Later, please. I just want to relax with you for a while."

"All right. Come here." He held his arm out, and I snuggled against his side. "You care what we watch?"

"Nope."

He flicked the TV on with the remote and found a movie. I closed my eyes and hugged him tight. I didn't care about the film. I just wanted to be close to Cole.

"I love you," I murmured into his chest.

I felt his smile against my hair. "I love you, too."

"Oakley?"

I frowned and opened my eyes.

"Hey, sleepy," Cole said, smiling down at me.

Sitting up, I stretched out like a cat. "Sorry." I looked up and saw Cole's parents and Mia were home.

Embarrassing!

"Hey," I said, smiling sheepishly.

"Hi, sweetheart," Jenna replied.

"Where's Leona?"

The house was too quiet, and there was no way I would have been able to sleep if she were around.

"I dropped her off at Chris's earlier. It's his night," Mia explained.

I knew she hated sharing Leona with Chris, but she did it because Leona loved her dad.

"Your mum called a little while ago. You should at least text her and let her know you're okay. I think she's worrying," Cole said, handing me my mobile.

I took it from him and started a new text to Jasper's phone since Mum's was still in Australia. "Thanks." I knew she worried, too much sometimes.

I'm fine, Mum. Spending the day with Cole and will see you tomorrow morning. You okay?

I didn't want to elaborate much more than that and get into a full conversation in case it turned into discussing tomorrow.

Mum replied from Jasper's phone a few minutes later.

Okay, honey. We're fine. Jasper is driving me crazy. Have a nice night, and we'll talk tomorrow. Love you.

Cole and I ate with his family and then went upstairs for an early night. Our shopping bags were beside his bed. I had no idea when he'd brought them up. It was probably when I had been sleeping on the sofa.

He closed the door and walked toward me. Something changed between us. It was like a surge of electricity. Neither of us said a word as we collided. His mouth was on mine, kissing me. We were a tangle of lips and tongues.

I woke up in Cole's arms again and managed to smile. Even on the day I'd been dreading for so long, he still managed to make me feel happy. He was already awake, and by the dark half circles under his eyes, he must have been up for a while.

"You didn't sleep well," I said, stroking underneath his eye.

"Not really," he whispered, pressing his lips to my forehead. "How are you feeling?"

"Sick and nervous. I just want it to be over already."

"You'll be fine though, and I'll be right there the whole time."

That was half of the problem. Having to spill every single detail in front of the people I loved the most would be awful. I didn't want them to know what I had gone through.

I kissed him and slipped out of bed, wrapping my robe around me. "I know you will be. Thank you."

Without another word, I went into the bathroom to get ready. I looked into the mirror and sighed.

You can do this, Oakley.

I wished the police could make Dad do a lie detector, so I, and his other victims, wouldn't have to stand up in front of him and talk about anything.

Mum, Jasper, Ali, and Lizzie were sitting on the sofa in Cole's lounge when I got downstairs.

How long have they been there?

They all looked up at me with the same forced smiles.

"How are you holding up?" Mum asked.

"Okay. You?"

She nodded. "Okay. Nan and Granddad are meeting us there. They said to say hello and good luck."

I smiled, not knowing what to say to that.

I wasn't sure if Dad's parents would be there or not. I'd understand if they didn't come. No one would want to hear what a monster their own child had turned out to be. It wasn't my grandparents' fault though. It was all Dad.

Ali stood up and hugged me. "My beautiful, brave niece. I'm so proud of you," she whispered in my ear.

"Thanks, Ali," I whispered back.

"Are we ready to go?" Jenna asked.

Numbness. That was all I felt as we parked outside courthouse. Absolute numbness. It was as if it was happening to someone else.

I looked at the front doors and was shocked to see so many reporters outside. It looked like something I had seen on TV when a celebrity was on trial.

My heart started beating too fast, and my lungs felt as if they were being crushed.

"We're going in on the side. Linda arranged it, so you wouldn't have to face that," Mum said, nodding at the large crowd.

I swallowed. "Okay."

Mum, Cole, and Jasper got out of the car, and I opened my door. I felt rooted to the spot. I wanted to lock the car and hide in the foot well until it was over.

Jasper knelt down. "Are you ready, Oakley?" He held out his hand.

You can do it. Just take your brother's hand. He won't let you fall.

Reaching out, I placed my hand in his and stepped out of the car. "I'm ready."

As soon as I was out, I was quickly being ushered into the building before anyone could recognise us. Linda was meeting us inside, so we stopped a little way in from the door.

I leant against the window and concentrated on breathing. My stomach was in knots. *I'm not ready for this.*

Cole wrapped his arms around me. It was as if he understood what I was thinking.

How on earth can I go in there and face him when even the thought of it makes me panic?

I mentally counted down the minutes until I would have to see him.

Everything came flooding back. I could see it all happening, as if I were watching a horror movie. I was on the outside, looking in at a terrified child as her dad allowed his friend to abuse her. Dad's face was burned into my memory, looking on with no emotion whatsoever.

My eyes stung, and bile rose up my throat. I pulled back, and Cole frowned.

"Where's Linda?" I asked. I wasn't going to last much longer, so I needed to just do it.

"Oakley?" Linda called, jogging toward me.

I turned and headed her way, leaving behind my confused family and friends.

"Are you ready?"

No, not at all. Nodding in a daze, I flattened my jacket.

"Would you like a minute with your family?"

"No, let's just go," I replied.

"Oakley?" Jasper called.

But I ignored him and followed Linda.

I couldn't look back. I forced my feet to follow her, and with every step, even the simplest thing, like breathing, became a challenge.

Linda took me to a small room that had a few chairs and a dark wood coffee table in it. "This is where we'll come if you need a break. Remember, you can have one whenever you need it. If it gets to be too much, just tell me, okay?"

"I will," I whispered.

Someone opened the door. I didn't look up, but I saw Linda nod and knew that was our cue.

Oh God.

Linda smiled reassuringly. "This way."

I followed her through the other door in the room and across a corridor into the courtroom. I stepped inside, and my hands started to shake.

I was on my own now. My family, Cole, Jenna, David, and Mia were all sitting in the public gallery somewhere. I wanted Mum with me, but I had to be strong and do this myself. My eyes immediately scanned the rows of seats in the public gallery. Finally, I found Cole sitting at the end, closest to where I would be.

"Are you okay?" Linda whispered.

I nodded once in response. Very soon, I would have to find my voice. Sitting at the lawyer's table was intimidating.

With a deep breath, I looked to my right. Dad was sitting in his seat, looking straight ahead at nothing. I felt as if I physically couldn't get enough air, like my lungs were too small to take in the oxygen I needed, and they quickly started to burn.

Someone was talking to me, but I couldn't focus. The only noise I could hear was my pulse crashing in my ears. A copy of the Bible was shoved in front of me, and I raised my hand, placing it gently on the worn book. Linda had gone through what would happen with me, so I knew what was being said to me, but I couldn't hear a word of it.

"I swear by almighty God that the evidence I shall give shall be the truth, the whole truth, and nothing but the truth," I said. I took a deep breath.

Out of the corner of my eye, I saw Dad staring at me. I *had* to look at him to show him that I wasn't afraid even though I was terrified inside. Very slowly, I raised my eyes and met his head-on.

I felt as if the air had been sucked from my lungs. This time, they refused to work at all. I gasped but took nothing in.

My lungs burst into flames, and black fog blurred my vision. The tips of my fingers tingled painfully. Someone stepped in front of me, but I couldn't see who it was. The room exploded into life. I heard voices, but somehow, they didn't sound real.

Someone, possibly whoever had stood in front of me, picked me up like a child. My head fell back, and then I felt nothing.

fourteen

COLE

I sat forward in my seat. *What's she doing?*

Oakley looked frozen. Her body was still, apart from her chest rising and falling rapidly. Linda rushed to her side along with someone else, and together, they helped her down.

Shit! What the hell's happened?

"Oakley!" I shouted.

Jumping up, I ran toward the door. I couldn't get to her from the public gallery, but I knew roughly where she would be. Dodging people as I ran, the only thing on my mind was getting to her.

I didn't care about the group of tracksuit-clad teens I almost knocked over or the old man shouting at me to slow down.

Oakley. She was all I could think about.

She was scared and nervous—of course she was—but I'd had no idea it was that bad.

As soon as she'd looked at *him*, it was like she'd just shut down.

I was out of breath by the time I got to where we'd left her earlier. Linda had taken her to a room just off the hallway, so that was the first place I planned on looking. I flew through the door, hoping it would be the right one.

I looked down and froze. Oakley was lying on the floor.

My heart stopped, and I dropped to my knees. "What happened?" I asked desperately. "What's going on? Oakley, talk to me!"

Behind me, some old guy was on his phone, calling an ambulance, and Linda was busy checking Oakley's pulse. I was so scared that I felt sick. My heart thumped against my chest.

"Oakley! What happened, Linda? Please wake up, Oakley. Don't do this to me," I begged.

"She just collapsed," Linda replied. She rolled Oakley onto her side. "She's breathing."

Oakley looked pale, and her skin was clammy.

"I think it was a panic attack. Did she eat this morning? That wouldn't help if she hadn't."

"Um…" I shook my head. "I don't know." Leaning down, I brushed her hair from her face. "Can you hear me, baby? It's going to be all right," I whispered in her ear.

"Oakley!" Sarah screamed.

Jasper dropped down beside me. "What the fuck? What's wrong with her?"

"Panic attack, Linda thinks," I muttered, stroking the back of her hand.

Paramedics rushed through the door seconds after them and rushed over. After firing off a string of questions and checking her over, they placed an oxygen mask over her mouth and laid her on a stretcher. Her eyes flickered, and I thought she was going to open them, but she didn't.

"Okay, let's get her out," one paramedic said.

They both lifted her at the same time.

I jogged alongside the stretcher as they carried her out to the ambulance. The place seemed bigger now. The second we stepped out of the side door, quick flashes of light flickered in my face.

We'd deliberately come in through the side for privacy. The trial was going on, so we had known it would only be a matter of time before they started hounding Oakley. They must have followed the ambulance.

Questions were fired out of the sea of reporters. Police officers stopped them from coming too close and slightly shielded Oakley. Their faces seemed blurred as I looked at them all at the same time, trying to see who was coming too close to her.

Anger rose inside me as they continued pushing forward to get a picture. *Hasn't she been through enough already?* None of them cared about her. As long as they got the good story and the best picture, it didn't matter what that would do to her. The extra stress and pressure of seeing her photo in the newspapers was the last thing she needed.

Sarah got straight in the ambulance, and I started to panic.

"Can I come, too?" I asked, staring at Oakley lying deathly still.

The thought of losing her was physically painful.

"Sorry," the paramedic said, smiling apologetically, before he slammed the door shut.

Just before he'd closed it, I'd seen Oakley's eyes flitter open. *Is she properly awake now? She might be asking for me.*

I spun around and sprinted back to my car. There was no point in trying to get them to allow me to come. Oakley needed to get to the hospital as soon as possible, and I wasn't going to hold them up.

Jasper's footsteps thudded behind me.

Ripping the door open, I jumped in and started the car before I even shut the door. Thankfully, Jasper moved just as quickly. My heart hammered in my chest. All I wanted to do was be with her already.

"What the fuck is going on?" Jasper shouted. His eyes had filled with tears, and he looked terrified.

"I dunno," I mumbled in response. "She was all right before she went in, but I saw her look at *him*, and then she seemed…I dunno." I shook my head. I didn't have any answers.

Jasper spit out a string of expletives, muttering about how much he hated his dad and wished he'd had the chance to "murder the bastard."

I couldn't disagree with that. If I could turn back time, I would have locked Oakley in my car, called Jasper to come and get her, and gone to find Max and Frank there and then. That way, she wouldn't have had to move halfway across the world. She wouldn't have to worry about ever seeing them again or panicking about the possibility of her dad calling her from prison.

"If anything happens to her…" Jasper trailed off, his face twisting in pain.

I couldn't even think about that. Nothing could happen to her. She *had* to be okay.

"I don't think she should carry on with the trial."

"What?"

"It's not worth this," he said, shaking his head. "They're going down with or without her testimony."

"Maybe, but they're more likely to get sent down with it. Especially Frank," I spit. Saying his name burned my throat.

"I don't give a fuck about them. I don't want Oakley anywhere near that court. If they get off, there are other ways of dealing with it."

The only other time I had seen him this angry was the night he'd found out what they had done to her.

I didn't reply. There was no point. He would just get angrier. If Oakley wanted to give up, I would understand completely, but I knew her better than that. She wanted to do it. She needed to.

Jasper wouldn't be happy about it, but Oakley was the most important person here. Whatever she needed to do to be able to move on, I was behind her one hundred percent.

The tyres screeched as I turned hard and came to an abrupt stop in the hospital car park. We jumped out of the car and sprinted to the entrance.

"Oakley Farrell!" Jasper shouted, slamming into the reception desk. "She was brought in a minute ago. Where is she?"

Following the receptionist's directions, we quickly made our way down the hallway to another waiting room. Sarah was pacing back and forth, waving her shaking hands.

"Sarah," I called. "What's going on? Where is she?"

"She came round in the ambulance and was talking, but they still have to check her over," she explained. "They couldn't tell me much, but with everything that's going on, it's not surprising. There's too much pressure on her. It's just too much for her. Too much." She started crying and leant against Jasper.

I sat down as Jasper comforted his mum. Mia had texted to say they were on their way, and Oakley's grandparents arrived shortly after we had. The waiting room didn't smell like the hospital. It smelt of a mixture of perfumes and the vanilla air freshener on the windowsill.

The clock slowly ticked by. We hadn't been sitting long, but it felt like hours. My chest was tight. Sarah had spoken to Oakley, and she was just being checked over, but until I saw her and saw that she was okay, I wouldn't be able to relax.

A doctor walked in, and before he could even call Sarah's name, we were all up out of our seats.

"How is she?" I asked, getting in there just before everyone asked the same thing.

"She's doing just fine now," he replied with a thick Scottish accent. "She had a panic attack. She's also dehydrated. When she collapsed, she hit her head against the side of the stand, and she has a mild concussion, so we'll keep her overnight and see how she's doing tomorrow."

"But she's okay? Can I see her?" Sarah questioned.

"We're monitoring her, but she's fine and awake, so you can see her. Not all of you though."

My heart dropped. No way was I staying in this room.

"Just family for now, please. Oakley needs rest."

Sarah looked between me and Jasper. "The three of us. Please?"

I waited outside while Sarah and Jasper went in first, giving them a few minutes alone with her. I paced back and forth, checking the discoloured clock on the wall. When five minutes had ticked by, I went inside.

Oakley was sitting up, talking to her mum. She looked up and smiled sheepishly as her eyes landed on me.

"We'll go and get a drink, give you two some time alone," Sarah said. "Do either of you want anything from the canteen?"

"No, thanks," I replied.

Oakley shook her head.

Jasper started to follow Sarah out. With a tight jaw, he looked back at his little sister in a hospital bed. "Get Cole to call if you need us sooner," he said. He let go of the door, letting it close behind him.

Perching on the edge of the bed, I pressed my lips to hers and kissed her as I stroked down her jaw. It was pure relief to see that she was okay and back with us.

"Don't ever do that again," I told her. "You scared me to death."

"I'm sorry," she whispered. Her cheeks turned a light shade of pink, and she diverted her eyes. She did look a little dazed and pale, but apart from that, she was the same perfect girl as always.

I sighed and lifted her chin, so she was facing me again. "It wasn't your fault. I need to take better care of you."

"What? This certainly wasn't your fault." She frowned and slightly pursed her lips, the way she did when she was annoyed.

"Oakley, the doctor said you were dehydrated."

"That's not your fault though! I should be taking care of myself. It's just, with everything going on, I've not really thought about eating and drinking properly. I'm fine now—apart from feeling like a complete idiot and being beyond embarrassed, that is."

"Don't feel like that; you couldn't help it. Everything's gonna be fine now."

Oakley nodded, but I knew she didn't believe it would be fine. I had to try and make her feel better though.

"Do you want to continue with the trial? You know you don't have to, right? We don't have to talk about that now actually. Forget I said anything." *Stupid!*

She gently shook her head and winced. "I want to. I just need to learn how to deal with seeing him again. I didn't cover that in therapy. I didn't think I'd ever be facing him again."

"Okay," I said, running my hand through her hair. "Whatever you want. Do you think speaking to someone will help?"

"I honestly don't know." She shook her head again, winced, and rubbed it.

"Careful. Are you okay?"

She smiled. "I'm fine."

"You have a concussion! You're not fine, fine."

"Fine, fine," she repeated, grinning in amusement. "And it's a *minor* concussion. I can't remember doing it. My head hurts a bit, but it's just like a little headache, so stop worrying."

"It's the boyfriend's job to worry."

"Wrong. It's the boyfriend's job to do the kissing." Her voice was light and flirty.

My Oakley is back, but for how long? She couldn't just push this to the back of her mind anymore.

Sarah and Jasper let us have ten minutes alone before they came back into the room.

"How are you feeling now, sweetheart?" Sarah asked.

Oakley smiled. "Better."

"I've just gotten off the phone with Linda, and the trial has been put on hold for three days."

Oakley bowed her head, cringing at how her collapse had delayed proceedings.

"It's okay," Sarah said soothingly. "After what just happened, they had to. We need to get you well before you return."

"It's a good thing, Oakley." I squeezed her hand. "It means you have a few more days to prepare."

She reluctantly nodded in agreement. I knew she felt embarrassed and just wanted it to be over, but she had to put her health first.

Me and Oakley met up with my family, Ali, and Oakley's grandparents in the café and filled them in on how she was doing.

Oakley had asked for an hour alone to rest. Everything had been going at a hundred miles an hour, and she needed a few minutes to stop and think.

I sat opposite Sarah and Jasper, absentmindedly running my finger around the rim of the coffee mug. Leaving Oakley alone felt wrong. Sarah was going to pop back up when she finished her drink, and if Oakley wanted company, she would text and tell us to come back.

"I still don't think she should go back," Jasper argued. "We should just book our flights back to Australia and get her the hell out of here."

"You can't spend your life running from things, Jasper. That's the reason she decided to be here. Oakley wants to do this. It's the only way she'll get closure and be able to move on," Sarah said.

I almost applauded.

He narrowed his eyes. "We'll let her decide."

"She already has," I cut in. "I asked her if she wanted to continue, and she's adamant that she does."

Jasper angrily shook his head and mumbled something under his breath. I wasn't even going to bother with trying to pacify him.

When the time was up, we quickly made our way back to her room. She was in exactly the same position, staring down at the thin sheet covering her legs.

"Oakley?" I called quietly.

Without even looking up, she replied, "Mmhmm."

"Are you okay?"

She nodded, still refusing to face us.

Sitting back down on the bed, I brushed her hair behind her ear. "What's going on? Has something happened?"

I knew she'd needed time alone, but it seemed to have freaked her out.

"I've just made everything ten times worse, haven't I?"

"What? No, darling, everything's going to be fine," Sarah replied, rubbing her arm.

"I have. They'll say I did it for attention, to manipulate the jury, and anything else they can think of. Me freaking out and ending up in the hospital is just going to back that up. Everyone is going to think I'm this dramatic little girl who makes stuff up, and Dad—"

"Enough, Oakley!" Jasper shouted, cutting her off. "They can say what they like, but the jury *will* believe you."

"Yeah," she responded with a fake smile. "Can you guys give me a minute with Cole, please?"

Sarah immediately stood up, but Jasper only left when I nodded toward the door. I knew he was only thinking about her, but I didn't think he realised just how important this was for her.

She waited until she was happy that they were gone and turned to me. "You're the one who will tell me the truth. They're too positive. I understand why, and I love them for it, but I need to hear it straight. Have I made this harder?"

I shuffled closer to her and wrapped my arms around her body.

"Am I going to lose, Cole?"

I shook my head, pulling her closer, and she snuggled into me.

"You're not going to lose. The defence is going to make up all kinds of shit, but we know the truth. Oakley, they can't make you slip up or pretend your silence was something else because you're telling the truth."

She nodded against my chest.

"Just tell the truth. That's all you can do. With everything they have against him, there's no way the jury won't believe you. I've backed you up in my statement. That day you called me, there was never any doubt in my mind that you were being honest. No one can act that scared."

"Thank you," she whispered.

"You need to be strong, baby. We'll do this. I promise."

"Yes. It's not impossible, right? Just harder."

Nodding in confirmation, I replied, "Just a little harder."

"I don't know what I'd do without you."

"You'll never have to find that out. I'm not going anywhere." Lifting her chin, I gently kissed her lips. "I love you so much."

She sighed happily before she whispered, "I love you, too."

fifteen

OAKLEY

I left the hospital after spending just one night there. It had taken the doctors all day to release me, as they'd wanted to keep an eye on me for a little while longer. I returned home at five in the afternoon with a bunch of leaflets and breathing techniques in case it happened again. Breathing deeply wouldn't help though. I couldn't breathe at all when I saw *him.*

The whole thing was humiliating—collapsing in court in front of everyone. What was worse was that it would back up the defence's argument. Surely, now, people would believe him when he said I was a selfish little girl just looking for attention.

It came as no surprise that my dad was trying to make the jury believe I was lying. Linda had filled me in on what he'd said and now it was my job to show everyone that I was the one telling the truth.

Whatever anyone said to make me feel better, I knew it would now be harder to prove that I was telling the truth. Mum seemed to think the jury would feel sympathetic rather than suspicious. I couldn't allow myself to think that though. *What if she's wrong?*

What the hell am I going to do now?

Cole ran his fingers through my hair. "Are you okay?"

"I think I'm going to get a tattoo saying, *I'm fine*, on my forehead."

Turning his nose up, he replied, "I'd prefer, *Property of Cole*."

"I'm sure you would. If I were paying to be repeatedly stabbed, I'd get my one true love's name though. Cam Gigandet."

"Being jealous of someone I'll never even meet is weird." Cole mumbled something under his breath that sounded like, *Blond bastard*. "Feed me," he said, changing the subject completely.

Okay.

"Hey, I just got home from the hospital. *You* be *my* slave!"

He smiled and stood up. "What do you want then? I'll get you anything."

"Anything?" I raised my eyebrow. "What if I want KFC?"

"Then, I'll go get KFC," he said.

Pulling the fleece blanket over my lap, I smiled. "You're sweet, but I think I'd prefer to keep you here. Maybe a cheese sandwich or something?"

"Salad cream, no butter. Gross, but it's coming up." He saluted and walked into the kitchen, making me smile.

He was the perfect boyfriend, and I was so lucky to have him.

I took a deep breath and tugged the blanket up just under my chin. I used to do that when I was little; the cover was a protection from *him*. I used to think, if it was covering me, then he couldn't get to me.

Since I'd gotten back from the hospital, I hadn't stopped worrying about giving evidence again. I knew that, if I hadn't collapsed, my part would be over by now; instead, I would have to start all over again and build up my courage once more.

I had called my therapist and been through a few things, which helped a lot. Talking to her had seemed to put everything in perspective again, but the anticipation was still killing me.

I couldn't change what had already happened. Things in the past were carved into stone, never to be amended. All I could do was go back in there and tell them the truth. After that, it would be completely out of my hands. The jury would decide if they believed my dad was guilty or innocent.

Dad had charm and charisma though. He was well liked and respected. I prayed that the jury would be able to see through that. If they found him innocent, I didn't know what I would do. He'd told me over and over that I wouldn't be believed if I ever did speak up. He couldn't be right.

My phone rang in the kitchen, and just as I was about to get up, Cole brought it through.

"Miles," he said, handing it to me. He went back into the kitchen to finish making our sandwiches.

Putting the phone to my ear, I smiled. Finally, he was calling.

"Hi, Miles."

"Oakley, how are you?"

"I'm doing okay. How are you?"

"I'm well, thank you. Is your mum all right?"

That, I have no idea.

Like me, she always said she was, but I thought she was lying, too.

"As all right as she can be. She doesn't talk about how she feels. Mostly, she just worries about me and Jasper."

"That sounds like your mum. Is she there?" He sounded nervous all of a sudden.

If Mum didn't give Miles a chance, I was going to have to slap some sense into her. He was kind, caring, and generous. What you saw was what you got. There was no ulterior motive or mystery about him. He was exactly what Mum needed and deserved.

"Not at the minute. She's at the supermarket." *Getting all my favourite foods to cheer me up.* I would prefer a happy Mum though. "I can ask her to call you…" I trailed off, realising that she probably wouldn't.

"Do you think she will?"

I cringed. I didn't want to say no and hurt his feelings. "Um…"

Miles laughed. "Me neither. Look, I called to get your opinion on something anyway, forget talking to your mum at the minute, okay?"

"Okay. What do you want my opinion on?"

Miles launched into the reason he'd called. My smile grew and grew as I listened. When he finished telling me his plan, we spent about twenty minutes talking about everything, from the trial to life back in Australia and his work. It was good to talk to him again.

Cole patiently sat beside me, rubbing circles on the palm of my hand with his thumb. My sandwich was probably starting to harden, but I didn't care. When we eventually wrapped up the phone call, I turned my attention back to Cole.

"Everything okay?" he asked.

I nodded. "Yeah, actually, everything's great."

He looked intrigued. "What do you mean?"

"You'll see," I replied before kissing him.

I spent the rest of the night doing nothing, but it was nothing with Cole, so that was plenty. We lounged on the sofa, watching TV. It was perfect. The only time we were apart was when he quickly went home to get a change of clothes for work in the morning. It had taken a lot of convincing to get him to go back, but I didn't want to get in the way of his job. Mum and Jasper would be with me constantly anyway.

"Let's go to bed." I yawned, pressing my face into Cole's shoulder.

He kissed the top of my head and helped me up.

"Night," I mumbled to Mum and Ali.

"Night," they called back at the same time.

Mum and Ali had two bottles of red wine and were determined to finish them off. I didn't blame them. If I liked red wine, I would have joined in after how the last few days had gone.

I changed, brushed my teeth, and got into bed. Lately, I had been exhausted all the time even though I hadn't done much. Lizzie had been spending most nights over at her *friend's*. I had a feeling she was using me as an excuse to stay with this so-called friend.

"I love you," Cole whispered.

I rolled onto my side and slung my leg over his. "I love you, too."

When I woke in the morning, I was filled with dread. Cole was going to work, and I would be left with Mum and Jasper fussing over me. I loved them both to death, but their worrying drove me crazy. I wasn't the only one who was having a tough time right now.

"I don't want to go to work," Cole complained as he rubbed the sleep from his eyes.

"I don't want you to go to work either, but you have to. You don't want to get fired."

"No, *you* don't want me to get fired. I could happily chill with you all day."

"We'd end up killing each other."

He pushed himself up and rested on his elbows, hovering over me. "I don't think I would. I quite like you."

I laughed and pushed him off me. He flopped back on the bed.

"Shut up and go to work, Cole."

He sighed heavily. "Fine."

I watched him hop off the bed and pull on his grey trousers and light-blue shirt. I felt so calm whenever I was with him, so long as he was in sight. He had this effect on me that just made everything seem a little better. When I was back in court, I was going to ignore my dad and focus on Cole.

He slumped back on the bed when he was dressed.

"Now, you have a good day and try not to get fired," I teased.

He beamed and kissed me. My heart soared as his tongue swept over my bottom lip. I tangled my fingers in his newly styled hair and pulled him closer.

Cole abruptly ended the kiss and said, "Bye."

"Oh, you're mean."

"Call me if you need anything." His voice told me it was an order and not an option.

"Yes, sir!"

He fought a smile but failed. "I'll see you tonight."

Once Cole left, I decided to get up and face my family. I walked downstairs, and the house was deserted. There was a piece of paper on the counter.

Jasper's scribble read, *Gone for breakfast with Abby. Be back later.*

Mum must still be asleep. I had prepared for an argument about not putting my health at risk for the sake of giving evidence in person, and now, I was alone. I filled the kettle and flicked it on, knowing Mum would need coffee as soon as she got up. When there was no sign of her after I'd made the coffee, I decided to do her breakfast in bed, and I made her some toast.

I carried the tray upstairs and pushed the door open with my foot. "Mum?" I called.

She groaned and looked up at me. *Oh, hangover, of course!*

"Breakfast."

A smile slipped on her face, and she sat up. "Thanks, sweetheart. That's just what I need."

"Polished off that wine then?"

She groaned. "Please, don't mention the W word."

I grinned and handed her the tray.

That afternoon, sitting in the lounge, watching daytime TV, I nervously checked the clock. Miles was due here any minute, and I still wasn't sure if I had done the right thing.

Mum put a mug of hot chocolate down in front of me, clearly having fought off the hangover. "Are you expecting Cole?"

"No. Why?"

"You keep looking at the clock."

"Oh. I don't know."

She frowned at me. I had been texting Cole throughout the day, and he was working an extra hour to catch up on a few things.

"Cole's working. I'm just waiting for a new top to be delivered."

"A new top?" she repeated.

"Yeah, ordered it yesterday." *Oh God, I'm the worst liar in the world!* I sighed. "Okay, that was a lie."

Mum grinned. "No. Really?"

Biting my lip, I considered whether I should just sprint out of the house and leave her to it.

"Miles is coming," I blurted out.

Her face dropped, and I leant forward slightly, ready to take off if necessary.

"Miles is what?" Mum asked, sitting down.

I cringed. "Coming here. Now."

She stayed perfectly calm, but she was probably planning on how she could kill me and dispose of my body.

"Mum?"

"Thank you," she whispered.

Thank you? What? "Huh?"

She smiled and replied, "I need him here."

Admitting that was hard for her, I could tell. She didn't trust men anymore, so it wasn't easy for her to let one into our lives.

"So, you admit it? You like Miles?"

"Don't get too carried away, young lady." She grinned sheepishly, which told me everything.

The doorbell rang, and Mum jumped.

"Wow, he has good timing," I muttered.

Mum slowly rose out of the seat and walked to the front door. I wouldn't answer the door now. The press were constantly outside, and I really didn't want to deal with them taking pictures and firing questions at me.

The door opened and closed so quickly that I almost missed Mum grabbing Miles's arm and pulling him inside. In shock, I sat still and stared at them staring at each other. I wasn't sure if I should sneak off upstairs and leave them alone or at least say hello to Miles. I felt awkward, watching them.

"Oakley," Miles said, finally breaking eye contact with my mum, "how are you?"

I stood up and gave him a quick hug. Mum didn't tense up like she did when other men were too close to me. She trusted Miles, whether she realised it or not. I trusted him, too, or I wouldn't go anywhere near him.

"I'm okay. Thank you for coming."

"Of course." His eyes flicked back to Mum, and she smiled, blushing lightly.

"Well, I'm going to go do that thing I have to do." I turned on my heel and practically sprinted to the stairs.

They needed some time to talk and, hopefully, finally admit how they felt about each other. I certainly didn't need to witness it.

Once in Lizzie's room, I debated on leaving the door open a crack and listening, but I resisted and dialled Cole's number instead.

He answered after the second ring. "She's not killed you then?"

I laughed and lay back on the futon. "Actually, she took it really well. She was pleased."

"Wow."

"Yeah. So, how's work going?"

"It's going. I've got about another five hours, and then I'm all yours."

That sounds good.

"I've been offered more money for my story again," he said.

I sighed. "I'm sorry, Cole."

Since the start of the trial, everyone close to me had been asked constantly for their side of the story. No one had given in, and I knew they wouldn't. I just hated the hassle they had been receiving.

"Not your fault," he said, completely dismissing the issue. "What are you doing then?"

"Staying in Lizzie's room until I know it's safe to go downstairs. I would read, but all her books are Katie Price's autobiographies."

"I'd read them."

I rolled my eyes. "Why am I not surprised?"

He laughed and then sighed. That meant he was wrapping up the conversation. "I have to go now, babe, but I'll see you after work."

I grinned. "Okay. I love you."

"Love you, too," he replied before hanging up.

Sighing happily, I pulled a *Cosmopolitan* magazine down off the end of Lizzie's bed. I hadn't even finished reading the "Eat Yourself Thin" article when Mum pushed the door open.

"How's it going?" I asked.

"We've just been *talking*," she said, a little too defensively for it to be entirely true. "Lunch is ready. We've made chicken Caesar salad."

"We've?"

"Yes, Oakley. Miles helped."

"Any kissing yet?"

Her face turned a deep shade of pink, and I gasped.

"You have!"

"I'm an adult!"

I laughed and stood up. "I know that. It's a good thing, Mum. No one deserves to be happy more than you."

She smiled, and her face softened. She replied, "I can think of one person. Now, lunch. You need to eat."

Miles would only be here for a week before he had to return to work. Thankfully though, he would be coming back again as soon as he could arrange the time off.

I sat at the table next to Mum while Miles was opposite her.

"How's work without me?" Mum asked.

I had a feeling this was a topic she'd saved for when I was with them. That was good. I didn't need to hear all the mushy stuff.

"Dull and busy. We're all looking forward to your return."

I frowned as they talked about going back to Australia, realising that, as much as I hated being here, I didn't want to leave Cole. I would have to eventually though, especially if Dad and Frank got off.

"Probably another eight weeks. I think we'll have to wait roughly three to four weeks for the sentencing of both. I'll be working from my laptop once Oakley's finished in court though," Mum explained.

Miles's dark eyebrows knotted. "That long?"

"Unfortunately. When they're found guilty, it should be dealt with then rather than making us all wait weeks for it to be over." Mum shook her head in anger.

I completely agreed with her; it would be better if it wasn't drawn out even longer, but there was nothing we could do about it.

"Thanks for lunch. I'm going back up to read," I said, taking my plate to wash it up.

"You don't have to hide out, Oakley. You can stay downstairs, too."

"Of course you should," Miles agreed.

I shook my head. Hanging around them and watching them smile at each other like teenagers wasn't my idea of fun. "Actually, I'm *really* fine with reading."

"Does Lizzie have a particularly wide variety of books then?" Mum teased.

"Oh, yeah, she has the whole series of *Vogue* and *Cosmopolitan*," I replied sarcastically. "There's a few things on the bookshelf that look pretty interesting though." I nodded to the bookcase out in the hallway.

"Only if you're sure, honey. You're more than welcome to stay with us."

"No, thanks," I replied, winking at her as I walked out of the kitchen.

No doubt she was blushing.

I grabbed the first book off the shelf and went back up to Lizzie's room, leaving them to it.

sixteen

OAKLEY

My heart was beating as fast as it had the last time I was standing in the courtroom. I could feel myself losing control, and all the breathing exercises I'd learnt went out the window.

Don't look at him, I told myself.

I kept my head straight and refused to turn to where he was. I couldn't handle seeing him again.

You can do this, for every girl he would go on to hurt if you didn't speak up.

Strangely, I felt more afraid of him now than I had as a little girl. Back then, I'd still had hope that he would change, that he would be a proper dad again. That hope was lost the day he had taken me back to Frank when I was fifteen. I saw him for what he was now—a sick, evil monster.

No matter how afraid I was, I would not give up. No matter how hard things got, I would stand up and tell everyone what he had done. He had to pay for what he'd done, and I was determined to make that happen.

Linda stood up and walked toward me. She stopped a meter away and smiled discreetly. "Could you please state your full name?"

My heart crashed in my chest. "Oakley Ruby Farrell."

"And how old are you?"

"Twenty."

I was asked a few more straightforward, everyday, factual questions like that.

Where did I live? Who did I live with? Where did I go to school?

And then things turned more serious. Linda straightened her back and glanced at the judge and jury.

No turning back now.

Taking a deep breath, I focused on the end goal—to make sure my father never got the opportunity to cause damage to anyone else and to get justice for those girls he had hurt, including me, and for my family.

"Miss Farrell, do you understand why we are here?" Linda asked. Her voice projected authority and confidence. The way she looked and moved was almost as if we had already won.

"Yes," I replied. My voice didn't sound like my own.

It was like when you heard your voice in a recording. I wanted to elaborate and tell her, tell them all, exactly why we were here, but I couldn't. I had to keep it simple, not go into detail, use one-worded answers whenever possible.

Linda nodded once. "Did you grow up here?"

"Yes."

"Where did you live when you were here?"

"Eighteen Turner Road."

"Whom did you live with at that address?"

"My mum, dad, and brother."

"And how long did you live there?"

Those questions were still easy. *Isn't it going to get harder?*

"Sixteen years," I said.

My parents had moved there when Mum was four months pregnant with me. It was the only house I had ever lived in before we'd moved to Australia.

"You just mentioned your father. Do you see him in the courtroom today? Can you point and verbally acknowledge that he is in the court room, so our stenographer can enter your response into the court records?"

I took a deep breath. "Yes. He's there," I said as I pointed to him. I was careful not to look directly into his eyes though. I could feel him watching me, burning a hole in the side of my head. It made me feel weak.

Linda half-smiled and briskly moved on. "Now, Miss Farrell, we are obviously here today because your father, Mr Farrell, sold you and other children to Mr Frank Glosser for the purpose of sex—"

"Objection," my father's defence lawyer, John Bee, cut in. He stood up and faced the judge.

The judge, a short, plump woman, leant forward a fraction. "Sustained."

Linda was told not to lead the jury to a conclusion when the charges were alleged.

Alleged. It made it sound like I was lying. *Does the judge think I'm lying?*

It didn't seem to faze Linda at all. She turned back to me and continued. She read out a list of the charges and asked if I understood them.

The charges were administering a substance with intent to commit sexual offences; trafficking within the UK for sexual exploitation; controlling a child prostitute or a child involved in pornography; causing or inciting child prostitution or pornography; production of indecent photographs of children; possession of indecent photographs of children; abuse of position of trust, causing or inciting a child to engage in sexual activity; and sexual assault on a child.

The last one in particular turned my stomach. While in university, where he'd met Frank, he had abused a little girl for the first time.

Gulping back the urge to sob, I straightened my back. I couldn't believe this man was my dad. "Yes. I understand the charges."

"Miss Farrell," Linda started again.

I wished she would just call me by my first name. I now regretted not changing my surname, but no one had ever called me by my father's name until now.

"On or around the twentieth of August 2008, did you make contact with the Clearview Police Department?"

"Yes."

"What was your reason for contacting them?"

"To report my father for offering me to his friend—"

"Objection," John roared. "The witness is being led."

"Overruled," the judge responded.

I wanted to stick my tongue out at him as he shrank back to his seat.

"Please continue," she instructed Linda.

Linda carried on but not before a small smile had flickered across her face at the judge's intervention.

"Miss Farrell, can you recall the first time this happened?"

"When I was five."

"How do remember that you were five since it was so long ago?"

"Because it was shortly after my teddy-bear picnic party, which was for my fifth birthday."

The side of Linda's mouth tugged so quickly that I almost missed it.

"Always make sure you link the time with an event, so the jury knows you're sure of your dates."

"And when did this stop?"

"After I turned thirteen."

"To the best of your memory, can you tell us exactly what happened?"

My stomach turned, and I squeezed my eyes shut. "Yes." I gulped. "At first, Frank would just join me and Dad when we went fishing." I took another deep breath and swallowed hard. I could hear the blood pumping in my ears. Clenching my hands into fists, I continued, "But, after a couple of times of joining us on trips, he started to get me to sit on his lap while he read to me, then he touched me over my clothes."

"Can you tell us where?"

I clenched my jaw and closed my eyes. *Tell them. Just do it.* When I opened my eyes again, I launched into every detail. I told them how I hadn't understood what he was doing at the time, but that it'd felt wrong, and I hadn't liked it. I told them how my dad had made it sound normal and like something that happened to everyone. I told them that, even today, I could still taste the amber drink Dad had given me that made me feel sleepy.

I explained that, when I'd told Dad I didn't like what Frank was doing he'd shouted at me for questioning him and slapped me. I had been scared and thought that I'd let him down. I'd thought he must be really disappointed and must have hated me for him to hit me.

I also told them that, when I'd attempted to tell my mum, Dad had arrived just in time to stop me from actually saying anything. When we had been alone in my room, he'd threatened some hideous things. He'd told me, if Mum found out, it would kill her, and at five years old, I had taken those words literally. As I had gotten a little older, he'd said no one would believe me, and I would be taken away if I dared to make any allegations.

I told them how, every time Frank had abused me, my dad was there, watching, that he had taken pictures. Lastly, I told them that, when I was ten, Dad had stood by and let Frank rape me for the first time and that I'd looked to him for help, but he'd just stared on with a blank expression I still didn't understand now.

I didn't have the courage to look up at the public gallery as I repeated everything that I had endured, not that I would have seen much, as my vision had become blurred. I'd done it though.

I was so thankful that I'd told Mum in private everything that had happened, but Cole and Jasper hadn't known the details. Nor did the rest of my family or Cole's.

I breathed out deeply. Going through it all again felt like being cut open, but I also felt about a stone lighter. It was such a relief when I finished speaking that I almost broke down.

Saying those words aloud, I'd finally heard them properly for the first time. None of the blame was on me. None of it was my fault. Letting go of the blame was hard, but it was the most incredible feeling in the world. Even if the jury didn't believe me, I had stood up to my father, and that counted for a lot.

"And was Mr Farrell present every time this abuse took place?"

I nodded. "Yes."

"Did he ever say anything to you?"

"No. He'd occasionally snap and tell me to do as Frank said, but after a while, I'd learnt that he wasn't going to help, so I'd just do what I was told to do straightaway."

Linda lowered her head, and I thought she was telling me not to elaborate too much. I bit my lip.

"Miss Farrell, why did it take you so long to come forward?"

It must seem odd to people that I hadn't spoken out earlier, but I knew this was nothing unusual for someone who'd suffered abuse.

"I was scared. Scared for my family and scared for myself." I ducked my head. "And I wanted him to change. I hoped he would change," I whispered.

A tear slid down my cheek, and I made no attempt to wipe it away. Admitting that was hard. After everything he had done, it was hard to admit that I had still wanted him to be my dad.

"And what changed your mind?"

"I realised that it hadn't stopped. When I was thirteen, he promised me it had, and when I was fifteen, almost sixteen, he said he was taking me away on a fishing trip to make up for what had happened. I believed that he wanted to make things right and move on. When Frank turned up, I understood then that nothing had changed, and there was no hope for my dad. And I couldn't go through it again."

Linda turned to the judge. "No further questions, Your Honour."

As soon as I stepped outside the room, I had a rush of oxygen fill my lungs. I closed my eyes and concentrated on relaxing my body, which was knotted with tension.

"You did great, Oakley," Linda said softly. "I think your family is waiting for us outside the door. We'll go out the side way again." She squeezed the top of my arm and smiled. "You really did do well. You should be so proud of yourself."

Pride wasn't something I usually felt, but I kind of did now. "Thank you. Let's go meet them."

I followed Linda out of the room and into the hallway. Mum, Jasper, Ali, Lizzie, and my grandparents were waiting for me. *Where is Cole?* Even his parents and Mia were here. I stopped and tried to force a smile onto my face.

"Oh, sweetheart." Mum grabbed me, pulling me into a tight hug. "You were amazing, darling. I'm so proud of you."

"I don't feel amazing. Not completely," I replied, clenching my shaking hands around her back.

Jasper hugged me next, practically pulling me out of Mum's arms. I sank into my brother's embrace, feeling safe and protected.

"You're okay now," he whispered in my ear.

I was—almost. There was still Frank's trial to go, but for now, I had half the weight gone from my shoulders.

"Ready to get out of here?" Jasper asked.

I pulled away and smiled in thanks. "Definitely." I looked around and noticed the one other person I needed to see wasn't there. "Where's Cole?"

"He's outside. He needed some air," Mum replied.

My heart stopped. *He needed air?* That meant he was freaking out. I should have told him everything.

"We'll go see him now." Mum's arm remained around my back as we walked to the exit.

Linda went out the front, so the press would think I would be following, and hopefully, that would give us enough time to get out.

Jasper walked stiffly. His whole posture was tense, and his jaw was clenched. I knew he was struggling with what he'd heard in there. Later, I would need to sit down and talk to him, apologise for the way he had found everything out, if he would even let me. Jasper was too strong for his own good. All he worried about was me and Mum. I desperately wanted him to open up to me.

Ali pushed the door open, and everyone instinctively moved closer to me in case there was any press lurking at the exit. That was when I saw him. Cole was leaning against the brick wall. A deep frown dominated his face. He looked so tortured that it made my heart sink.

Swallowing the lump in my throat, I pushed past everyone that was in between us. He looked up and shoved himself away from the wall, practically running toward me. Within seconds of us catching sight of each other, I was in his arms, being lifted.

"Cole," I whispered, clinging on to him.

He gripped me, as if he thought he was the only thing keeping me from shattering. I finally cracked and sobbed into his neck.

"I'm sorry. I'm so, so sorry," he mumbled into my hair.

"For what?"

"For letting that happen to you. I should have known. I should have stopped it."

I pulled back from him a few inches, enough to look directly into his eyes.

"Don't. None of it was your fault. Cole, you were just a child yourself. Please don't ever blame yourself."

His eyes filled with tears, and in that moment, I wanted to run back inside and tell them I had made it all up. I wanted to take it all back. I would have done anything never to see him look that painfully sad ever again.

"He took pictures of you."

I nodded slowly. "Yes, but it's going to be okay now."

"Okay?" he repeated.

"It has to be. I won't be the victim anymore, Cole. There are millions of people in worse situations than I was. I got out, and I survived it. I'm the one who has a future. Even if they get out, everyone will know what they did."

He shook his head, staring at me with such intensity that it made me self-conscious. "You're amazing. I don't know how you can be so calm. I want to kill them both."

I shrugged. *What other choice do I have?* Falling apart wouldn't solve anything, but it would make me a victim again. I never wanted to be back there. I was going to do everything I could to get them both locked up, and then I was going to carry on with my life and be happy. They were not going to control any part of me ever again.

"Can we go now?"

"Of course we can." He kissed my damp lips and stroked the side of my face. "I have questions I don't know if you'll want to answer. I don't even know if I want the answers to them."

"I'll answer whatever you want to know, but right now, I just want to get back to Ali's and have a hot chocolate—or a vodka. Please, don't let them get inside your head. Fuck 'em."

Cole almost smiled, his eyes flicking in shock. "'Fuck 'em?' Wow, that was so un-Oakley."

I laughed. "I know, but it made you smile."

"Oakley, Oakley!" My name was being screamed by a number of different people I didn't know.

The press was running toward us, holding up cameras and microphones.

Before I could blink, a car door was opened, and I was being shoved inside. Cole got in and slammed the door.

"Go," Mum barked at Jasper.

He slammed his foot on the accelerator. I almost laughed at the theatrics; it felt like we were in an action movie.

"Easy, Jasper," Mum said after we'd sped out of there like a bat out of hell. "We want to get back in one piece."

"I just want to get her away from that. And, anyway, you were the one who ordered me to go!"

"Well, I meant, go, but go responsibly."

I laid my head on Cole's shoulder and smiled at how normal and petty their argument was. Under Mum's revised instructions, Jasper drove *responsibly*, and we arrived home twenty minutes later.

"I'm going to lie down for a bit," I said as we walked into Ali's house.

No one argued.

I climbed straight into my futon bed and pulled the cover over me, needing to hide from everything for a while. My makeup and clothes were still on, but I just didn't care. I rolled into a ball and allowed the tears to fall. Dragging up those memories had made me feel dirty all over again. I hated it.

Why can't I have just had a normal dad? That was all I wanted. Even when it'd stopped, I'd still wanted my dad.

I'd really believed it was over and that everything was going to be okay again.

I'd wanted him to love me, as strange as that sounded. I'd just wanted the man back who had carried me on his shoulders and played hide-and-seek with me. I should have known that he hadn't changed. I should have done so much differently, but I had been stupidly hopeful.

"Oakley?" Cole's voice made me cry harder.

Go away! I curled into a tighter ball and tensed.

The bed dipped, and the covers shifted. His smell filled my lungs, and I needed him more than ever.

I rolled over and snuggled into him, clinging to his body, as if it were my lifeline. He wrapped himself around me, protecting me.

"Don't cry," he pleaded.

"Do you want to ask me questions?" I whispered.

"Shh, not now. You're not ready to talk about it."

I had a feeling he mentally added, *And I'm not ready to hear it.*

"I love you so much, Oakley."

"I love you, too." I snuggled even closer and let the quiet thumping of his heart sing me to sleep.

seventeen

COLE

"Are you ready for this?" I asked Jasper as we stood outside the courtroom, waiting to be let inside.

"Not really," he replied. "This is a bad idea."

Yeah, probably.

Thinking about Max made me want to go postal, so fuck only knew what I was going to be like while hearing him lie.

"Cole, do you think she's really okay with us being here?"

"I think so. She would've said if she wasn't."

She wouldn't have though because she'd never tell anyone what to do, especially not Jasper when it came to *their* dad, but I didn't want to tell him that. This seemed like something he had to do. I still wasn't sure why I was here. It was either to hear his side and see how he was going to try swinging it or to support Jasper since Oakley and Sarah were dead against coming.

We'd only decided late last night that we were going to attend. A spur-of-the-moment decision. Probably a stupid one, too.

The door to the courtroom opened, and people started filtering in.

"Well," I said, "we should go in, I suppose."

"Yeah." He nodded, but neither of us moved.

I slapped his back and took a step toward the door. "Come on."

Jasper followed. Tension radiated from him. He was about to hear what bullshit his dad was going to spout to make his sister look like a liar.

There were too many charges against him, some already proven, but his lawyer seemed determined to knock the ones relating to Oakley off the list. So, who knew what bullshit was about to come out of his mouth?

We sat side by side, and I wondered if I could leave. I didn't want to be here, but I wanted to be able to prepare Oakley if Max's version of events changed anything, if the jury seemed like they were believing him.

Max looked like he'd aged more than just four years, but he still appeared every bit the respectable man. He wore a smart, expensive-looking black suit, crisp white shirt, and pale blue tie. His hair was neatly combed, and he was clean-shaven. He sat confidently, back straight and chin up.

My hatred grew. How dare he sit there and pretend he wasn't a monster after everything he'd done.

Jasper's fists were clenched on his knees, and he glared at his dad, as if a look could murder him.

Max spoke fluently and calmly, the way he'd done when he was running the town committee to raise money for the new park and the church roof. I remembered watching him when I was young, hero-worshiping him because he was the reason our village was getting a skate ramp.

"Mr Farrell, how did you feel when you first heard the claims your daughter had made against you?" Linda asked.

She carried herself as if she'd already won the case. I wasn't sure if that confidence would bite us in the arse or if it was good and would show the jury that she was certain Max was guilty.

"Devastated. Shocked. Confused. One minute, we're setting up for a weekend camping trip, and the next, she's taken off, and I'm being arrested. It still feels like a nightmare."

"Why did you take only Oakley camping? You have two children. It seems rather strange that you'd only take your daughter."

Max nodded and swiftly replied, "I would have taken both, but Jasper didn't want to come in the end."

"What do you mean 'in the end'?"

"To begin with, Oakley didn't want him to come. She wanted me to herself, the way she only wanted Sarah—her mother—to take her to gymnastics. Camping became my time with Oakley, and my son's time was football on a Sunday morning."

"Liar," Jasper growled under his teeth.

The football part was true; the rest was Max's fantasy.

"You allowed your five-year-old daughter to dictate who was going on these trips?"

Max smiled his award-winning smile. "She needed one-on-one time, and so did Jasper. Every child does. We had plenty of times together as a family, too, but they each needed occasions where they had my undivided attention."

I ground my teeth.

"Mr Farrell, why did you not tell your wife that an old friend, Mr Frank Glosser, would join you on your most recent trip?"

Sarah and Jasper had written statements so they would prove that Max was lying about either of them knowing Frank was alone with Oakley.

"It was last minute. Frank called me to say he'd just arrived in town and was about to check in to a hotel. Within an hour, he was with us. Sarah knew Frank and knew he'd visited us at the campsite before. I knew she wouldn't have an issue with it, and Frank always stayed in a separate tent."

"You took a spare tent?"

"He hired one from the campsite. They have a record of the booking."

Linda smiled briefly. She had known that already. "Of course. And why did Mr Glosser continue to join you on these trips after Oakley had stopped talking? Did it not seem odd to you that she'd stopped soon after you'd been camping?"

"Frank is an old friend, and he'd been joining us for a while. My son and daughter liked him and had no issues with spending time with him. Frank had been around them both long before Oakley had stopped talking, and she'd never expressed any unease in his presence."

"So, it never crossed your mind that someone could be forcing her to stay silent? In your statement, you said that you spent many hours researching and visiting doctors."

"It was a consideration, of course, but we trusted everyone we had around our children."

"Still, the one person who saw more of your daughter than your son on a one-on-one basis was Mr Glosser."

"Frank had spent time with just myself and my son over the years," Max replied smoothly. He was a picture of calm, as if the questions being asked now were about the weather.

Linda smiled briefly. "How did Oakley's silence affect you?"

"It was difficult, to say the least. Oakley's other and I were desperate to help her, and we put everything in to finding out what was wrong. As a result, we suffered physically, emotionally, and financially. I lost work because I was so preoccupied in finding out what was wrong with my child. My now ex-wife and I fought, both lost as to what to do for the best. We didn't know how to help. I hadn't had a full night's sleep since the day she stopped speaking."

"Probably worrying she'd speak up," Jasper muttered in disgust under his breath.

"You suffered financially?" Linda asked.

"Yes."

"Mr Farrell, did you take money in exchange for allowing Mr Glosser to sexually abuse your daughter?"

"No," Max replied, appalled. "Absolutely not."

"How was your relationship with Oakley affected once she stopped talking?"

His eyes tore from the lawyer, and he blinked hard a few times. Jasper glared.

"It was never quite the same. I still loved her just as much, but part of her had closed off to us all. She no longer squealed in delight when I threw her in the air or ran around the back garden with her on my shoulders. We couldn't talk, and I stopped hearing her say, 'I love you, Daddy.'" He paused and took a deep breath. "It broke my heart."

I gripped the seat, fingertips digging into the wood. *Don't believe it,* I prayed in my head to the jury.

Linda rocked back on her heels. "Mr Farrell, why do you think Oakley stopped talking?"

"I believe she has histrionic personality disorder."

What?

Jasper's head snapped to me, and he frowned, his dumbfounded expression mirroring mine.

Linda didn't look at all surprised by the disorder Max had just thrown out of his mouth. "People with histrionic personality disorder—HPD—typically have extravagant and lively personalities, Mr Farrell."

She had been ready for it.

Max tilted his head to the side. "Sufferers tend to have dramatic behaviour," he corrected. "Oakley was a very lively child, but with a sibling, she could never have the majority of our attention—until she stopped talking. People with histrionic personality disorder also act out a role, that of a character or a victim."

I looked to Jasper, panicked. *Shit, he's found something that could explain her behaviour.*

Jasper stared at the jury with wide eyes, willing them to see through Max's crap.

This isn't good.

"Mr Farrell, you state that you've spent the best part of fifteen years trying to figure out what was wrong with your daughter. Is that correct?" Linda asked.

"Yes."

"Hmm, then it seems rather odd that you've only come across this disorder *after* your arrest."

Max said nothing.

"I've been looking over your police statements, and nothing was mentioned then."

"My ex-wife and I spent hours on the Internet, searching *muteness.* We visited countless doctors and specialists in that field, and not one of them mentioned histrionic personality disorder. When Oakley went to the police with her claim, I realised there was something more to it, that she had *chosen* not to speak. My searches changed, and that was when I found HPD."

"Hmm. So, why do you think she spoke out then? You say you believe that Oakley fabricated this story to gain attention but she was away with you, getting your full attention, so surely, she wouldn't have needed to act out?"

"I told her that Mr Glosser was coming for the weekend, and she was unhappy, to say the least. I hadn't seen Frank in almost a year, and he was in town. Oakley didn't want him to come. She'd thought it was just going to be us. I assume that was when she created her story. She had been excited about the trip, put the tent up almost completely by herself, and brought two backpacks full of marshmallows. When I told her that Frank was coming, she dumped the marshmallows in the bin and wouldn't make eye contact with me. Rapid shift in emotion is very typical in HPD."

I looked at Jasper again, and he stared at his father with hatred. He also looked as terrified as I felt.

The jury couldn't fall for that. Please.

I gulped. *This is bad.*

eighteen

OAKLEY

My father's lawyer, John Bee, was such an intimidating man. He made me feel like a child. His face was hard with angular lines and a pointed jaw. Everything about him screamed, *I'm going to break you.*

Cole and Jasper hadn't said much about watching my father give evidence, and I wasn't sure if that was a good or bad thing. Whatever it was, I didn't want to know. I had enough stress at the minute, and I didn't know how much more I could take.

John stepped in front of me. He wasn't even that close, but it felt as if he were just an inch from my face. I looked at him straight-on, determined not to show how scared I was.

"You claim that your father first took you to meet Mr Glosser, alone, when you were five years old. Is that correct?"

"Yes," I replied.

Without blinking, he fired off the next question, "And how soon after that did you stop talking?"

"I can't remember exactly. About a month, I suppose."

He started walking back, away from the jury. "So, there was a gap between the start of the alleged abuse and when you stopped talking?"

"Yes."

"I see." He clicked his tongue, turned to the jury, and held his hand up, extending his index finger. "And you claim that you were forced to remain silent *forever* because your father did not want anyone to find out."

"I never said *forever*. He never said forever, but yes."

He never mentioned a time limit, and I never really thought about it. I had been too afraid to talk again, so I'd tried living a new kind of life.

"So, between the start of the alleged abuse and when you stopped talking, there was nothing in your way of speaking out. Is that correct?"

I shook my head. "No. That's not true."

"You claim your father threatened you. Is this correct?"

"Yes."

"And what did he say?"

"That the truth would kill my mother. I was terrified that it was true."

"You believed *words* could kill her?" He cocked his head to the side.

Patronising, word-twisting bastard.

When I was five, I believed my dad, every word he'd said. I had no idea what could or couldn't kill a person then. I hadn't understood any of it. All I had known was that I loved my mum and didn't want her to die.

I said nothing.

"Miss Farrell, did you like playing games as a child?"

What kind of question is that? "Yes, of course," I replied. *What child doesn't play?*

He nodded and swiftly moved to his next question. "Did you play make-believe games?"

"Yes," I replied cautiously, knowing this couldn't be leading anywhere good.

Jasper, Cole, Mia, and I used to play all sorts of games, pretending we were our favourite TV show characters from *Power Rangers* and programmes like that. Every child did.

"Mmm. And, when you stopped talking, you liked the attention you got, didn't you?"

My face fell. That was where he was going. "No, that's not how it was."

"You said you liked to play make-believe games."

Keeping calm was almost impossible. *What kind of a person would make up something so evil?* I hated that anyone could even suggest that I was lying about it. All I'd ever wanted was a happy, normal family. I never wanted any of this.

"I did not make that up."

John turned on his heel and took a few steps toward the jury. He had been walking around the whole time. He seemed so at ease here, as if this were his house and we were guests.

"Miss Farrell, you state that, from the first time Mr Glosser accompanied you and your father, he would be there every occasion after that. Is that correct?"

"Yes."

"Did he meet you at your house?"

"No. My mum and brother were never aware he was with us on the fishing trips."

"He was waiting for you?"

"No, he always came after we'd set up and been to the local shop."

Being on the stand meant that I was slightly higher than him, so I used that to my advantage and straightened my back, forcing him to look up at me.

"You said your father took payment from Mr Glosser?"

"That's correct."

"Could that have merely been Mr Glosser paying for his half of the food bill? You said he showed *after* you'd shopped."

"No," I growled through my teeth.

Linda looked up and widened her eyes, warning me to remain calm. I needed to, but I couldn't help it. He was twisting everything I had said to make it look like I was lying.

"How did you know what the exchange of money was for? Were you told?"

"No, but—"

"So, it could have been his share of dinner. Miss Farrell, you've also alleged your father took photographs during the abuse even though no pictures of you have been found."

I narrowed my eyes. "They should look harder."

I didn't even bother looking at Linda's face. No doubt she would be wincing at my knee-jerk response, which was exactly what the defence wanted.

The photos existed. I *knew* they did.

"Every phone, tablet, PC, and laptop in your father's position has been searched, Miss Farrell. I can assure you that there aren't any pictures to back up your claim."

I didn't know if I should be pleased they were gone and no one would ever see them or frightened that them being gone backed up Dad's story.

"It happened," I whispered. I looked to the jury. *Please believe me.*

"Miss Farrell, could you at least tell me what camera was allegedly used?"

I shook my head. "I don't know. It was silver, but I don't know which make."

"Of course," he replied. "And was this the family's camera?"

I coldly looked at him. "My father's sick, not stupid."

Linda stood up. "Can we please have a five-minute break?"

John the Arsehole objected, but the judge agreed and called a recess.

I followed Linda out of the room in a daze. The world was spinning around me but I felt like I was dead still. We went into another room to talk privately.

"I'm sorry," I mumbled, dropping to the seat in the little room where I'd passed out a few days ago.

"Oakley," Linda said, sitting down beside me, "you're doing great, but you need to try to keep your cool. Their whole argument is that you're a troublemaker who craved the attention. Unfortunately, any sign of anger or temper from you—however understandable in the circumstances—will mean that you're playing right into their hands. I know it's frustrating. I've been sitting there, wanting to throw my briefcase at him, but I can't. You *have* to stay calm."

I nodded and roughly ran my hand through my hair. "I know."

She was right. If I let John get to me, blowing this chance of getting Dad and Frank sent down, then I would mess up the whole reason I'd spoken out in the first place. For me and all the other girls, I had to do this.

"I'll be fine now. I won't let Dad get away with it."

She smiled. "Good girl. You can do this. Just stay calm. He can't trip you up because you're telling the truth."

"Okay. I'm ready."

Linda squeezed my hand and stood up. "Let's get back in there."

"Welcome back, Miss Farrell," John said almost sarcastically.

I wanted to give him the finger. I'd never given anyone the finger before, but he would be a good place to start.

"You said the alleged abuse lasted for eight years—until you turned thirteen?"

"That's correct," I said.

"And how did that make you feel?"

My heart dropped. I had to talk about that. "Dirty, worthless, and broken."

"So broken that you started a relationship with your childhood friend and neighbour, Mr Cole Benson?"

With shaking hands, I gripped the bottom of my top. "That was completely different."

Why is he doing this? No one had the right to tell me when I could have a relationship or my reasons for doing so. There was no set time for everything to be okay. None of this would ever be okay, but I had to keep going on. I would never apologise for my relationship with Cole. It might have been too soon to other people, but it was right for me.

I found a little bit of courage buried deep.

"I wasn't aware there was a time limit on when I was allowed to be happy again."

I mentally kicked myself and refused to look at Linda. I knew she would be giving me a warning stare. I couldn't help it. He was getting under my skin.

He ignored my comment. "So, your physical relationship with Mr Benson started at the beginning of summer in 2008?"

How does he know that?

My heart stuttered. I had known he might bring Cole up, but I'd had no idea he would be so personal. "Yes."

His eyebrows shot up. "And when did you turn sixteen?"

Oh God. My eyes flicked upward to Cole. *No! Am I going to get him into trouble?* I couldn't. We hadn't done anything wrong.

Cole nodded, telling me to continue.

"August."

"Hmm. Your physical relationship with Mr Benson started relatively quickly, wouldn't you say?"

"No. I'd known Cole my whole life. I trusted him, and it felt right. For the first time in my life, something felt right, and it was completely different to what Frank had done. I chose it."

Someone barged into the room and approached the judge, interrupting John's line of questioning. I looked to Linda to see if she knew what was going on, but she wasn't looking at me. Her eyes were also on the judge. The room fell deathly silent. I tried to listen but could only hear muffled voices.

What's happening?

"We're going to take a break," the judge announced. "Mr Bee and Mrs Rake, please approach."

John and Linda walked over.

Walter, Linda's colleague, came over to me and gestured toward the exit. "Follow me, please."

I stepped down and followed him into the room I'd fainted in before.

"What's happening?" I asked Walter.

"I'm not sure. We'll just have to wait for Linda. Can I get you something? Tea or coffee? Water?"

"No, thank you," I replied. *This is bad. Why would they have stopped? Dad must be getting off.*

It wouldn't surprise me. He was so well liked and respected. Everyone believed him and looked up to him. *Of course he's getting off.*

I sank into the worn chair, and my heart dropped to my feet. Pulling my legs up, I pressed my face into my knees. *This can't be happening. What am I going to do now? Run. I want to escape back to Australia. Coming here was a mistake.*

A stray tear rolled down my cheek, and I angrily swiped it away. I was so stupid. *Who's going to believe me over a well-respected businessman?*

At least he couldn't deny the other charge though. There *was* evidence of him abusing a little girl when he had been in university. Evidence of him and the other people in the paedophile ring. And evidence of him having images of little girls on his computer.

Even if there were now nothing linking him to me and what Frank had done, he would still go to prison. He *had* to go to prison.

I closed my eyes and breathed in for five seconds and out for five. Those familiar feelings of panic were threatening to take over again.

Time slowly ticked by as I waited for news. No one else came in, so I assumed everyone was still in the public gallery or were not allowed to come in. Walter had left to find out what was going on, but all he knew was that Linda and John were no longer in the courtroom.

The door opened, and Linda walked in. It had been almost two hours. Her face betrayed nothing. I couldn't tell if the news was good or not.

"I'm sorry I was gone for so long," she said.

"He's getting off, isn't he?"

"No," Linda replied.

What? "No?"

She shook her head. "They found a folder on his laptop. It had been very well hidden and was only just found by one highly determined man who had known this was his last chance. He had to call someone else in to assist; it had been that well hidden. We've had them reexamining the evidence all week. They found it, Oakley, and brought it straight here."

She still has people looking over evidence? I'd thought all that would have been left alone by now. They'd kept looking and looking.

"What folder?" I asked even though I knew what folder she was talking about.

She placed her hand over mine. "The pictures of you."

I felt like I had been hit by a bus. *That folder.* I closed my eyes and took a deep breath. I didn't even want to think about it. "So, what does that mean?"

"It means your story is proven to be true, and your father is exposed as a liar."

My eyes filled with tears. "What happens now?"

"The public gallery has been closed. The jury will be shown the photographs, and then the trial will be wrapped up. I see no reason to call your father back to the stand. The pictures speak for themselves, and, surprisingly, John is not calling for him to take the stand again, the new evidence will only make things worse for him if he tried giving his side."

"Do I have to go back in there?"

She shook her head. "No, I don't think so. It seems unlikely that his defence will call you back in now that this new evidence has come to light. I've got to go back, but Walter will take you to your family."

Walter escorted me to the café where everyone was sitting. I paused at the entrance to the café and watched my family and friends for a minute, all these amazing people who had stood by me. They sat around two pushed together tables in silence. Mum stared at her mug. Her face was pale.

Cole spotted me first and jumped up, so I took that as my cue and walked toward them.

I sat in the chair Jasper had pulled over for me between him and Cole.

"How are you doing, honey?" Mum asked. She hadn't moved an inch. It was as if she were made of stone.

"Um, I don't know. Do you all know what's going on?"

Mum nodded. "Yes. We were told just a few minutes ago. We wanted to come and find you, but we were told you were with Linda."

"Okay, good."

Why isn't Jasper at least celebrating? This is good, right? They'd found the one concrete thing that backed up my version and proved that I was telling the truth. I didn't want to celebrate because it felt wrong, but I'd thought they would. *Do they think something's going to happen? The evidence could somehow be dismissed? That couldn't happen.*

Cole gripped my hand, and we fell silent again. There was so much to say but the enormity of it was overwhelming so we just sat united.

I felt sick. I didn't like them being happy about any part of this trial, but the fact that they weren't petrified me.

After one hour and forty-seven minutes, I saw Linda walking toward us with purpose. She'd told me to wait around. In that time, we had quietly drunk too many hot drinks and entered into a few light conversations.

"The jury has reached their decision," she said.

Mum jumped up. "Already?"

Linda nodded once. "If you all want to make your way back."

I stood up and was about to follow Linda when Mum pulled me into a hug. "It'll be fine."

"Yeah, it will," I replied. For the first time, I truly believed it would be.

I walked back with Linda and entered the courtroom. I would be allowed to sit with my family, but Linda quickly ran through what would happen and how the judge would ask for the jury's decision on each individual charge.

Stepping into the public gallery, I found my mum and brother and sat in the seat between them. I made eye contact with as many members of the jury as I could. There was no way they could believe him over me now, but I was still terrified.

"Have the ladies and gentlemen of the jury reached their decision?" the judge asked, her voice businesslike and intimidating.

A tall lady with long grey hair and bright red lipstick stood up. "Yes, we have, Your Honour."

I took a deep breath. My palms started to sweat.

"On the charge of administering a substance with intent to commit sexual offences, how do you find the defendant?"

"Guilty."

The air left my lungs in a rush.

"On the charge of trafficking within the UK for sexual exploitation, how do you find the defendant?"

"Guilty."

"On the charge of controlling a child prostitute or a child involved in pornography, how do you find the defendant?"

"Guilty."

"On the charge of causing or inciting child prostitution or pornography, how do you find the defendant?"

I held my breath and watched the lady's red lips say, "Guilty."

"On the charge of possession of indecent photographs of children, how do you find the defendant?"

"Guilty."

"On the charge of abuse of position of trust, causing or inciting a child to engage in sexual activity, how do you find the defendant?"

"Guilty."

"On the charge of sexual assault on a child, how do you find the defendant?"

"Guilty."

A sob erupted in front of me, and a woman fell against a man, who I assumed was her husband. She must have been one of the women my father had abused.

I let out a breath that I felt I'd been holding for years.

Guilty on all charges. The jury believed me. They believed all of us.

nineteen

OAKLEY

I watched Cole pour the paint into the tray and couldn't help picturing this as *our* house rather than just his.

"Ready?" he asked, passing me a paintbrush.

After briefly pressing his lips to mine, he dunked his brush in the paint and slapped it on the wall.

"Cole?"

He looked over his shoulder. "Hmm?"

"I don't think I like this colour anymore."

His face dropped, making me laugh.

"I'm joking."

"Oh, good one," he replied flatly. "Get to work you."

His whole posture was casual, and he had been playful all day.

Tomorrow, my father was going to be sentenced. Since I'd given evidence three weeks ago, Cole had been deliberately keeping me distracted. He let me cry, promised everything would be okay, whatever the sentence, but he always had something planned to take my mind off the waiting and worrying.

I dipped the paintbrush in the Caramel Blush paint and started on the living room wall.

Mum was right when she had said that helping Cole would take my mind off Dad's sentencing. I hadn't been convinced at first, but I was enjoying doing it now.

The muscles in Cole's arms flexed as he moved the brush up and down. Painting with him took so long, but somehow—between the kissing, flirting, and play fights—we managed to get the first coat in the living room done.

I smiled at our work. The room looked so warm and inviting already. I couldn't wait to see it completely finished with the sofas, coffee and TV tables, and large rug.

Cole sighed and flopped his arm over my shoulder. "Well, we're done for today. Shall we go get ready?"

We were going to dinner at his parents' tonight along with Mum, Miles, and Jasper.

I leant against Cole's side. "Yep. I need feeding soon. Want to share a shower? Save water and all."

And I needed the comfort and normality of us.

"Best offer I've had all day." He kissed the side of my head and grabbed the paint tray and brushes, so we could wash them before we left.

"Oakley." Jenna smiled warmly, giving me a hug the second I walked into the house. "You don't bring her here enough," she scolded her son.

Cole held his hands up. "We've been busy, and you're often very embarrassing."

"Please, I watched you pee your pants when you were a kid. How much more embarrassing can it get?" I teased.

He pretended to take offence. "I was five, and I'd had a load to drink."

"Uh-huh." Jenna laughed and pulled my hand, leading me through to the kitchen.

Cole followed behind, grumbling.

That was one of my earliest memories. I was only just three. We had all been visiting the Lake District and had taken a long walk. We had been told to keep drinking water because it was hot. Cole had needed the toilet but refused to do it outside in case a bee stung his *winkie*. Bless him, he'd had to walk back commando in my white shorts—the only spare clothing we'd had.

Mia sat at the kitchen counter, staring at her laptop.

"Hey, Mia," I called.

She jumped up and off the seat, pulling me into a tight hug. "How are you?"

"I'm good." And I was.

Well, I was certainly doing a lot better since Dad had been found guilty. The jury believed me and not him. Whatever the sentence was, I would always have that.

"What are you up to?" I sat down beside her.

"Looking for a place. I want a two-bedroom flat with a nice big garden for Leona to play."

"Where is Leona?"

Mia smiled. "It's Chris's weekend again, so she'll be driving him up the wall instead of me."

"Do you and Chris get along more now?"

She shrugged. "Most of the time. We're arguing at the minute because he wants to introduce his new girlfriend to Leona, but I refused. This is the third one this year, and it's not been that long. I don't want random women walking in and out of Leona's life."

I nodded. That sounded reasonable. Mia didn't have men coming and going, so Chris shouldn't have women. It would only be upsetting to Leona if she got attached to whoever the woman was, and then they broke up.

"What did he say?"

"He didn't look that happy when I said no, but he's agreed to wait. I don't care if he's happy about it or not, to be honest."

"You don't think he would just do it anyway?"

"No. He wouldn't do anything that could hurt Leona. We agreed that she wouldn't meet anyone either of us is dating until we've been with them for at least six months. Oh, look, this one is nice." She pointed to a semi-detached bungalow. It was quaint and pretty with cream-rendered walls and colourful flowers hanging in baskets.

I grabbed her mobile from the counter and handed it to her. "Call the estate agent."

Jenna gasped. "You found somewhere?" She rushed over to look at the pictures. "Oh, good. It's not too far. Closer to me than your house, Cole."

"Cut the cord, Mother," he replied. His arms wound around my waist, and his chin rested on my shoulder as he took a peek at the house on Mia's laptop.

I snuggled back against his chest and smiled. *Should it even be possible to love him as much as I do?* It was overwhelming sometimes. How I'd managed four years without seeing or touching him, I didn't know.

"Oh, shut up." Jenna slapped his arm and turned her attention back to the laptop. "It's gorgeous, Mia."

What will Jenna do when they've all moved out? She loved having a full house. I was sure they would visit a lot, and she would have Leona to sleep over whenever Mia would let her, but it wouldn't be the same.

"You all right?" Cole whispered against my neck.

His breath tickled my skin, and I closed my eyes, gasping.

"Yeah," I mumbled. I felt his lips turn up into a smile against my skin. He knew the effect he had on me.

"Are we painting the bedrooms soon?"

I felt him shrug against my back. "If you want."

"I do want. You need to decide what colour to do your study though." The fourth room upstairs was too small to be a bedroom, so it was going to be his study. I doubted he would use it much.

"Light blue?"

I didn't know why he asked for my opinion so much. This was his place. He didn't need me to agree on anything.

"Light blue sounds good. We can pick some up in the week."

"Sounds good."

I'd learnt that early wall-painting sessions, or any painting sessions actually, were not something Cole enjoyed. In fact, they made him whine like a four-year-old.

"There's something I need to do first thing anyway. I'll pick you up after."

I frowned. "What do you need to do?"

He shook his head and chuckled. "So nosy. It's a surprise, so you'll have to wait."

I looked at Jenna and Mia. "Do you two know?"

Jenna grinned. "Nope."

Liar. I let it go because I knew Cole wouldn't tell me.

"Fine. I can wait."

Mum, Jasper, and Miles arrived twenty minutes later. Miles's hand slid down Mum's back as they walked into the kitchen, and I couldn't keep the smile off my face. She was letting him in, trusting him, and allowing herself to be happy again.

About time!

"Wine and beer are in the fridge, and red is on the counter. Help yourselves to whatever you like," Jenna said, stirring something on the hob while playing with the timer on the oven.

"Good day?" I asked Mum. Clearly a loaded question.

She glared. "Yes, thank you."

We sat in the living room to eat the home-cooked Chinese food. I loved lounging around at their house and chatting about nothing important. No one mentioned the sentencing tomorrow or Frank's looming trial, and I was thankful for that. I just wanted to chill for the evening with friends, family, and the man I was crazy about.

"So..." Cole said, resting his chin on my shoulder as we sat with my back to his chest on the soft carpet. "You know I love you, right?"

I frowned. "Yes..." *Where is he going with this?*

"Good."

"Good?" I repeated.

He nodded.

"You're strange," I said.

"Happy and in love actually."

"So cheesy," I teased, wrapping his arms around my waist.

Cole spent the night, as usual, and I woke up to him sleeping next to me again. He rarely woke first.

Reaching out, I gently stroked my fingers down his cheek. "Cole," I whispered.

He groaned. "No."

I laughed. "We have to get up soon. We need to be at court in a couple of hours."

His eyes flicked open, and he rolled onto his side to face me. He looked wide-awake now. I wished I were able to forget like him. From the second I'd opened my eyes, I pictured Dad standing in that room, waiting to hear his fate.

"How are you feeling about today?"

What am *I feeling?* Too many things at once made it impossible to figure out what the main emotion was. I was happy, scared, sad, relieved, exhausted. The list went on.

"I'm not sure. I never thought I would be doing this."

"You never should have had to."

No, he was right. I shouldn't have to, but paedophiles, murderers, and rapists had families, too. They didn't always live alone. They didn't have distinguishing features or a tattoo on their forehead. They could be anyone, in any seemingly normal house. They might be charming, lovable, and known and liked by everyone around them. And I was unfortunate that my father happened to be one of them.

I smiled at Cole to acknowledge his words without having to reply and got out of bed to get ready.

Jasper opened the bathroom door just as I got to it.

His face was sombre. "Hey," he grumbled.

"Hey. You all right?"

"Nope. You?"

"Nope."

He leant against the doorframe. "I hope he dies in prison."

"Jasper…"

There was a time when Dad had been Jasper's hero. I knew he hated what Dad had done, but he had to feel more than anger and hatred. Emotions were never that straightforward.

"Don't, Oakley. I'm okay. Get ready, yeah? We need to go soon." Jasper walked back into his room.

I felt awful for him. Sighing, I walked into the bathroom and closed the door. *Let's just get this over with.*

I sat between Mum and Jasper in the public gallery. Cole was on the chair in front of me, and the rest of my family was dotted around. I wanted to be between Mum and Jasper, rather than Cole, because I wanted to show Dad that he hadn't broken us.

My heart felt as if it were going to burst right out of my chest. I wanted him to get the maximum sentence, but at the same time, I felt wrong for wanting that.

Separating who he was from knowing he was my dad was hard. I wished he could have been different, but now, all I could hope for was that he wasn't ever given the opportunity to hurt another girl.

Dad seemed older and smaller. He stood with his shoulders hunched over and looked at the floor. His hair had greyed so much that he looked ten years older. Looking at this man in front of me, I couldn't believe that I had ever been afraid of him. But appearances were deceptive.

The judge stood up in what felt like slow motion. I took Mum's and Jasper's hands and prayed that my father would spend the rest of his life in prison. When the judge opened her mouth, I couldn't hear a thing, just a ringing in my ears.

My head felt light, and I could just about lip-read. I caught a few words.

"Gross abuse of trust," and, "danger to young children," were the only things I could pick out.

I blinked rapidly, spilling my tears. *Please.*

Jasper sucked his breath through his teeth and gripped my hand.

What?

The courtroom burst into life, but I hadn't heard what the sentence was.

"What happened?" The shrill ringing in my ears and distant murmuring was still all I could hear.

Mum gripped my arms and cried. "Life, Oakley. He will never hurt anyone again." Her voice sounded muffled, as if I were hearing her from underwater, but I'd made out every word.

My father had received a life sentence.

Breathing in sharply, I collapsed into Mum's arms. *He's got life. How will he cope in prison? Why do I even care?*

Oh God.

I pulled back from Mum and looked down at him again. His eyes were wide with shock. The dad I had known had left fifteen years ago. I felt the air rush to my lungs as I finally let go. He wasn't my dad, and I didn't ever want to see him again. He was nothing to me now.

As he was being led away to start serving his sentence, he looked up. Our eyes met, and there was nothing. No remorse. His expression was empty.

My heart was beating at a hundred miles an hour, and I wanted to run, but I held his gaze, refusing to back down.

Mum and Jasper both put their arms around me. The last image he would have of his family would be of us standing strong together, watching him being hauled away.

Good-bye, Dad.

"Honey?" Mum whispered.

"It's okay now, Mum," I whispered. "We're going to be okay."

Back at Ali's, I went up to Lizzie's room for a few minutes to clear my head. Downstairs, a celebration had started, but I couldn't bring myself to raise a glass to helping put my father behind bars. I had gone through too much to be able to celebrate anything connected to what had happened to me.

I sat on the futon and took a calming deep breath. Letting him go felt as if a huge weight had been lifted off my shoulders. I no longer had a dad, but that was good because I no longer had an evil one.

Cole pushed the door open. "Hey," he said, kneeling in front of me. He pulled a little red velvet bag out of his pocket. "Open your hand."

"Okay," I replied, frowning, as I did as he'd instructed.

He tipped the bag over, and a small egg-shaped orange-red gemstone fell into my hand. A black lace was threaded through a hole cut into the top, creating a necklace. "Fire agate," he said.

"Fire what?"

"Agate." He grinned. "Energy, warmth, strength, and courage. You have so much already, but I know you struggle sometimes."

My heart swelled as I ran my thumb over the smooth stone. I definitely could do with a little more of all of that. "Thank you. It's perfect." I turned and kissed him. "You chose this yourself?"

"Well, I wanted to get you something, but it was Mia who suggested a stone. Shall I?"

Nodding, I handed him the necklace and pulled my hair out of the way. With it hanging around my neck, I felt stronger. I knew it was all in my head, but that didn't matter.

I leant forward and softly kissed him. "Let's get down there."

He smiled and stood up. I followed.

Down in the living room, my grandparents were sitting with Ali on one sofa while Jenna and David sat on another. Lizzie, Miles, Jasper, and Mia were dotted around the floor.

I sat on the carpet between Cole and Jasper. There was a space on the sofa near Ali, but that must be where Mum was sitting.

"Where's Mum?" I asked.

Jasper's eyes flicked to the floor. "Just on the phone."

What's he hiding? "On the phone with whom?"

He shrugged.

"*Jasper*?" I insisted.

"Linda, okay? She's on the phone with Linda."

Why is she on the phone with Linda so soon? Frank's trial was a few weeks away, and Dad's was completely over.

"Don't freak. It's probably nothing," Jasper said.

"Then, why were you trying to keep it from me?"

"Because I knew you would freak."

Mum walked into the room, clutching the phone. "You don't have to go through it again," she said straightaway. "Frank's changed his plea to guilty. He's admitted to everything."

My eyes widened in surprise. I felt my mouth pop open. "Really?" *Frank is pleading guilty now?* "So, that's it. It's all over?" Relief conflicted with disappointment. I'd wanted to stand up to him, but by him changing his plea, he was admitting that I was right anyway.

She grinned. "Yes, sweetheart. It's over."

"Good," Jasper said. His voice was as hard as his posture. "He can rot, too."

"What happens next?" I asked.

"Linda said the judge will set a date for the sentencing. She'll let us know."

I blinked. "Oh."

David stood up. "Well, this definitely calls for the other bottle now."

"Thank goodness," Nan said, standing to hug Mum.

I looked over at Cole, ready to tell him that I was a little disappointed I wouldn't get to look Frank in the eyes when I told my side, but he looked so relieved. And that was how I would ultimately come to feel. I wouldn't have to go over what had happened with Frank again.

Cole had heard what Max had watched and allowed, but he hadn't had to hear what it all had felt like, how painful and sickening it was. My family and he would be spared that at least.

"To justice and moving on," Granddad said, raising his champagne.

Everyone lifted their glasses and repeated his words. I lifted my glass, but deep in my heart, I didn't feel justice had been served. There was no sentence that could take back what either of those men had done. But, finally, they were going to be in a place where they could never do it again.

twenty

COLE

Oakley had been too quiet all day. I wanted to celebrate that the bastard Frank was going down as well as Max, but she didn't seem to want to. When I'd watched Max give evidence, I had almost been convinced that the jury believed he was innocent when it came to Oakley and that she'd stopped talking for attention or because of some condition.

She sipped on her vodka, lemonade, and lime while staring down at the table.

Not for the first time, I couldn't think of anything to say. *It will be okay.* It already was in the sense that they would spend a lot of time in prison, but for her, it wasn't okay. Oakley still had to live with the memories.

She looked up and gave me a small smile, her fingers gripping the necklace I'd bought her. I questioningly nodded toward the door, and she stood up. I followed her out to the porch and wrapped my arms around her tiny body. I loved how perfectly she fit against me.

She pressed her face into my shoulder and gripped ahold of me. Her hair tickled my face.

"What are you thinking?"

"I don't know," she admitted. "Just looking forward to when I don't have to worry about trials and sentences. I'm so tired of it all."

"Yeah, I know. Not long now, and it'll be done. Soon, there will be no more worrying about what will happen."

Oakley laughed humourlessly. "Unless he gets a short sentence."

"Don't worry about that. Whatever happens, he will never come near you again."

She pulled back, frowning, as she ran her finger down the side of my face. "It's not me I'm worried about. I've got nothing he wants now."

I bit down hard on my lip and swallowed. Now, she wasn't a child.

I gripped her tight. No one would ever hurt her again. "Want to get out of here? I'll let you drag me around home furnishing shops."

"Okay." She smiled. "Start the car for a quick getaway. I'll let them know."

"I feel like I'm in an action movie. We should blow something up, too."

She rolled her eyes. "I'll get right on that."

I started the car, and seconds later, she got in. *That was quick*. "To the boring shops," I muttered.

At least it would take her mind off everything.

"Whichever one you want," I whined. *What the hell does it matter what coffee table I get anyway?* It would just end up cluttered with video games and empty bottles of beer.

Oakley turned to me and sighed, exasperated. "Cole, just choose a fucking coffee table."

My mouth dropped open. I could count on one hand the amount of times I had heard Oakley swear. It was so alien but weirdly sexy.

"I'm serious," she said threateningly. "Pick one."

Blinking, I pointed to the table we were standing by. She'd picked out four that were the same wood as the window and doorframes, but it was my job to choose which I preferred.

She smiled. "Good. I'll go get someone to help."

I watched her walk away, delighted by her increasing confidence.

When she returned, she was arranging delivery to my place. The guy was grinning and looking at her in a way that made me want to smash his face into the effing table.

"Oh, and do you have any end tables?" She turned to me. "You could have one beside the corner sofa."

"What do I need two tables in the living room for?" The happy glint in her eyes made me give in immediately. "Fine, where are they?"

"What about that mirror for the hallway?"

"Yeah, that, too."

Maybe she didn't know it, but I was decorating the house for us both. All I had to do was get her to stay with me.

"What about photo frames? I promised Leona I'd put her picture up, so I wouldn't forget her." Like I could ever forget my beautiful, crazy niece.

"I think I saw some in the first or second aisle. We can go back in a minute."

Great, back to the start. Why the hell did I say anything? I scowled at how stupid I was.

"Aw, stop the frowning." Oakley rubbed her thumb over my forehead, as if erasing frown lines, and smiled. "We're almost finished, and then you can take me home to bed."

I was sure my eyes lit up when she'd said that. "You know, we don't really need to get the frames now."

She stopped walking and grinned up at me. "Oh, really? You have a better idea?"

I nodded. I had a *much* better idea.

"We're getting them. I think you can wait an extra five minutes."

"Can't," I grumbled. "How the hell am I going to concentrate on picking stupid photo frames out when all I can think about are those legs of yours wrapped around me—"

"Cole!" Oakley scolded, ducking her head to hide her blush.

I laughed and nudged her forward. "All right, just hurry up. The sooner I get you naked, the better."

She giggled and pulled my hand toward the stupid lamps. I was going to pick the closest one and then the closest frames, and then I'd be getting her home.

"Oakley…" I said when we had been looking at two very similar-looking lamps for seven minutes.

She frowned. "Cole, what you buy for your house is important. You have to live with it every single day."

"I can live with either of those. What I can't live with is not being—"

She gasped and slapped her hand over my mouth, her cheeks turning a dark shade of red. I would never get bored with making her blush like that.

"You're such a prude, beautiful."

"And you're such a…" She paused and frowned. "Whatever the opposite of prude is."

"Oakley!"

We both turned around at the sound of her name. Marcus, her old gymnastics coach, bound toward her, and she stepped into his outstretched arms.

"Oh my God, I haven't seen you in years," he said.

"I know. It's been too long."

He gasped and pulled back. "How have you been?"

She smiled. "Good. You?"

"Fabulous. Listen, you should drop by the gym sometime."

"Yeah? I'd love to. I can come next week."

"Perfect. Drop me a text?"

She nodded, took his phone, and started tapping her number in.

"Cole, how's it going?"

I shook his hand. Marcus had always been really good to Oakley; therefore, I liked him. "Good, man. How's Jack?"

Marcus shrugged. "The same—gorgeous and possessive." He'd been with Jack for as long as I'd known him.

Oakley handed his phone back. "Here. Text me your number, and we'll meet up next week."

"I absolutely will." He kissed her cheek and shook my hand again before gliding off toward the kitchens.

The man didn't walk like normal people. The only part of him that moved were his legs; his upper body was that solid.

"Nice to see him again," Oakley beamed.

Marcus hadn't spoken about those bastards like everyone else did, and I thought she appreciated that.

"Yeah, he's a good guy. Now, can we please finish in here and go?"

When we finally got out of the damn shop, I was ready to burst—from boredom *and* sexual frustration.

"Straight to bed?" I asked as we got in my car.

She smiled shyly and nodded.

"Good, because you're getting it."

"Who said romance was dead?" she muttered sarcastically.

"Please. I can do romance. You want roses on the bed?"

"Not really. Don't fancy thorns stabbing me, to be honest."

My parents' car was in the drive when we got back.

I let out an exasperated sigh. "Why can't they leave us alone?"

Oakley opened the car door. "This is their house, Cole."

"Whose side are you on?"

She laughed and got out. I traipsed behind in a bad mood. All the house crap was still in the boot, apart from the big stuff that was getting delivered. We still had to get it over to the new house and store it in the spare room. All I wanted to do was lock myself in my bedroom with my girlfriend and forget everything else, but the universe hated me today.

The front door opened right before we reached it. Mum and Dad stepped out. Mum had her bag, and Dad was holding his car keys. It was all looking positive.

"Oh, hey. Did you get everything you needed?" Mum asked me as she gave Oakley a hug.

"Pretty much. You guys going out?" *Please say for a while.*

"Yeah, dinner at Judy's," Dad grumbled.

Judy was my aunt, Mum's sister, the lady who criticised everything.

"Oh, stop moaning, David. I endure your mother, so the least you can do is put on a smile for my sister."

"My mother is *nowhere* near as bad as your sister," he argued.

"All right, parents! As fascinating as this is, we're going to go inside. You two enjoy your dinner." I pushed Oakley inside and shut the door before they could say anything else.

"Rude," Oakley said.

"I know. Sorry about them." I chose deliberately not to understand her.

"I wasn't talking about them."

"I know," I replied, grinning. "Come on. Bed, you."

She giggled and grabbed my arm, pulling me toward the stairs.

The second I closed my door, I gently pulled her top over her head. "I love you," I whispered against her lips as I moved us both down onto the bed.

Oakley yawned and lay back. "I'm so tired." She yawned and pressed her face into the pillow.

What? I groaned internally. "Okay, get some sleep then." *Be understanding.*

She looked up and grinned.

"Oh, stop teasing me!" I dived down on top of her, making her squeal and laugh. I kissed her hard, gripping her face between my hands.

She wasn't going to go back to Australia. There was no way we would be apart again.

twenty-one

COLE

"Do you want to sit with your mum and Jasper?" I asked as we stepped inside the public gallery.

I swore, if Frank didn't get sent down for the rest of his pathetic little life, I was going to murder him.

She shook her head. "No, it's okay."

I gripped her hand and led her to the end of the first row of chairs.

"You've got me. Always," she said.

We still hadn't had that what's-going-to-happen-when-this-is-all-over conversation. I had no idea where she was on that score.

Not going back to Australia, I hoped and prayed.

Sarah sat on the other side of Oakley, and Jasper was beside me. He muttered something under his breath that would probably turn the room blue.

I glanced at him.

He whispered, "I wish I owned a gun," in my ear.

I couldn't agree more.

There were a few reporters in the room; they all turned to look at us. The case had become so high profile that it had been in the national newspapers every single day. Even *my* family had been featured. The press were like vultures, hovering around, waiting to dive on you the second they got the chance.

Oakley had been offered so much money for her story; most of her family and friends had, too. Of course, no one had taken up the offers. I really hoped they never did that to her. The last thing she needed was someone she cared about profiting from the trauma she'd lived through. The attention was mental, but if it made the world see what disgusting fucking monsters those bastards were, then it was worth it.

"It's almost over," Oakley whispered, seemingly to herself.

I squeezed her hand. This was the only part that would ever be over. We could all try to forget, but it would never happen—especially not for Oakley. I couldn't even imagine what it was like for her.

I looked to my side, knowing where Frank was. As my eyes locked on his face, I felt my stomach turn. Oakley had once referred to his eyes as "beady," and I saw what she meant. Looking at him, I saw her as a child, scared and confused, and I could see how cold he might have looked as he stared back at her.

It was only when my jaw ached that I realised I had been clenching it. My muscles ached. Everything ached. I wanted to jump over everyone and beat the shit out of him. I hoped someone in prison would kill him. It shocked me how readily these thoughts came to me and how much I meant them.

Oakley kept her eyes ahead, watching the judge. Her body was stiff and tense. This was the first time she had seen him in four years—since the day she had run and called me. I wanted to say something to her to make her feel better, but what could I say?

I didn't have a damn clue what to say. There weren't any words that would make it okay. I could never take back the years of pain and betrayal she'd suffered. I hated it, but there was *nothing* I could do.

Her breathing became heavier. I wrapped my arm around her waist and pulled her against my side.

Is she going to pass out again?

"Do you want to leave?" I whispered.

She shook her head.

Should I just pick her up and take her out? Is it worth her staying if she's going to suffer?

"Oakley, you're not okay—"

"Fine," she muttered, leaning heavily against me.

I was aware that the judge had started to speak, but I couldn't concentrate on anything other than Oakley. She looked like all the blood had drained out of her. I was terrified she was going to collapse again. Her breathing was heavy and laboured. Sarah had realised something was wrong and turned to Oakley, running her hand over Oakley's forehead to check her temperature.

"Honey, are you all right? Baby?"

I caught part of what the judge had said. Oakley breathed a sigh of utter relief and fell against me.

"Fifteen years imprisonment."

"What?" Jasper roared, leaping out of his seat. "How the *fuck* is that justice? The dick needs to rot—"

"Enough," I growled as I pulled him back.

This was not good. There were no cameras allowed in the room, so thankfully, no one could take pictures, but the press were going to love this.

"Let go!" he shouted, snatching his arm out of my hand and turning to Frank. "Just wait until you get out, you sick bastard." Jasper's face was red in anger. His eyes looked so dark; rage had completely taken him over. "I'm gonna kill you, I swear."

Oakley stood shakily, but she managed to push past me, shoving Jasper toward the door. I was mad at him. Yes, the sentence was shit. Frank would probably be out in eight, but Jasper's reaction was not helpful for Oakley.

"What is wrong with you?" Oakley hissed at him, throwing her arms up.

Jasper spun around and faced her. His tortured face was the only thing stopping me from laying into him.

"Do you really want to go to jail for *that*? That piece of…" She trailed off.

He frowned. "I don't care about me. I want to kill him. I want to *fucking* kill him."

"Stop it, Jasper. Just stop. You can't change a thing. It's over; it's done. Do you really think that, even if you did kill him, it would make anything better? Do you think throwing your life away and going to prison will magically make this go away? The justice system isn't always fair but there's nothing we can do about that!" she shouted at him. "Stop. Please. I don't want to lose you."

His face softened, and I knew Oakley had gotten through to him.

Linda appeared next to us and grimaced. "Jasper, there will be no action taken for your outburst, but I suggest that you leave immediately. Go home, and cool down."

Sarah pushed Jasper toward the door. "I'm so sorry, Linda. Out, Jasper. Come on, Oakley."

"One minute, Mum."

Sarah looked between Linda and Oakley and then walked through the door, her hand firmly on Jasper's shoulder.

Oakley turned to Linda. "Thank you so much. For *everything*."

Linda smiled. "You're welcome. You take care of yourself."

"Thank you," I said.

Thank you seemed too weak for what Linda had done for Oakley.

She nodded.

I took Oakley's hand, and we walked to the exit. "How do you feel about the sentence?"

She shrugged. "I wanted it to be longer, but there's nothing I can do about it. I'm not going to dwell on it. He'll be on the sex offenders' register for life and, hopefully, closely monitored when he gets out."

Hopefully, he'll be murdered in prison. I didn't say it out loud.

"And it's officially over. No more court."

"You did it, babe."

"Yeah, I guess." She shook her head. "Whatever. It's done. I'm tired of being that poor little girl. I just want to move on now."

I was so happy to hear her say that. No more making herself sick, worrying about whether people would believe her or not. It was time for all of us to put it behind us and think about the future.

"What do you want to do now?"

"Lunch at your parents', remember?"

"We don't have to."

"I want to. Normal stuff now, okay?"

I smiled and kissed the side of her head. Normal felt good.

"Sounds great to me."

"Oakley! Oakley." A chorus of her name was screamed the second we were out of the building.

Our plan of getting out with as little attention on her as possible was—well, impossible now.

I pulled her close against my side, and she pressed her face into my shoulder to shield herself. They had a job to do, but I wished they would leave her alone. She didn't need this to be any harder than it already was.

"Oakley, do you feel justice was served?"

"What are you going to do now?"

"How do you feel about the sentence?"

"Ignore them," I whispered in her ear.

Jasper held the back door of the car open for her, and I pushed us both through the crowd to get her in.

Jasper ran around to the driver's side as soon as Oakley was in. I jumped in after her and slammed the door shut.

"Okay?" Sarah asked as we sped off.

"Yeah. I'm looking forward to this dying down," Oakley mumbled.

I hoped that it would be over soon, but I wasn't going to hold my breath.

Sarah reached to the back of the car and took Oakley's hand. "It'll be fine, sweetheart. There will be another big story soon enough, and they'll leave us all alone."

"I'm sure when they realise that you don't want to tell your story or give a statement, then they'll get bored," Jasper added, briefly turning to look at us.

"Yeah." Oakley agreed.

I wasn't sure if she believed that or not though; she hadn't sounded sure.

"Where to, Oakley?" Jasper asked.

"Cole's," she replied.

I frowned; he had known where to.

Oh, he was giving her the option of skipping, I realised.

Sometimes, he wasn't as stupid as he looked and acted ninety-nine percent of the time.

"If you want to go back to Ali's, that's fine," I said.

She raised her eyebrow, and I knew I was about to be in trouble. She didn't want to be babied.

I held my hand up. "Okay, just checking."

For the first time in a while, there were no reporters outside my house—although they were probably on their way either here or to Ali's from court.

"Anyone else see anything wrong with this picture?" Jasper said.

Sarah snorted in disgust. "They'll probably be here soon, so we should get inside."

"Untle Ole!" Leona screamed, running out the front door at me.

Shit. I managed to cover my area just in time. You only needed to have the collision *once* to automatically protect yourself forever more.

I missed being greeted like that though. With everything going on, Leona had temporarily spent more time with Chris, and it was good to have her around again.

I ruffled her hair. "Hey, what ya doing?"

She flashed me her cheesy toothy grin. "Watchin' Fifi."

What else?

"Can Oaley watch it with me?"

"You'll have to ask her."

Leona leant across, as if she wasn't suspended in the air, only being held by my arms. Kids had so much trust.

"Of course I'll watch it with you," Oakley said, taking her from me. "You'll have to tell me everyone's names though."

Leona's face lit up. "Well, there's Fifi and..."

I stopped listening to her. One, because I already knew them all. And, two, because the programme drove me nuts.

I ushered Sarah into the kitchen where my mum had already started getting the fresh pizzas out of the fridge. Mia was getting the full report from Oakley's grandparents and my dad. They didn't waste any time.

Sarah questioningly looked at me.

"She's doing as well as can be expected, I guess," I said, knowing what was going through Sarah's mind. "She just wants to move on. She's been under their control for most of her life and then had four years of waiting around and preparing for the trials. I think she wants to be the one in control of her life now."

"I have no idea how she does it. I feel like a mess most of the time. She's so positive and always looking forward." Sarah had said the words, but it didn't look like she believed them.

Oakley was nearly always positive on the outside because she worried about the effect falling apart would have on everyone else. We all knew the truth though.

"She deserves the future she wants. And so do you," I said.

"Thank you, Cole. I'm so glad you two found each other again. You're perfect together."

I grinned like an idiot, like an eleven-year-old girl who had just seen One Direction. It meant *that* much to hear her say it.

"Well," she said, exhaling deeply, "let's do what Oakley wants and move on. I think we *all* deserve a bit of happiness now."

If Oakley had heard her mum say that, she would probably burst; she wanted her mum to be happy so much.

"Okay, so we've got about a hundred pizzas, garlic dough balls, and crispy chicken strips. Anyone want salad, too?" Mia offered, looking in the fridge for something.

"Who the hell wants rabbit food when we have pizza and meat?" Jasper said. With a look of horror, he rejected the lettuce in Mia's hand.

I nodded. "He's got a point."

"I second that," Lizzie said.

Mia chucked the lettuce back in the fridge and closed the door. "Good, because I can't be bothered to make it. But I can be bothered with this," she said, holding out two bottles of champagne to Dad.

"Celebrating again?" Oakley asked from the doorway. She chewed on her lip.

"We're celebrating new beginnings," Sarah said, leaning into Miles.

I waited for Oakley's reaction. She had been less than enthusiastic to celebrate before, and I understood why.

Her lips pulled up into the faintest smile. "I'll drink to that."

"An I have some, too?" Leona asked, pointing to the glasses on the counter.

Mia smiled. "Of course you *can*."

She handed Leona a champagne glass that was clearly filled with lemonade, but from the goofy grin on Leona's face, she thought she was drinking champagne, too.

"To new beginnings," Miles said, raising his glass.

The celebration was going well. At last, we were all together and having a laugh rather than the serious talks and tension. People were laughing—at Jasper mostly, but still laughing.

"Come on, Oakley! You must remember those hot twins! They were at the Christmas beach party!"

Oakley sighed. "No, Jasper, you made them up."

"I did not make them up. They were hot and *all* over me."

"Yeah, that definitely sounds like a lie," I said.

"Dude, why would I make that up?"

"To prove how big your balls are?"

He huffed. "I don't need to prove anything. You all know."

Oakley put down her drink. "Okay, we need to change the subject before I'm sick."

"I'm so glad Leona dragged Dad and Miles outside," Mia added.

"You don't need to make up stuff like that, Jasper. We all like you, ya know," Lizzie said.

Jasper blankly stared at her. "Well, thanks for that, Peroxide, but it happened. Believe me, that's not something you forget. But, anyway, I don't care what you lot think."

I rolled my eyes and went through to the living room. The others followed.

The doorbell rang, thankfully. I thought Lizzie was seconds away from reacting to the peroxide comment.

It fell on me to open the door since Mia had laid back and kicked her feet up on the coffee table.

"Don't move. Yeah, I'll get it," I said sarcastically.

I pulled the front door open, and my face fell as I saw two police officers.

One of them frowned. "Cole Benson?"

"Yeah."

"Can we come in?"

I stepped aside, and they walked in. The room fell silent.

My dad, who had come back inside, asked, "What's going on?"

"I'm sorry to do this," the taller officer said, turning to me. "Mr Benson, I'm arresting you—"

That was all I heard because Oakley shouted, "No!"

She stared at me in horror. Her face was as white as a ghost.

Shit, is she going to be okay?

I turned around as one of them held out handcuffs.

"Is that really necessary?" Dad shouted.

Oakley wasn't moving. The only things that made her still look alive were the tears rolling down her face. I looked at Jasper for help.

"You can't do this." Mum sobbed.

They can do this. I'd had sex with Oakley when she was fifteen. They were *supposed* to do this.

"It's okay. It's going to be fine," I said as I was pulled toward the door.

Oakley fiercely shook her head. "No! No, please. You can't do this. Please. Please?"

Jasper caught her as she fell toward me. I wanted nothing more than to grab her and wrap my arms around her, but I couldn't do a fucking thing.

"Oakley, it'll be fine," I repeated.

She shook her head. "No. Please, don't do this," she pleaded with the police officers.

It broke my heart. I hated seeing her like that. *What the hell can I do to make it better though?*

First, I needed a damn good lawyer. In my head, I was mentally planning the worst-case scenario and what I should or shouldn't say.

As we approached the car, I noticed the neighbours' curtains being pulled back, and some even came outside.

"Leave him the hell alone," Mr Gregory, from across the road, shouted.

I flashed him a grateful smile.

"They've been through enough. How dare you!" he roared.

Shit. The whole street was getting involved.

By the time the officer had opened the car door, at least ten more people had come out of their houses to protest. As the car door was slammed shut, I looked back at Oakley. Sarah grabbed her as her legs gave way. My heart felt like it had just been ripped out of my chest.

I love you, I mouthed as the car pulled away.

twenty-two

OAKLEY

I lay in bed, staring at the ceiling in a zombie-like state. *Arrested. Arrested because of me.*

The night Cole and I made love was the best night of my life. It was the night when I had felt so loved and safe and normal. *How could that possibly be wrong?*

Wiping my face again, I noticed nothing was there anymore. *Have all my tears dried up?* I felt as if I had nothing left inside me to come out. It had been almost thirty-five minutes since Cole was arrested, and I just wanted to be with him.

"It wouldn't look good if you went to the station," had been the officer's words.

Wouldn't look good? Surely, it'll show that I love him?

The only reason I was still in the house was because I was too scared of making it worse for him.

There has to be something I can do? Deny it and say I lied in court?

But then why would I lie about sleeping with him in the first place?

I could say we hadn't gone that far. That Cole had stopped it just before we'd actually had sex.

I pressed my face into the pillow and whimpered. *What could I do?*

"Oakley," Jasper said softly, sitting on the edge of the futon.

I hadn't even heard him come in.

"Oakley?"

Squeezing my eyes shut, I pretended he wasn't there. I felt bad for ignoring him. He was only trying to help, but I just couldn't talk to anyone. The only person I wanted to talk to was Cole.

Jasper sighed and got up, making me roll a little as the mattress sprang up. "I'll be downstairs. David and Jenna have gone to the station. We'll get him a good lawyer and figure this out."

We'd left Cole's parents' place when he was arrested and his mum and dad rushed after him.

As the bedroom door closed, I sat up and gasped. *Linda. Of course! She helped me, so she can help Cole, too, surely?*

I called her straightaway.

"Oakley?" she said, picking up on the second ring.

"Linda, I need your help. They've arrested Cole."

"They've what?" She sighed, as it obviously sank in why. "Oh. Okay," she said, changing to her businesslike tone. "I assume they've taken him to the station already?"

"Yes, half an hour ago," I whispered. A strangled sob escaped my throat, and I clamped my mouth shut. *What the hell will I do if he's actually charged? His whole life would be ruined because of me.*

"All right, they might offer him one of their lawyers, but I'll call now and tell them I'm on my way. Don't worry. I'll do everything I can."

Hearing her say that gave me hope. She was the only person I would trust with this. No other lawyer would be good enough.

"Is there anything I can do to help?" *There must be something. I can't just sit around and wait.* "What if I said that I made it up?"

"Oakley, no. You'll undermine everything you said in court."

"Please, Linda. I *need* to do something. Please?" My heart dropped. I felt so useless.

"Well…" She trailed off, sounding unsure if she should tell me or if what she was going to suggest would be right.

"Please, I just want to do something. I'll do *anything*," I promised. And I would. There wasn't anything in the world I wouldn't do to get him out of that station.

"I've not looked at the TV, but I assume it's news."

"Yes," I confirmed.

Two people from the press and most of the neighbours had witnessed the arrest. They would be having a field day, writing their stories for the papers, reporting half-truths with their own messed up fantasy twists.

"I thought so. Well, since it's already news, it might be a good idea to get the public behind Cole. This isn't something I would usually suggest, but then this isn't your usual situation." She let out a shallow breath. "Oakley, I think you should go to the local press with the truth before they put their spin on what they *assume* to be the truth."

I froze, automatically shrinking from the idea of speaking to journalists. Then, I shook myself, remembering what was at stake here. "Okay. I can do that."

There was still a large gathering of people out in the street. There would most likely be one or two members of the press still out there.

I heard Linda's car door slam, and the engine roared to life. "One second. I'm just putting you on hands-free," she explained.

I waited, listening to her press a button.

"All right, I'm now on my way to the station. Before you go out there, we need to run through a few things you should and shouldn't say."

For the ten-minute drive to the station, with one two-minute break as Linda called the police to say she was on her way, we spoke about what I should say. Linda promised she would call the second she had any news, and I was happy that she had given me something to do that might actually prove to be helpful.

Mum and Jasper were with me, giving their support even though they had reservations about me going. I had to do something and they understood that.

I was scared though. Actually, I was terrified.

What if I say something wrong? What if people think Cole deserves to be arrested for it?

I just prayed that they would see our point of view. Yes, I had been underage but barely, and there wasn't a huge age gap between us. It was nothing like what Frank had done to me, and to think other people would be making it out to be the same made me feel sick.

Five minutes later, and I had mentally prepared myself, getting everything I needed to say straight in my head. This was all happening so quickly. I hated not having control over the situation.

Taking a deep breath, I opened the front door. Jasper stood beside me on high alert with his chest puffed out. The rest of my family was just inside, behind me all the way.

My name was shouted over and over. The sea of noise was deafening. I held my hand up, and surprisingly, they all shut up. I guessed they really wanted to hear something from me.

Deciding to get straight to the point and not hang around, wasting time, I said, "I really need your help."

The second I finished my sentence, questions were yelled at me all at once.

"Stop! I'll answer some questions but one at a time."

"Oakley, what's happening with Cole?"

Jasper stepped closer and wrapped his arm around my shoulder.

"I'm okay," I whispered to him before addressing the reporter who had asked the question, "Cole has been arrested because we slept together when I was fifteen."

Another round of questions started, and I wanted to scream. *Can they not just let me finish?* This was so important.

I wanted the whole country behind Cole, but they were making it so difficult.

"Please!" I shouted, sighing in exasperation. "Cole doesn't deserve this. We were both teenagers, both in school, and both made the choice to be together. What happened between us was completely different to what my father and Frank had done. Cole is *nothing* like them. This shouldn't be happening."

Words of support and disgust at the situation buzzed around the crowd, in which neighbours outnumbered press. Talks of a campaign and protests made my head spin. They really were willing to help. Most of the explicit words were spit by my old neighbours, the people who had known me and Cole since we were born.

I opened my mouth again, and the crowd paused.

"Please, I need your help."

Launching into the details I could say, I prayed they would follow through and help.

"Oakley, are you sure you know what you're doing with drawing this much attention to Cole?" Jasper said, frowning as he debated internally with himself. He locked the front door behind us.

I was overwhelmed by the support everyone was showing and just needed to keep going. "I can't sit around and do nothing. It's already all over thc news, and I want people on Cole's side. And if Linda thinks it's a good idea…"

I pushed past Jasper and headed back up to Lizzie's room to get my phone, so I could try calling Linda for some news.

Lizzie was in her room for the first time in weeks. She looked up, startled. "Oh, sorry."

"Lizzie, this is your room. Don't be sorry. I was just getting my phone."

"You don't have to go, you know?"

"You don't have to stay over at your boyfriend's every night either."

She shook her head and shrugged. "He's not my boyfriend." But she wanted him to be; that much was clear.

"Maybe not yet." I grabbed my phone and headed to the door before I realised we'd just had a normal conversation. She really wasn't that bad. "Lizzie, tell him how you feel. You never know; you could just get everything you want." I did, and I hoped with everything that I hadn't lost it again.

"Oakley," she called.

I turned, poking my head around the door.

"You'll tell me if there's anything I can do, right?"

"Yes. Thanks." I closed her door, giving her some privacy. "Jasper!" I shouted, running down the stairs.

He jumped up and spun around, looking up at me, confused. *What has he been doing?* I didn't even want to know.

"Can you take me to the station, please?"

"Are you sure that's a good idea?"

I nodded. "Yes."

Now that I'd told the world and asked them to get behind Cole, I needed to do the same thing.

Jasper frowned as he considered what would be the best thing to do. Finally, he gave in with a grunt of exasperation. He found it hard to say no to me, and I tried not to use it to my advantage too much, but this was different.

"We leave if we need to though. If it's best for Cole, we leave, okay?"

Of course that was okay. "Yes, I promise. Let's go. Mum, can you—"

"We'll keep calling and researching. You go." She waved her hands, dismissing us, and went back to the computer. She was looking into laws and calling our local Member of Parliament with Miles and Mia.

Jasper and I arrived at the station and headed straight to the front desk. A short woman in a police uniform sat behind the window, drinking from a takeaway cup.

"Hello?" I snapped to get her attention.

She looked up at me and sighed.

Oh, sorry, am I disturbing your break?

Putting down the cup, she scooted her chair to the opening. "How can I help?"

"I need to know what's happening with Cole Benson. Please?"

"He's still being questioned. That's all I can tell you, Miss Farrell."

She knew who I was then, not that it was a surprise.

I sighed. "Please?"

Jasper pulled my arm. "Go and sit down, Oakley. I'll try talking to someone who knows what's going on."

She made a face at him but didn't comment. She just looked away at her computer screen.

"David!" I pushed past Jasper and ran to Cole's dad, who had just appeared from around the corner. "Where is he? Is he okay? What's going on?" I questioned, speaking too fast.

He held his hands up. "Calm down. It's okay. He's still being questioned. Linda's with him. I don't know anything else, but Linda assured me that she would do everything she could. We didn't get time to speak properly, but I think she'll be able to get him off."

David looked stressed and worried. He was usually a closed book, hiding his emotions well, but right now, the book was lying wide open.

"Really?" *Oh God, please!* My heart started pounding in my chest.

"We just have to wait. Come and sit."

I let him lead me to the black fake-leather chairs, and Jasper followed.

Just have to wait. How long for though? What do they have to ask?

Yes, we'd slept together when I was underage, but we'd *both* wanted to; we were *both* kids. It wasn't the same. They were turning it into something sick and twisted, and that wasn't what it was.

We all sat in silence for what seemed like an eternity. The mahogany clock on the wall ticked loudly with every second. Watching time pass was never a good idea. Time was different in here, it seemed. Every second lasted a minute.

"What the…" David trailed off, looking out the window.

Turning in my seat, I gasped as my eyes fell on what he was looking at. *Oh, wow.*

Outside were most of our neighbours. Some of the press, I recognised, and others, I didn't. It was hard to hear what they were shouting, but a few people had *Free Cole* banners. They'd really listened. My heart leapt into my throat, and I ran for the door.

There was a round of applause when I stepped outside, and the all too familiar flashing of cameras. I didn't mind the cameras this time. They were there because I'd asked them to be, as well as just wanting a story.

"Thank you all so much," I said.

My eyes filled with tears. It was so overwhelming to see all these people here for Cole.

"Oakley, what's happening now?" someone from the crowd shouted.

I couldn't see who it was, so I replied in their general direction, "Cole's being questioned, so at the minute, we're just waiting."

Jasper pulled my arm. "We appreciate you all coming, but we need to get back inside. Thank you," he said. He dragged me back into the building. "Just stay in here, okay? You've done your bit now, but you can't get too involved."

"Yeah. Okay," I agreed, nodding.

He was right. If I stayed around out there, I could mess something up, say too much.

Jenna paced the reception area.

"What's going on now?" I asked.

She shrugged and rubbed her hands over her face. In the short few hours that Cole had been here, Jenna had developed dark circles under her eyes.

Does she hate me for what happened? I anxiously gazed at her.

"Come and sit, sweetheart," she said as she finally sat down. "How are you holding up?"

"I don't know," I replied, sitting next to her. I was just about holding it together. I wanted to scream and cry. "Why are they doing this to him? I'm so sorry, Jenna. I should never have said—"

"Oakley"—she grabbed my hands—"please don't blame yourself. Everything will be fine."

"How do you know?" I whispered.

"Because I won't let anything happen to my son."

I smiled and prayed she had the ability to do that. *Of course she wants to protect her child, but is there anything she can realistically do?*

"You should go home, Oakley, especially now that there's so much media attention. There's no use in you waiting around here, too."

I started to panic. My stomach turned. "I don't want to leave him."

"I know, and I understand that. I do think that, while he's being questioned and we're not sure if they'll charge him, you shouldn't be here though. Please don't think it's because I don't want you here. I just need to make sure everything is done properly to give him the best chance, and I don't know if the press following you and getting wind of what's happened is the best thing here."

Her eyes filled with tears. I couldn't even imagine how she was feeling.

"Okay. I'll go," I agreed. If that was all I could do now, then I would. "When you see him, tell him…" *Tell him what?* "Tell him I love him."

"I will. You know he loves you, too, don't you?" Jenna rubbed my arm, and I nodded.

"I'll take you back," Jasper said. He turned to Jenna and David. "Call when you know anything?"

Jenna nodded. "Of course we will."

"Come on," Jasper whispered, wrapping his arm around me. "Walk quickly to the car, and don't stop to talk. Let me handle the questions, okay?"

I nodded. David smiled as we passed him, but I couldn't bring myself to smile back.

As soon as the door opened, the deafening noise returned. It had only been a few minutes ago when we had told people we were going back inside to wait, and now, we were leaving. I was all over the place.

"Just walk, Oakley," Jasper instructed. He held his hand up as he ushered me to the car. "There hasn't been any news, but we will let you know as soon as there is. Now, I'd appreciate it if you let me get my sister home. Thanks," he spoke so confidently and calmly, so unlike Jasper.

He practically pushed me into the car and ran to the driver's side.

"You should be Prime Minister." I smiled at him.

He grinned and shut his door, already starting the car. "I should."

We drove in silence until we were almost back at Ali's house.

"He'll be okay, won't he?" I asked desperately, needing reassurance.

"He will."

Jasper's sudden cry of complaint pulled me out of my thoughts. The crowd outside our house had easily doubled since we'd left. The drive was barely visible.

"Let's just run for it," I said.

"Good plan," Jasper agreed as he carefully drove the car through the parting crowd.

He got out first and ran to my side. My hands were shaking as I got out. It was all so surreal. Jasper bundled me under his arm and propelled me through the door.

"Any news?" Mia questioned, stumbling over her words.

No news. Unable to hold it in, I started crying. It was like I'd opened the floodgates again, and everything came pouring out. Jasper picked me up like I was a little child, but I didn't even care. I curled up in his arms and cried until my throat was sore.

Later, I lay on the sofa, staring at a pinhole in the ceiling left from the Christmas decorations. I had returned to my zombie state of numbness.

"Oakley!" Mum shouted.

I jumped. She ran into the living room as I shot up.

"What?" My stomach lurched in anticipation.

She held her hand up as she listened to someone on the phone.

I looked at Miles, and he mouthed, *David.*

David. Oh God, please say Cole's coming home. Please.

When Mum gasped and smiled, I felt a pang of hope.

"Okay, bye," she said. She hung up the phone. "They're not pressing charges."

"They're not? Really? You're sure?" I questioned. My heart soared.

It was going to be okay. Cole was going to be okay.

She smiled and hugged me, her arms squeezing me in celebration. "Yes, he's coming home now. They're already on their way. David said everyone at the station was less than happy at the arrest. Because of Cole's and your similar ages at the time, the charges against him have been dropped."

I gripped Mum, sagging against her body with relief, as she stroked my hair. I stayed there, hugging my mum like a child, until I heard the front door open. I dried my tears just in time to see Cole walk in, closely followed by his parents and Linda. His eyes scanned the room and settled on me.

For a second, I couldn't move. He was really back. His face fell, and he took the few steps toward me.

"Cole," I sobbed, stumbling to him.

He wrapped his arms around me and held me tightly.

"I'm so—"

"Don't," he said.

I closed my eyes and buried my head in his neck, needing to be close to him.

"We're gonna be okay now," he said.

"Are you okay? They've definitely dropped charges for good?" I took a shaky breath and blinked back tears of relief.

He nodded and squeezed his arms around me. "I'm fine. It's over. I promise."

"Definitely?"

Cole smiled and pressed his forehead against mine. I closed my eyes, savouring the moment.

"Definitely. They were so apologetic after they'd finished the questioning. Nothing will go on my record. Think we can maybe keep our private life private from now on?" he teased.

All that mattered was that he was home and was staying home. "Think we'll get a break now?"

He pulled a face. "Now, where's the fun in that?"

"Cole, man, good to have you back." Jasper ripped Cole away from me and gave him a man hug before pushing him my way again. "You can go back to feeling up my little sister now."

I rolled my eyes. Hugging was hardly feeling up.

Jasper turned to Linda and said, "So, love, before we all sit down, is there *anything* else *any one* of us could be arrested for?"

She laughed a little and shook her head. "No. Well, just me for murder if you call me *love* again."

"Awesome!" Jasper exclaimed, clapping his hands together. "I'll crack open the JD."

"Yes, do you want to stop for a drink?" Jenna offered Linda. "It's the least we can do."

"Thank you, but I have a lot to do." And she probably needed to lie down after dealing with me and my family. "Now, don't take this the wrong way," she said to me and Cole, "but I hope I don't see either of you for a while."

I stepped closer to her and smiled. "Me, too. Thank you again, so much."

"You're very welcome."

We hugged and said good-bye. I tried to think of something I could do to repay her, but nothing would ever be enough for what she had done for me, Cole, and the other girls along with the ones who would have been at risk had my dad and Frank been set free. She had given me freedom by putting Max and Frank away and made it possible for me to move on.

As we closed the door behind Linda and the crowd still hanging around the house, I felt lighter. We were done and could just live our lives now.

Smiling, I turned to Cole.

"Wine?" Mia said, giving Cole a sideways hug. "I could drink some wine."

Cole feigned disapproval. "What kind of example are you setting for Leona?"

Mia pointed at him. "A good one. Mummy only drinks in the evening when it's Leona's bedtime."

Jasper fake coughed. "Apart from yesterday."

"Oh, please, Jasper. You're the worst role model ever," Mia argued. "What would you show your son, huh? That Daddy can get laid by a different woman every night of the week?"

He grinned widely, and I was glad all our parents had gone in the kitchen. "Yeah, 'cause Daddy's the boss."

Cole laughed and wrapped his arms around my waist, resting his chin on my shoulder. I loved it when he did that; I felt completely protected.

Mia rolled her eyes. "Daddy's an idiot."

The three of them started bickering about who was the best role model.

I smiled to myself.

twenty-three

OAKLEY

Things were normal—finally. In the sixteen days since Cole had been released, I spent time with my family, went shopping, played princesses with Leona, and been with Cole at his new house. He had moved in two days ago and loved having his own space. Well, apparently, he loved having me invade his own space.

Since Max and Frank were locked away, I felt free. The memories couldn't be locked away, but I was doing much better. It would take time still. I had a lot to work through, but I could finally feel myself healing.

After having a long conversation with Cole about the things in my old life that I missed, I decided it was time to revisit gymnastics. Cole wanted to come, but he was working, and I wanted to go alone anyway. There was no need for anyone to escort me everywhere anymore. I felt safe while being alone for the first time in fifteen years.

Even the press had gotten a little bored of me. Well, most of them had. A few still occasionally hung around, and I was contacted almost daily, asking for my story. But phone calls, I could ignore easily enough. I was able to leave the house without people running at me.

I parked Mum's hired car as close to the door as I could and walked through the familiar building. Apart from new posters and flyers pinned to the blue boards on the walls, everything was the same. Even the walls were still the same dull cream with dark marks and chips in the paint.

Of course, everyone in my old gymnastics group had left, so the people would be different with the exception of my old coach, Marcus. I was so eager to see him. I couldn't stop smiling. It had been far too long.

"Oakley!" Marcus shouted. A grin spread across his tan face as he jogged over to me. His crushing arms held me against his hard chest. "I'm so glad you came. How are you doing?"

"I'm great. Having breathing issues right at this second, but great."

He chuckled and loosened his arms a fraction.

"How about you?" It was really, really good to see him again.

Marcus grinned wider. "I'm good. The gym's not doing too well though. Mary's moving, so we have no one to teach the under fives on Tuesdays and Thursdays. So, I was wondering…" He trailed off, pouting his lips, the way he did when he wanted something.

Wow, he wasted no time at all, but then he always did get straight to the point.

"I would love to, Marcus, but I don't think I can."

"No! You're going back? Screw Australia! Stay here with Cole, and teach the kids. Oakley, you've got nothing to run from anymore and a few huge reasons to stay. You know that."

I knew that, but I was the one who had made Mum and Jasper move halfway across the world four years ago. *How can I tell them to go home without me?* Mum had Miles now, too. "I know."

"Just think about it. I need to replace Mary in four weeks. I'll keep the job open to you for two, and then I'll *have* to advertise."

"Thanks, Marcus. I'll definitely think about it." I was already thinking about it. Staying here *was* a possibility now. I had enough money to support myself for probably five or six months, but after that, two days' work wouldn't be enough.

"I'm sure you'll make the right decision," he replied, giving me a cheeky schoolboy wink. "Wanna get a drink? I have a while before practice."

The drinks in the canteen were disgusting, but I actually missed that, too. "Drinking that crap again?" I smiled and linked my arm through his. "You bet!"

Marcus nudged me and nodded to a table. "You sit. I'll buy the liquid shit."

I sat in my favourite spot by the window. Marcus sat down and handed me a hot chocolate; he'd remembered my drink of choice.

I wrapped my hand around the mug. "Thanks. Hey, you remember when Silas broke his wrist doing a backflip off that table?"

Marcus laughed. "Yeah. What an dick. You just stood there, looking at him like, *Did he really just do that?* He was too cocky."

I smirked. "He wasn't after that. Anyway, so what's going on? Why are things so bad for the gym?"

He sighed. "I don't know. Something's going on, but no one seems to know a damn thing, or they do, but they're not saying. Some guys in fancy suits have been wandering around. I think the place is in trouble."

And that would be why he desperately wanted the gymnastics to work; he was scared the business was in trouble.

"Have you asked Greg?"

Greg was the owner of the centre and a total idiot. He cared about money, not people. I'd always hated him. There was trouble with him every year about raising the prices too high, and none of the extra money ever went into improving the facilities.

"I did. He made it sound like it was all in my head. Of course, he wouldn't tell me the truth. He's said so much bullshit in his time that I don't even think he knows what the truth is. Enough of that crap though. Has the media circus died down?"

"Took a little while, but I think they've finally realised that I don't want to talk about it. Well, most of them; some still hang around."

Marcus nodded. "It'll stop before too long. Don't let the paps be a factor in deciding where to live though." He thumped his heart and said, "Team England."

"Team England?" I repeated, laughing. "You've clearly never been to Australia!"

There was no way I would let the press decide anything for me. The house I had grown up in was still a huge problem, however. I couldn't drive past it without feeling sick. I wasn't sure if that was something I would be able to get over or not. Every time I was at Cole's parents' house, I could feel its proximity. It might as well have been a hundred feet tall and lit up in neon lights.

"Want some advice?"

I smiled. "Do I have a choice?"

"Why no, you do not!" He winked. "Look, Oakley, they took too many years of happiness from you. Don't let them have another second longer."

"Hmm. All right, I'll give you that one. That's actually good advice. I expected you to say something crude."

"I can if it'll make you feel more comfortable?"

"No, thanks. Anyway, I should really get going."

"Already?"

"Yes, but I'll come back soon."

Marcus stood up as I did. "Okay, just remember, *Team England.*"

Nodding, I grabbed my cup. "I will. It was really good to see you, Marcus. Thanks."

"See you *soon*," he called.

Laughing to myself, I waved over my shoulder and threw the plastic cup in the recycling bin. I felt happier for seeing him, and everything else seemed a little clearer now.

I got in the car and dialled Ali's mobile. Marcus had good advice. Advice I wasn't going to ignore because he was right. Max and Frank were not going to stop me from being happy for another second.

Hanging up the phone from speaking to Ali, it rang immediately. I smiled as Cole's name flashed up on the screen.

"Hi," I said.

"Hey. How'd it go with Marcus? You on your way home?"

"Good, and yes. How's work? You're not busy, right?"

"Hmm, are you insinuating that I'm not busy because you think I do nothing all day, or are you asking?"

Giggling, I replied, "Asking!"

"Well, no, not really."

"Of course you're not," I teased. "Sorry. I know you're very important."

"Was there anything in particular you wanted?" Cole asked. His voice was laced with sarcasm and a hint of amusement.

"You called me," I pointed out. "And nope." My heart danced in happiness. I loved our playful conversations. "Want me to go?"

"Nope," he replied. "I want you in my bed."

"Cole, you'd better be alone in your office!"

"No, I'm in a conference," he muttered dryly. "Of course I'm alone. No one really comes in my office."

"I'm playing a sad song on a tiny violin."

He chuckled. "I'm gonna hang up."

"No, you won't. Are you coming to Ali's after work?"

"Do you want me to come to Ali's after work?"

I shook my head, laughing softly. "You know I do."

"Then, you know I'll be there at quarter past five."

I pulled into Ali's driveway, right by the front door because a few people were hanging around outside. They didn't come onto her property anymore, not since Jasper had threatened to call the police and report them for trespassing.

"I've just gotten back to Ali's. I'll see you tonight, okay?"

"Okay. Love you."

"I love you, too." I hung up the phone and took it out of the cradle. My house key was in my pocket. I grabbed it, so I could get in as quickly as possible.

"Oakley, a few words?" a deep voice shouted.

Ignoring the questions being shouted at me, I shoved the key in the lock, keeping my head down.

"Oakley, how do you feel about—"

I slammed the door shut, cutting out the noise. Australia became more appealing whenever I had to run into a house to escape the cameras and questions.

I flopped down on the sofa.

"Hi, honey," Mum said, carrying two mugs in her hands. She sat down on the sofa, and from the look on her face, she was trying to figure out how to tell me something.

"You okay, Mum?"

"Yeah, fine. I booked the tickets. We leave in two days."

"Okay. Good." I sat up and wrapped my hands around the mug. "How's Miles?"

He'd had to go back to Australia for work, and I knew Mum was missing him. It wouldn't be long before they were together again though.

"I spoke to him last night. He's fine."

"You'll see him soon."

She smiled and nodded.

"I'm glad you're happy, Mum."

A ghost of a smile touched her lips "So am I."

"But?" I prompted.

She sighed. "I don't know really. Miles is an incredible man and a good person. I just find myself doubting things. Doubting him. I guess I'm afraid."

"Mum, that's understandable, but Miles is nothing like Max. After…everything, I found it hard to trust men, too. I wasn't sure what they wanted from me or what they were going to do."

Mum scrunched her eyes shut; her jaw clenched in what almost looked like pain. I swallowed the lump in my throat and continued because I needed to say it, and she needed to hear it.

"It took time, but I realised that Max and Frank were the minority. You can trust Miles, Mum. I do. He really loves you, and hard though it is to believe it, he's willing to take you on when you have Jasper. Marry him!"

"Oakley, I'm so s—"

I held my hand up. "Don't apologise. We didn't do anything wrong." I sounded like a therapist, but it was true.

"I really wish you would take your own advice, honey."

I should, but it was hard sometimes. There was still a lot of guilt weighing on my shoulders even though it lessened every day. "I'm trying to. It's getting easier."

"Good," she said, wiping her nose on a tissue. "Okay. I'm okay." She wiped a stray tear from under her eye and smiled. "No more dwelling on the bad things. We look forward from now on. Deal?"

"Deal." That was all I'd wanted her to say. It wouldn't be as simple as she made it seem—we both knew that—but as long as we were willing to work on our issues, we would be fine.

"Good. Now, what time is Cole coming over? I assume it will be the second he gets off work," she teased.

I smiled. "Yes, from work. He'll be having dinner with us tonight. Do you think that would be okay?"

He'd been over most nights, and Ali had said it was fine, but I worried she was just being polite.

"Of course. Ali loves having a full house. Lizzie will be moved out in a few years, I imagine. I'm a little worried that Ali will be lonely here by herself."

I bit my lip. "We should set her up."

"She'd kill us, and we don't really know anyone here anymore!"

"Well, *we* don't, but…"

"Cole," she said, grinning.

Cole had mentioned that he worked with a load of men in their forties and fifties; he was the youngest one there.

"Someone around her age, single and trustworthy," she said.

"You had to specify single?"

"Less of the sarcasm. Oh, I'm actually excited now. I can't wait to see her reaction."

I laughed at her. She really did seem like a fifteen-year-old girl, but I loved seeing her so carefree.

"We can demand a list of eligible bachelors when Cole gets here."

I'd been so wrapped up in myself, Mum, and Jasper that I hadn't really thought about Ali. So, I hoped I could do something for her. Loneliness was awful, and Ali had said she hoped to find someone special. She deserved to.

"Hey," Cole greeted me, flashing the smile that still gave me butterflies.

"Hi." I closed the distance between us as quickly as I could and kissed him. "I'm glad you're here. We need your help."

"What with?"

"Finding Ali a man."

Cole grinned. "Sorry, I'm taken."

"You sure about that?" I goaded him.

"Uh-huh. So, you want me to set Ali up with randoms from work?"

"They're not randoms; you know them. Just do as you're told and in a couple months when the drama from the trial is behind us find a nice guy who will treat my auntie right."

Cole saluted. "Yes, sir."

I patted his cheek. "There's a good boy." I led him to Lizzie's room. At least I would be out of her room soon. "Sit," I instructed, pointing to the futon.

"I hope you're going to do a striptease, bossy," Cole teased.

He looked ridiculously hopeful. *Does he know me at all?*

Rolling my eyes, I sat down next to him. "So, Mum booked our tickets back to Australia today."

His face fell, as I'd expected.

"We leave in two days."

"No," Cole replied, getting up and kneeling in front of me. "Not again, Oakley, please. I can't lose you again. Stay here with me—"

I placed my index finger over his lips. "I have to go back—"

"No," he said fiercely. His eyes were wide with panic.

If he would just let me finish!

"Will you let me talk?" I shook my head. "I'll be gone for a total of three days. Ali's already said I could have the spare room until Mum sells the house and moves back here."

"No," he repeated.

I frowned as his whole face lit up with the most perfect smile.

He doesn't want me to come back?

He was smiling though.

Huh? "No? What?"

"You're not staying with anyone else. You're living with me."

He can't be serious?

We had only been back together a few months—although it had felt so much longer, like we hadn't been apart for those four years. But still…

"Cole, you—"

"I've spoken!" he said like a caveman. "Seriously though, Oakley, you're mine now. Suck it up, and move in with me."

Oh my God, he is being serious! He wants us to live together.

Squealing, I threw my arms around him and hugged him tight, probably crushing his bones, but he didn't complain.

"I love you."

"I love you, too," I murmured against his neck.

Wow, I'm going to be living with Cole. Living in that beautiful house we're decorating together.

It didn't seem real. It was like it wasn't happening to me. I never thought I would have that—a proper relationship with someone who wanted me, someone who didn't care about my past.

"And I'm coming to Australia with you."

I shook my head. "You have work, Mum, Jasper and Miles will be with me, and it's only *three days*."

"We'll argue about that later." He lowered us down onto the futon. "I fucking love you," he whispered. And then he kissed me senseless.

twenty-four

OAKLEY

I got into the car and closed my eyes. Finally, it was done. No more revisiting the past—outside of therapy anyway. I wanted to be finished with therapy already, but I had learned not to give myself a timeframe. I would go until I felt I didn't need to anymore, and I just wasn't there yet.

"How'd it go?" Cole asked, squeezing the top of my leg.

"Good." I had just finished the last interview I'd agreed to do, and it was such a relief. Selling my story had been the last thing I wanted to do—until I'd realised the money would fund a sports and hobby centre at the gym.

After speaking to countless therapists and other people who had been in my situation, I'd discovered that a lot of children who had been abused were able to use hobbies as an escape. Through therapy, so far, I'd met people who painted, sang, played music, danced, and cycled. For me, it was gymnastics.

When Marcus had told me how bad the gym was doing and that the owner was cutting his losses and turning it into a fitness gym with a swimming pool, I knew I had to do something.

The thought of someone going through a similar thing to what I had without having access to that tiny bit of normality was painful. So, I'd sold my story to a major magazine, had one interview with a national newspaper and a women's weekly, and done three TV appearances.

Dredging everything back up was hard, but I knew that it would be worth it in the end. The centre would help so many people, and I was going to donate a cut of the yearly profits to a charity that helped victims of child abuse.

My last interview with a magazine marked the end of the *fundraising* and meant I could afford the finishing touches for the centre. I'd officially named it La Fuga, which was Italian for *the escape*, but we mostly just called it the centre.

"I'm proud of you. You've done all this by yourself."

I shook my head. "Not by myself. Marcus has been with me every step of the way. So have you and both of our families!"

"All right, well, it was all your idea."

"That one, I'll take credit for."

Cole chuckled and took the exit that would take us home. "So, tomorrow's going to be ridiculously busy, huh?"

I nodded. "Yeah, we've got so much to do. The electricians are coming at one. The mirrors are being installed in the ballet room at two thirty. There's a huge delivery of football and rugby balls coming sometime in the morning, and I have to call some companies about vending machines and a cleaning service. Oh, and we really need to get those liability insurance forms signed."

"You have a list, right?"

"I have about a thousand lists."

"Right. Well, don't stress over it. We'll get it all done. Jasper and Abby are picking up the art easels and stools next week, and apparently, the company agreed to throw in a bunch of paintbrushes, too."

"Yeah? That's great! How is the shack looking?"

When word had gotten out about what we were doing, the whole community had gotten involved. An online sports shop had donated football goalposts. An arts-and-crafts company had donated the easels, stools, and now brushes.

I'd had a load of gymnastics equipment donated to the centre, which would replace a lot of the used stuff from the old gym. Tables and chairs for the cafeteria had been donated from a manufacturing company. Also, I'd already gotten a stack of job applications back.

It was a little overwhelming, but I had a lot of support.

Cole laughed. "It'll look great when it's done. Have faith!"

We had a huge old summerhouse at the back of the surrounding gardens at the centre. It was right out of the way and overlooked the little stream that ran from one end to the other. Eventually, it would be for people who wanted to explore their artistic side. I thought they would probably want peace and quiet to draw and paint.

At the minute though, it looked like a run-down old shed. It needed new glass in the doors and windows and repair work to the roof and sides along with new floor and clad walls with wood inside. The project was for Cole, David, Miles, and Jasper. They'd promised me it would look brand-new when they'd finished. Miles decided to take a chance on love and moved to the UK. He and Mum were deliriously happy.

"I have faith. I know it'll look amazing."

It'd better anyway. I'd put everything into this, and so badly, I wanted it to work and change people's lives. If I hadn't had gymnastics, I honestly didn't know what I would have been like.

"It will. Your mum's there now, feeding the decorators in the ballet room."

Until we'd got the call that the mirrors were coming tomorrow, we'd been decorating ourselves, but there was no way we'd get that gigantic room done in time.

"Good. How's it looking in there?"

Cole shrugged. "Big and pink."

It wasn't pink-pink. It was an off-white pink that looked fresh. I wanted the whole building to be light and inviting.

"I'm so tired." I yawned, covering my mouth with the back of my hand. "Can we just drop in quickly before we go home?"

"You still want to go? I'm sure everyone will understand. They have it all under control."

"Five minutes. Just to make sure everything's all right."

Cole smirked and nodded. Yes, I was probably a nightmare, but I needed it to be right.

Cole really did let me stay for only five minutes. I had just about finished speaking to everyone when he grabbed my hand and pulled me back to the car.

"You're staying in for the rest of the day. I shall be at your service," he said.

"Hmm, that I can get on board with."

"Oakley, no!" Cole said. "I'm serious. You're gonna make yourself ill. Stay at home today." He pointed to the sofa. "Sit. I'll make you some breakfast and call your mum. She can check in on the centre today. Everyone else will be there, and Ben promised to help with some of the deliveries."

I groaned. Cole was going to work, and I'd thought I would have a day's peace to get a few little things done at the centre. When he left, I would just go anyway.

"Cole, I'm fine. I'm just a little tired."

"Then, sleep," he replied, giving me a smug smile. "You're not going out today."

"You're being ridiculous."

"You're being stubborn. Oakley, you're doing too much, and it's making you ill. I like healthy Oakley. Please, for me, just stay in, and relax today."

I held my hands up and sank back into the sofa. "Fine. Today, I'll be lazy."

He grinned. "Good. Now, toast or bagel?"

"What if I want an omelet?"

"I can undercook one and poison you if you'd like."

"Bagel, please."

"Eat. Sleep. Watch crap on TV. Just don't leave this house," he said, raising his eyebrow as he handed me breakfast.

"Thank you. I'll stay in and behave."

It took about two minutes after I'd finished eating for me to plunge into boredom. I desperately wanted to go to the centre and check on things, but if I left the house, Cole would probably have a heart attack, the overprotective fool.

I dialled Mum's number and decided that the only way I would be able to relax was to know everything was okay.

"Hi, love," she greeted.

"Hey, Mum. How are you?"

"You mean, are you at the centre?"

"Okay, yes, but you first."

"I'm fine. Just pulled up. Jasper and Miles are here. Cole called me already. We'd better not see you here today. He's right; you do need to take a break. Promise me you'll relax and take care of yourself."

"Yes, I promise."

"Okay, good. I'd better go. I'll give you a call in a bit, and I'll send Jasper over with some lunch."

"I can make myself food, Mum."

"Jasper's getting KFC for everyone."

"Around one-ish?"

Mum laughed. "Sure, honey. Speak later."

"Bye." I hung up the phone and switched the TV on. *Daytime rubbish it is then.*

I chose a movie instead, but I just couldn't get into the film. Sitting around and doing nothing when I had so much to do made me feel anxious.

What if I don't get everything ready in time because I'm lounging around on the sofa?

The front doorbell rang, and I got up, eager to answer it and have something to do. Mia stood at the door with a box of Thorntons chocolates.

"Cole told me you're on house arrest, and I was to come over and make sure you didn't leave."

I narrowed my eyes and stepped aside, so Mia could come in. "Of course he did." I was glad to see her though.

"I'll put the kettle on, and we can catch up," she called over her shoulder as she headed into the kitchen. "So, what's going on? Besides the centre."

I shrugged and grabbed two mugs from the cupboard. "Not much really."

"No ring yet?" Mia pouted, looking at my hand. She was obsessed with Cole proposing.

It hadn't been that long since we'd gotten back together, and we had already moved in together. I was happy with how things were.

"Not yet, but there's no rush!"

She sighed dramatically, her forehead creasing in a frown. "He needs to hurry up. I've seen a lovely dress for your wedding."

"Buy that for someone else's wedding. You'll be wearing a bridesmaid's dress at mine."

"Really?" she squealed as her eyes widened in surprise and excitement. "Oh my God! You're serious, right?"

"Of course I am. You're Cole's sister! I want to have Leona, too, if that's okay?"

"If it's okay?" she repeated, staring at me like I was stupid. "Oh, he needs to propose soon!"

I held my hand up. "Okay, calm down. Let's talk about you."

Mia groaned and threw a tea bag into each mug with a little too much force.

It made me grin. "Date went well then!"

"You're enjoying this, aren't you?"

I laughed. "Absolutely. It was that bad?"

"God, you should have seen him, Oakley. He looked so nice at the gym, running on the treadmill, and he was so polite and interested in what I was saying. Turns out that he's a twat."

Reaching for the milk in the fridge, I laughed at her bluntness. "What did he do?"

"He spoke about cars the whole night. I couldn't care less what engine his car has or how many of those horse things it has! I was so bored that I texted Mum and made her call, lying that Leona wouldn't settle without me. I'm done with men."

"Don't give up. You'll find someone. You know, I could—"

"No way," she hissed. "You are not setting me up."

"Fine, be stubborn."

She glared at me. "I don't want to talk about this anymore."

I carried the mugs to the table, and Mia brought the chocolates.

"You're annoyed because I'm right," I said.

"Change of subject. If your arsehole ex wanted your child for one extra day a week, would you let him?"

"Chris wants another day?"

She turned her nose up. "Yep."

He already had Leona on Fridays and Saturdays and every other Sunday, which was how it had been since she was born.

"He wants a mid-week day, too. I don't really know what to do. Leona would love it, and I would be able to get more done. When it comes to Chris though, I just want to stick my tongue out and give him the finger."

I laughed, almost spilling my tea.

"I know I should be an adult about it though," she said.

"You probably should. It's horrible you have to sacrifice another day with her, but if it's what's best for her."

Mia nodded. "Yeah. I'll give him the extra day but just until her bedtime."

I couldn't imagine how hard it must be to share your child with an ex, especially one who had hurt you so much over and over again.

"Tell me about your wedding again."

"I'm not getting married yet," I said.

"Yet."

"I'm so setting you up."

She glared and grabbed a chocolate.

Mia stayed with me for the whole day. We had a KFC lunch, courtesy of Jasper, and chatted about everything. As much as I wanted to be at the centre, it was really nice to have a relaxing girlie day. We made a plan of doing it one morning a week on Leona's new day with Chris.

At five o'clock, when Cole would be leaving work, Mia left.

I curled up on the sofa. The energy seemed to drain from my body. I felt as if I could sleep for a week.

"I love coming home to you every night," Cole said, lying down beside me.

I frowned and looked up, half-asleep. "Hmm, I love you coming home to me every night." I pressed my lips against his and curled my fingers into his hair.

He wrapped one arm around my back and the other under my legs, holding me bridal-style.

I gasped. "Cole!"

"Shh," he whispered as he headed to the stairs.

epilogue

OAKLEY

Taking a deep breath, I stepped forward, closer to the red ribbon that stretched from one side of the double doors to the other. Everything was done, and it was time to officially open La Fuga.

"I'd like to start by thanking every one of you for coming today and showing your support. Four months ago, when I was just playing around with the idea, I had no clue so many people would get behind me. Without the people and companies donating money, equipment, and their own time, this would not have been possible."

Out of the corner of my eye, I saw Mum crying.

Already!

I smiled. "I want this to be a place where everyone can come and do something they love. This centre is for you to come to and escape. So, I'd like to declare La Fuga officially open." I cut through the tape with a huge smile on my face.

We did it!

I stepped to the side as the crowd applauded and walked forward.

"Welcome! Come on in!"

Children bounced around in excitement, running into the building. A sea of people streamed past me, giving their congratulations as they looked eagerly inside.

"I can't believe it's really open," I said, rushing into Cole's arms, as the final people made their way through the door.

"Feels good, doesn't it?"

I nodded against his neck. It felt incredible.

"We should get inside and speak to people. Hanky-panky later," he said, wiggling his eyebrows.

The classes weren't starting until tomorrow, but everyone was looking around today. The over-fifties painting club, as they called themselves, were going to bring along their supplies to use the shack. I was hoping that younger people would use it, too, once they saw it wasn't just all about painting still life outside. It was a quiet space for them to paint whatever they wanted.

Cole held the door open for me, and we were immediately greeted by Mia holding out two glasses of champagne.

"Welcome to *La Fuga*," she said in a fake Italian accent.

I'd picked Italian because it was in Italy where Cole had given me hope for having a normal life. It was where he'd made sex about love and trust and when I'd realised that I wasn't too broken to be in a relationship.

"Oakley!" Kerry shouted, bouncing her way over to me. "This is amazing! I want to work here! I love it. You've done such a great job."

Laughing, I gave her a one-armed hug, being careful not to spill my champagne. "Thank you. Wanna be a receptionist?"

Lizzie was doing it until I could find someone suitable, someone with experience, and someone whom I trusted.

"Are you being serious?"

"Yes. Look, we'll talk later. I really should mingle." I left a beaming Kerry gazing after me. "Who first?" I asked Cole.

He shrugged. "Why not go to one of the bigger rooms? There will probably be more people we can get through at once."

"Sounds like a plan. Gymnastics room?"

Cole smirked and pulled on my hand, leading me there. Of course that was going to be where I wanted to go first. It was the room that meant the most to me.

Cole was right. It was full. I could barely see through the crowd of people. Children were already playing on the equipment. I didn't mind though. They were being supervised, and hopefully, it would encourage them to sign up for classes. Plus, we had the insurance.

After spending the whole day talking to hundreds of people, giving interviews, and having my picture taken, I was exhausted and beyond ready to go home. I felt light-headed and dizzy even though I'd been eating canapés throughout the afternoon.

The place had a buzz about it. Mum and Jenna had lists of people's details and what they were interested in. Not all would follow through and come to classes, but I hoped a fair few would. David and Miles had been talking to people from local businesses and handing out a lot of leaflets for them to put in their shops.

"Thank you all so much," I said once the centre was all locked up and we could leave.

Mum, Miles, Jasper, and Abby all gave me hugs and got into one car, and then I said good-bye to Cole's parents and Mia.

"Take me home, please?" I asked Cole, leaning against him.

"My pleasure." Cole smiled and leant in, kissing me deeply.

I gripped his arms, and the whole world disappeared. The entire way home I stared at Cole like he was some grand prize. To me, he was. He was my forever.

We pulled into the drive and he raised his eyebrow. "Get inside, you perv!"

Practically crawling into the house, I kicked my shoes off the second I was inside. My feet hurt, and I just wanted to sleep.

Cole followed me a step behind as I climbed the stairs and headed straight for our room. He was concerned. Whenever he thought something was wrong he barely left my side.

"I don't feel good," I muttered, pressing my face into one of the pillow as I collapsed into bed.

Cole sat beside me. "You've been saying that a lot recently. Are you okay?"

I nodded. "Yeah, just tired from being so busy."

"Let's just go to bed then."

There were no arguments from me. I climbed under the cover and laid my head on Cole's chest.

"Night," I whispered. My eyelids were so heavy that I fell asleep before I could even hear his reply.

I woke up early. The clock on my bedside table showed seven thirty in the morning. I groaned.

Jasper and Abby, who were very much back on, were opening the centre, so Cole and I could go to Leona's nursery school fete for a few hours. I hated not being there the first morning it was open, but family came first. We didn't have to be at the nursery until ten, so I had hoped to sleep in until about nine.

Groaning, I pressed my hand to my throbbing head.

Cole stirred beside me. "You okay?"

"Fine," I lied and then said, "No." I jumped up and rushed to the bathroom. Oh God, I was going to be sick.

Cole ran in after me and dropped to his knees just as I threw up in the toilet.

I stood up and flushed the toilet when I'd finished. My head was pounding, and I felt like I was going to faint.

"Oakley, you don't think you could be pregnant, do you?"

My heart stopped. "No. I'm just run down." I was on the pill.

Cole frowned. "You're going back to bed, and I'm going to get a test. We need to make sure."

Please, no. I can't be pregnant.

Nodding my head, I turned on the tap and rinsed my mouth with the cold water.

Turning around, I stumbled out of the bathroom. Cole's arm kept me upright. I felt so weak and fell back into bed.

"You relax. I'll get some water and then go to the shop."

I mentally rolled my eyes and snuggled under the cover. Cole left the room, and I started to panic.

Pregnant. I can't have a child. What the hell am I going to do if I am?

Perhaps it's just food poisoning?

Although no one else was sick, and Cole and I ate the same things.

My heart was in my throat as I waited.

How can I protect a child when I couldn't even protect myself?

I curled up and pulled the cover over my head, hiding from reality. Placing my hand over my flat stomach, I tried to feel a connection. *Shouldn't I just know if I'm carrying a little life inside me? Shit! No, no, no, no!*

I gulped as my eyes stung with tears.

"Oakley," Cole called softly.

I pulled the cover down and looked up at him.

"Hey, come on, let's go and do it now, yeah?"

I took the box from him and got out of bed. The sooner we knew, the better.

"It'll be okay, whatever the result," he said.

Nodding, I walked out of the room and to the bathroom. *Would it?* I read the instructions to make sure I would know what the result meant and sat down to pee on the stick.

As soon as I finished, I washed my hands and opened the door. *A tiny person, half-me and half-Cole. The idea is perfect, but the reality? What if something happens to the child?*

Cole paced outside the bathroom, wearing a hole in the carpet.

"I'm scared," I admitted, gripping the stick in my hand.

A little blue cross would change our whole lives forever. He opened his arms, and I eagerly stepped into them.

"What if I'm pregnant?"

"Then, we'll need to finally sort that second bedroom out."

That's it? No freak-outs? Just, we'll need to decorate?

"Oakley, I want to spend the rest of my life with you. I want to get engaged, married, and have kids. I don't care what order that comes in."

I laughed through my tears. "You're greedy."

"Never said I wasn't. Please don't worry. Whatever happens, I'll always be here to protect you and any children we have. Should we look now or…"

"Will you?" I croaked, holding the test out.

He nodded and took it from me. Cocking his head to the side, he frowned. *What does that mean?*

"How do you tell? It doesn't say anything. There's a line in the Test window and a cross in the other one."

I gasped and grabbed it out of his hand. *A cross!* It was positive.

"What does that mean, Oakley? Negative? Why can't it just say *Pregnant* or *Not Pregnant*? Where are the instructions?" He looked behind me into the bathroom for the box.

"Cole," I whispered, "a cross means positive."

His mouth dropped open.

Oh God, I'm pregnant!

"We're gonna have a baby? Wow." He leapt forward and scooped me up in his arms, spinning me around. "Shit, I'm gonna be a dad!"

I couldn't help laughing, getting caught up in his celebration. When he put me down, he had the biggest smile, one that lit up his whole face and showed his dimple. He stroked the side of my face. I took a shaky breath; my knees felt weak.

We were going to be parents. In that instant, I knew that I would do anything to protect this little life inside me. It would be okay because the baby would have us.

"We're having a baby," he repeated.

Cole's hand trailed down my neck and chest and rested on my stomach. I bit my lip. It seemed like a dream. Smiling, he slowly bent his head and softly pressed his lips against mine.

Jasper's story,
Players, Bumps,
and Cocktail Sausages,
is a stand-alone companion
novel to the Silence series.

BOOKS BY NATASHA PRESTON

THE SILENCE SERIES

Silence
Broken Silence
Players, Bumps, and Cocktail Sausages
Silent Night (A Free Christmas Short Story)

THE CHANCE SERIES

Second Chance
Our Chance

THE BAND SERIES

With the Band

STANDALONES

The Cellar
Save Me
Awake

www.natashapreston.com

19088509R00160

Printed in Great Britain
by Amazon